"Victoria Thom[...]
Anne Perry and Cal[...]
—Tam[...]

"Victoria Thompson's Gaslight Mysteries are first-rate
with a vivid historical setting and a hero and heroine
that will keep readers eagerly returning
to Sarah Brandt's New York City."
—*The Mystery Reader*

Praise for
MURDER ON LEXINGTON AVENUE

"Thompson expertly weaves in details about the history of
the era and the educational system without detracting from
the well-paced and suspenseful story. Despite a potentially
confusing plot with too many suspects, Frank and Sarah's
investigation makes for a compelling and quick read with
believable twists and a satisfying conclusion. Series fans will
be thrilled with this latest entry."   —*Booklist*

"[Thompson] skillfully balances several unusual plot
lines . . . [She] embellishes her beautifully constructed mysteries with little-known historical tidbits; her long-running
series will offer rewarding reading to fans of Rhys Bowen
and Cordelia Frances Biddle."   —*Library Journal*

"Thompson illuminates a battle in the deaf community that
continues even today."   —*Kirkus Reviews*

"Thompson does a solid job bringing the past to life."
—*Publishers Weekly*

continued . . .

"A terrific entry that uses the background-like references to Bell to set the era while also providing insight into the two predominate education theories of teaching deaf students. The whodunit is complex . . . Readers will appreciate the latest Victoria Thompson's historical investigate tale."

—*Futures Mystery Anthology Magazine*

"A suspenseful murder mystery that will have readers holding their breaths until the very end . . . Scandals galore erupt in this post-Victorian era mystery as Victoria Thompson once again delights her readers with a fascinating whodunit . . . Thompson's keen eye for detail give these novels the old-fashioned intrigue that keeps her readers coming back for more."

—*Fresh Fiction*

"This book should come with a warning: Pick Up at Your Own Risk! Start it in the morning and read as much as you can because you will not willingly put it aside in the night. *Murder on Lexington Avenue* has a main storyline and a multitude of side ones. Each page will reveal a new twist. Each chapter will leave you in awe of life at the turn of the century. Each character leaps from the pages in such detailed description that you feel part of the family. I wanted this story to never end, only to roll into another mystery involving Malloy and Sarah. Great job, Victoria Thompson!"

—*The Romance Readers Connection*

"Throughout the mystery, Thompson effectively describes some of the period's very real conflicts between economic classes, trendy philosophies, and an inherent mistrust by the poor and innate disrespect by the rich for the police who try to solve the plentiful crimes of the period."

—*New Mystery Reader*

MURDER ON
LEXINGTON AVENUE

A Gaslight Mystery

Victoria Thompson

BERKLEY PRIME CRIME, NEW YORK

THE BERKLEY PUBLISHING GROUP
Published by the Penguin Group
Penguin Group (USA) Inc.
375 Hudson Street, New York, New York 10014, USA
Penguin Group (Canada), 90 Eglinton Avenue East, Suite 700, Toronto, Ontario M4P 2Y3, Canada
(a division of Pearson Penguin Canada Inc.)
Penguin Books Ltd., 80 Strand, London WC2R 0RL, England
Penguin Group Ireland, 25 St. Stephen's Green, Dublin 2, Ireland (a division of Penguin Books Ltd.)
Penguin Group (Australia), 250 Camberwell Road, Camberwell, Victoria 3124, Australia
(a division of Pearson Australia Group Pty. Ltd.)
Penguin Books India Pvt. Ltd., 11 Community Centre, Panchsheel Park, New Delhi—110 017, India
Penguin Group (NZ), 67 Apollo Drive, Rosedale, Auckland 0632, New Zealand
(a division of Pearson New Zealand Ltd.)
Penguin Books (South Africa) (Pty.) Ltd., 24 Sturdee Avenue, Rosebank, Johannesburg 2196,
South Africa

Penguin Books Ltd., Registered Offices: 80 Strand, London WC2R 0RL, England

This is a work of fiction. Names, characters, places, and incidents either are the product of the author's
imagination or are used fictitiously, and any resemblance to actual persons, living or dead, business
establishments, events, or locales is entirely coincidental. The publisher does not have any control over
and does not assume any responsibility for author or third-party websites or their content.

MURDER ON LEXINGTON AVENUE

A Berkley Prime Crime Book / published by arrangement with the author

PRINTING HISTORY
Berkley Prime Crime hardcover edition / June 2010
Berkley Prime Crime mass-market edition / June 2011

Copyright © 2010 by Victoria Thompson.
The Edgar® name is a registered service mark of the Mystery Writers of America, Inc.
Cover illustration by Karen Chandler.
Cover design by Rita Frangie.

ISBN: 978-0-425-24187-5

BERKLEY® PRIME CRIME
Berkley Prime Crime Books are published by The Berkley Publishing Group,
a division of Penguin Group (USA) Inc.,
375 Hudson Street, New York, New York 10014.
BERKLEY® PRIME CRIME and the PRIME CRIME logo are trademarks of Penguin Group (USA)
Inc.

PRINTED IN THE UNITED STATES OF AMERICA

10 9 8 7 6 5 4 3 2 1

To Keira,
the very newest Thompson!

I

DETECTIVE SERGEANT FRANK MALLOY PUSHED HIS WAY through the crowd gathered at the entrance to the modest office building. Murder always drew a crowd in New York City, even in respectable neighborhoods. Even on a peaceful, autumn Saturday afternoon. The uniformed copper guarding the door nodded and admitted him, causing much outrage to the curious onlookers, who had been fruitlessly demanding admittance for quite some time.

Inside, the building wasn't so modest. Marble floors gleamed in the late afternoon sunshine, and rich, dark woodwork gave the place a distinct air of respectability. Not the kind of place where people usually got themselves murdered, Frank thought as he scanned the loitering figures for whoever was in charge of this investigation.

The man in question had already spotted Frank, and he disengaged himself from the men he'd been speaking with and made his way across the marble floor. Frank recognized him immediately. They'd crossed paths before, and Frank knew he wasn't the kind to resent Frank's involvement in the investigation. In fact, he'd be glad to be relieved of the responsibility.

"Malloy," he said, reaching out a hand. "Good to see you." He was one of the ward detectives. His main job would be collecting bribes and blackmail money from the crooks and the madams and distributing it to the right places. But he was also responsible for reporting crimes in his ward to Police Headquarters and getting one of the detective sergeants down to investigate as quickly as possible. Today, Frank was the one called down. For some reason, he'd been asked for by name.

"Sullivan," Frank replied, shaking the outstretched hand. "What's going on?"

"Some fellow got his skull cracked open. Blood everywhere," he added with obvious disapproval. "Not so bad when it's in an alley, but in a place like this . . ." He shook his head again. He looked like he hadn't shaved in a few days, and his suit had probably been slept in. Frank could smell the whiskey on his breath, but his bloodshot eyes betrayed his intelligence. Sullivan might be a drunk, but he was no fool. "Come on, I'll show you."

"Have you sent for the medical examiner yet?" Frank asked as he followed Sullivan down a hallway.

"Yeah, as soon as I saw what happened, but nobody's come yet."

Frank heard an exclamation of surprise as they passed an open doorway, and a moment later, a round man with a shiny bald head popped out. "Mr. Malloy, is that you?"

Frank turned in surprise. "That's right," he said, thinking the man looked familiar but unable to place him.

"Edward Higginbotham," he said, taking Frank's hand and shaking it vigorously. "I'm the one who found Mr. Wooten." He still looked a bit shaken, and his face was beaded with sweat, but that could just be because it was warm on this September afternoon.

"Mr. Higginbotham said he knew you," Sullivan reported. "Asked me to send for you special." Which explained a lot.

"Because of your son, you know," Higginbotham said.

Frank frowned at the mention of Brian. Who was this man and how did he even know Frank had a son?

"You spoke to me about putting your son in our school," Higginbotham reminded him eagerly. "The Lexington Avenue School, or rather the Institution for the Improved Instruction of Deaf Mutes. The name's so long, we just call it Lexington Avenue, but you already know that."

Now Frank remembered. He'd visited the place when he'd been trying to decide whether to send his boy to school at all. Finding out Brian was deaf had been a shock, but not as much as it might have been. Until then, he'd believed Brian was simpleminded and would have to be cared for his entire life. Now he'd enrolled him in a school where he would learn to read and write and eventually be able to learn a trade. But it wasn't Mr. Higginbotham's school.

"I remember now," Frank said, deciding not to mention that he'd decided against the Lexington Avenue School. "Is that why you asked for me? Because we met before?"

"Well, yes, but . . . well, I mean, I thought you might be more . . . I mean . . . Mr. Wooten, he was very interested in our work. A great champion for the deaf. Tireless. And now—" His voice broke, and he pulled out a handkerchief and pressed it to his lips.

"You were friends with Mr. Wooten?" Frank asked.

"Oh, yes," Higginbotham said, using the handkerchief to mop his face. "Well, not friends exactly. Not socially. Acquaintances, I suppose you would say. His daughter is one of our students, and he has been a great supporter of the school. He serves on our board, and he's been an advocate for—"

"Mr. Higginbotham found the body," Sullivan reminded Frank, eager to get on with it.

"How did you happen to do that?" Frank asked with interest.

"We had an appointment," Higginbotham said. "And when I went to his office, there he was . . ." He grew even paler than he had been.

"Why was he in his office on a Saturday afternoon?" Frank asked.

"He would come in at all hours," Higginbotham said. "Especially if he was seeing people about the school. He didn't want it to interfere with his regular business hours, you see, and he didn't want his family bothered at home."

"Did you see anybody else when you got here?"

Higginbotham's eyes grew wide. "Oh, dear, I didn't think of that! I could have seen the killer!" Now he was chalk white, and Frank wouldn't have been surprised to see him keel over in a dead faint.

"Why don't you go sit down and wait for me. I've got to . . . to look around, and then I'll be back to ask you some more questions," Frank suggested.

"Oh, yes, yes, of course," Higginbotham agreed weakly. "I'm only too happy to help."

Sullivan was calling a uniformed cop over to escort Higginbotham back into the room where he'd been waiting. Frank could see now that it was some sort of conference room, with a large table surrounded by chairs. Higginbotham didn't object to the assistance the cop offered, and Frank and Sullivan were finally able to continue on their mission.

"I already questioned him," Sullivan explained as they moved down the corridor. "He didn't see anyone in the building, and he said the body was cold when he got here, so I'm guessing the killer was long gone."

"You're sure he didn't do it himself?"

Sullivan shook his head. "If you'd seen him when I got here, you wouldn't even ask. He was almost crying, and white as a sheet. Had some blood on his shoes, from stepping in it—you'll see the footprints—but none anywhere else, and the killer would've had some blood splashed on him, at least. See for yourself."

They'd reached the last door at the end of the hall, and Sullivan stood back and allowed Frank to enter first. He could smell the blood the instant he stepped through the doorway, the sharp, metallic scent that you never forgot once you'd smelled it.

The body lay on the floor in the middle of the room, in a heap just where the man had fallen. A pool of blood had formed around the ruined head, congealing now in the autumn heat, and flies were buzzing, settling on the red-streaked face. A few bloody smudges marked the floor where Higginbotham had stepped in the pool and tried to wipe his shoes clean on the carpet.

Beyond where the body lay sat a large desk made of dark, polished wood. The kind of desk an important man would have. He'd sit there behind it and intimidate those who came to see him to ask a favor or beg for business.

Two chairs had been positioned in front of it for visitors to use. They weren't comfortable chairs. The dead man hadn't wanted to encourage his visitors to linger. One now lay on its side. Frank studied the tableau, taking in every detail.

From the way the blood had splattered, he could see that the victim had been standing, probably talking to or arguing with his killer. What had he said to enrage someone enough to pick up . . . ? What had the killer picked up? Or maybe he had been carrying the weapon with him. He thought of the weapon that had killed another man whose murder he had recently solved: a silver-headed cane. Many men carried canes, and just about any of them could bash a man's head in if wielded correctly.

"That's what he used," Sullivan said, pointing.

A brass loving cup lay on the floor where someone had dropped it. Frank walked over and hunkered down beside it. Blood and a few hairs clung to the rounded, marble base. The sunlight streaking through the windows glittered off the metallic finish, highlighting the engraving. Mr. Nehemiah Wooten had won first place in sculling at Harvard University over thirty years ago. Maybe if he had lost on that long-ago day, he'd still be alive.

"It was sitting over here," Sullivan informed him, pointing to a credenza that sat against the wall. Sullivan was enjoying being the one with all the information, Frank noted.

When Frank stood up, he saw that the credenza was covered with various large and heavy trophies from Mr. Wooten's athletic youth. His killer would have had his pick.

"Is anything missing?" Frank asked, looking around for signs of a robbery.

"He didn't have any money in his pockets, but his watch is still there," Sullivan said with a shrug.

Which meant that the beat cop who got there first probably took whatever ready money Mr. Wooten had on him. He'd have left the watch, since it would be too hard to get rid of without attracting attention. A real thief would have taken the watch and anything else of value. Frank could see some fancy pieces on the desk that looked like they might be silver. A real thief would've taken that stuff, too.

"I don't suppose anybody else was working in the building this afternoon," Frank mused.

"Not that we know of yet."

Frank walked around to the other side of the desk. Wooten probably had an appointment book. Maybe he'd noted the name of this killer in a neat, businessman's handwriting that would make Frank's job very easy. He rummaged through the drawers.

The top one contained several sheets of paper with columns of numbers written in a neat hand, added up with some of the sums circled. Beneath it was a ledger of some kind. Wooten must have been looking at the accounts. Beneath the ledger, he found what he was looking for, an appointment book, but the page for today contained only one entry—an appointment to meet Higginbotham at two o'clock. Frank sighed and tossed it back into the drawer where he'd found it, and replaced the ledger and the papers. The desk yielded nothing else of interest except a half-empty bottle of very good Scotch whiskey. Frank tossed it to Sullivan, who caught it deftly.

"For your trouble," Frank explained. Sullivan grinned, and dropped the bottle into his baggy coat pocket.

Frank rose from the chair and started back around the desk when his foot hit something on the floor and sent it rolling. "What's this?" he asked, bending to pick it up. It was a small tube that appeared to be made of ivory with a brass tip on one end. The other end appeared to have been broken off something.

"What is it?" Sullivan asked, coming over to examine it.

"Looks like part of a mechanical pencil," Frank said, giving it to him.

"Broke in half. Where was it?"

"Here on the floor," Frank said, looking down to see if he could find the other half.

"Wooten didn't seem like the type to leave broken pencils laying around on the floor," Sullivan observed.

"No, he doesn't. Help me look for the other half."

Sullivan found it on the other side of the room where it had rolled up against the wall. "That's funny," he remarked, handing it to Frank. "How did it get way over there?"

"It's almost like somebody threw it there," Frank said, "but why throw part of it in one direction and part in the other?"

"If you wanted to get rid of it, like this," Sullivan said, pretending to toss something away in opposite directions with both hands.

"Funny way to get rid of a broken pencil, though," Frank observed, examining the broken ends. It had separated where the brass top fitted into the ivory grip.

"You're right. Maybe he broke somebody's pencil, and they got mad and clocked him in the head," Sullivan joked.

"Yeah, that's probably what happened. I'd kill somebody for breaking my mechanical pencil," Frank agreed, dropping the pieces into his pocket. "Do we know where Wooten lived?"

"Higginbotham gave me his address."

"He have any family besides the deaf daughter?"

"A wife and son. Somebody needs to break the news to them."

"I'm surprised Higginbotham hasn't done that already," Frank said.

"He wanted to, but I made him stay here."

"Thanks," Frank said sincerely. Seeing the family's initial reaction to a murder could tell a lot.

A commotion in the corridor heralded the arrival of the medical examiner. Doc Haynes appeared in the doorway and stopped, taking in the entire scene with his world-weary eyes. "What have we got here?" he asked of no one in particular.

"Just what you see," Frank said. "Sullivan here will fill you in. I have to question a witness before he decides he wants to go home."

He left the two men to examine the body and found Higginbotham in the room where he'd left him. Somebody had brought him a glass of water, but he looked like he needed something a lot stronger. Frank began to regret giving the whiskey to Sullivan.

"Oh, Mr. Malloy, have you found out how this happened yet?" Higginbotham asked eagerly, half rising from his chair.

Frank motioned him to stay seated, and pulled out a chair for himself. Seated at a right angle to Higginbotham, he'd be able to watch his every expression. "It's too early to know anything for certain yet," he said, taking from his pocket a pencil and the small notebook he used to jot down important facts. "What can you tell me about Mr. Wooten?"

"I . . . I'm not sure what you need to know," Higginbotham said uncertainly.

"What did he do for a living, for instance?" Frank looked around for some indication of what sort of business was conducted in this building, but saw nothing helpful.

"I'm not sure," Higginbotham said. "He called himself a broker. I believe he helped companies who made products find customers to buy them."

"It must pay well," Frank observed.

"Oh, Mr. Wooten was always very generous to the school. And his family wanted for nothing, I'm sure."

Frank nodded. "Do you know if he had any enemies?"

"Oh, no, I wouldn't know anything about that," Higginbotham assured him. "Everyone who knew Mr. Wooten loved him. He was a kind and generous man. Very good to his family. Did I mention that?"

"Yes, you did," Frank said dryly, not bothering to point out that at least one person who knew Mr. Wooten hated him enough to murder him. "Mr. Sullivan said you didn't see anyone else in the building when you arrived."

"No, no, I didn't. I didn't expect to, you see. It's Saturday and the office closed at noon."

"How did you get in?"

"The front door was open. It sometimes was. I didn't think anything of it then."

"I don't suppose you know if Mr. Wooten was supposed to meet with anybody else this afternoon?"

"Oh, no, he wouldn't have confided that to me."

"What was your meeting about today?"

Higginbotham hesitated, and Frank's instinct told him he'd finally found a subject that might be worth pursuing. "I . . . Nothing that would have anything to do with his death, I'm sure."

"I don't think we can be sure of that just yet," Frank said, "since we don't know who killed him or why. So what were you going to discuss with him?"

Higginbotham shifted uneasily in his chair. "Mr. Wooten . . . Well, he was concerned about his daughter, Electra."

"Electra?" Frank echoed in surprise. "That's a funny name."

"It's Greek," Higginbotham said a bit defensively. "Mr. Wooten was a Greek scholar in his youth."

Frank nodded, mentally dismissing Wooten's youthful scholarship. "Was the girl having trouble in school?"

"Oh, no, not at all. Electra is an excellent student. A lovely girl. Everything a father could want in a daughter."

"Except she's deaf," Frank reminded him.

Higginbotham bristled at that. "I'm surprised to hear you say a thing like that, Mr. Malloy."

"I didn't mean it as a criticism," Frank said mildly. "I'm sure if Mr. Wooten had his choice, he'd choose that his daughter not be deaf."

"I can't speak for Mr. Wooten," Higginbotham said stiffly.

"I'm not asking you to," Frank reminded him. "So if this Electra is such a good student, why were you meeting with her father today?"

"She . . . Oh, dear, I hate to break a confidence."

"Mr. Wooten was murdered," Frank reminded him. "He doesn't have any privacy anymore. If we're going to find out who killed him, we have to know everything about him, even if it's embarrassing to him . . . or to his daughter."

"But I'm sure it had nothing to do with his . . . his unfortunate death."

"Then you don't have to worry about telling me, do you?"

Higginbotham wrung his plump hands in an agony of indecision. "If it really has nothing to do with his death, will you promise not to tell anyone else?"

"Of course," Frank lied. He never knew when a piece of information might come in handy to frighten another suspect into confessing.

"Well, you see, Electra, she . . . she is a lovely young lady, as I believe I mentioned."

"Yes, you did," Frank said, encouraging him.

"Naturally . . . I mean, quite naturally, because nothing could be more normal in young people, no matter what their situations, and I'm sure no one can place any blame at all because young people will find each other, no matter what—"

"Mr. Higginbotham," Frank snapped, losing patience with him. "No one is going to blame you for anything. Just tell me what you were going to talk to Wooten about."

"Oh, dear, please forgive my rambling. I'm quite unnerved, I'm afraid. I've never seen a murdered man before."

"I'll forgive it if you stop doing it," Frank offered sternly.

"Oh, yes, of course. Well, what were you asking me?"

"What you were going to talk to Wooten about . . . ?"

"Yes, yes, of course. Electra, you know. She is so young, only sixteen, although in my time, I've seen girls marry at that age and be perfectly happy, but of course, Mr. Wooten didn't approve—"

"Are you saying that Electra wanted to marry somebody her father didn't approve of?" Frank tried not to betray his excitement. Frustrated lovers were very likely suspects for murder.

"I can't say he didn't approve, not exactly," Higginbotham hedged.

"What did he do, then, exactly?"

"He . . . Well, you see, the young man Electra wished or rather *wishes* to marry is also deaf."

"And Wooten didn't want her to marry a deaf man?" Frank asked, a little surprised. He'd met some deaf couples in the past year who seemed very happy together.

"It was more than that," Higginbotham hastened to explain. "Mr. Wooten was a student of eugenics."

"What is eugenics?"

"I'm not sure of the exact definition, but Mr. Wooten believed that the human race should be improved by eliminating people with certain . . . certain flaws."

"Flaws? You mean like being deaf?"

"That is one, yes," Higginbotham reluctantly admitted.

Frank considered this. "Are you saying that Wooten believed deaf people should be killed?"

"Oh, no, not at all!" Higginbotham hastily explained. "His own daughter is deaf, after all!"

"Then what did he want to do to 'eliminate' them?"

"He didn't think deaf people should marry each other, so they wouldn't produce deaf children. His fear was that the intermarriage of deaf people would produce an entire race of deaf people."

That made a certain amount of sense to Frank, except for one thing. "Do deaf people mostly have deaf children?" His son, Brian, was the child of two people who had normal hearing, and he knew at least one deaf couple who had produced two children who could hear perfectly well.

"I have to say that I have not observed this to be true," Higginbotham said carefully. "In fact, only a few of the children in our school have even one deaf parent, and only one has parents who are both deaf. Even your own son has at least one hearing parent."

"Two. My wife wasn't deaf either," Frank informed him. "Then why do you think deaf people shouldn't marry?"

"I don't think any such thing," Mr. Higginbotham said, a bit exasperated. "I was merely explaining to you what Mr. Wooten believed."

"Then you don't believe in this . . . what was that word?"

"Eugenics," Higginbotham supplied.

"Eugenics," Frank repeated. "You don't believe in it?"

"No, I do not."

"Where did Wooten get an idea like that, then?"

"From Mr. Alexander Graham Bell. He attended one of Mr. Bell's lectures on the subject."

"Bell? The man who invented the telephone?" Frank asked. "What does he have to do with this?'

"Mr. Bell is very interested in helping the deaf. Both his wife and his mother are deaf, you see. In fact, his research into hearing devices was what led him to invent the telephone."

"The curse of modern life," Frank said in disgust.

"Indeed, although it can be handy sometimes."

"Sometimes," Frank conceded. "So Bell set out to help the deaf, and now he wants to stop them from marrying each other so they don't make more deaf people."

"I don't mean to sound critical of Mr. Bell . . . or of Mr. Wooten, for that matter. They are both good men, and they only want the best for deaf people. It's just . . . Well, I'm sure you understand how headstrong young people can be."

"Especially when they think they're in love," Frank agreed. "What did Wooten expect you to do about his daughter's romance?"

"I'm not sure," Higginbotham said. "We were going to discuss it today, but . . ."

"Who is this boy she was in love with?"

"I don't know his name."

Frank looked up from his notebook in surprise. "Isn't he a student at your school?"

"No, he . . . He's actually a teacher at another school, the New York Institution for the Deaf and Dumb."

Brian's school. "That school teaches sign language," Frank said.

"Yes, it does." Higginbotham obviously disapproved.

Frank had done a lot of investigation before choosing a school for Brian. The Lexington Avenue School taught their students to speech-read and speak and didn't allow them to use signs at all.

"How did this girl, Electra, meet somebody from that school?"

"I'm sure I don't know," Higginbotham said. "All I can tell you is that Mr. Wooten did not intend to allow his daughter to marry a deaf man. Not just this deaf man in particular, you understand. He objected to the very idea that any two deaf people should marry. This is why he sent Electra to our school, so she would learn to speak and to understand the spoken word. Hearing people can understand her, and she can understand them. She can make her way in the world, Mr. Malloy. That was Mr. Wooten's wish."

Frank understood that very well. He'd had the same wish for Brian.

"Malloy?"

Frank looked up to see Sullivan in the doorway. "Doc Haynes is ready to take the body. You want to talk to him before he goes?"

"Yeah, I'll be there in just a minute."

"May I go now?" Higginbotham asked. "I'm really feel-ing rather ill and——"

"Just give me your address, in case I need to speak to you again." Frank took the information and sent the man on his way just before the orderlies carried Wooten's body out on a stretcher. Frank was glad Higginbotham didn't have to see that.

"Did you find out anything?" Frank asked the medical examiner.

"Somebody bashed his head in with a loving cup," Haynes said. "I guess you already knew that, though. I'll let you know if I find out anything else, but I didn't see any other injuries, so that's probably what killed him."

"Did he die right away?"

"The blow would have knocked him unconscious. From the amount of blood on the floor, he lived awhile, but not more than half an hour and probably a lot less. He never moved once he hit the floor."

"Thanks, Doc."

Frank watched as Doc and his orderlies took the body out and loaded it into an ambulance. The crowd around the front steps parted for the procession and gawked curiously at the shrouded body, asking questions that the orderlies ignored.

"Do any of those bums work here?" Frank asked Sullivan.

"No, but I managed to find the name of Wooten's part-ner. Terrance Young. Here's his address." He handed a page ripped from a notebook similar to Frank's with an address scrawled on it. Or rather two addresses. "The other one is Wooten's. Somebody needs to notify the widow."

"I'll do that," Frank said. "And the partner, too."

Frank thought Sullivan looked relieved. "Let me know if

you need anything. I'll clear everybody out of the building and lock up. I found Wooten's keys in his pocket."

"I'll tell this Young fellow you have them," Frank said by way of warning. If anything went missing from the building, Sullivan would get the blame. "Make sure they get back here to him on Monday morning."

"I will," Sullivan promised.

Frank took his leave, wondering grimly if he might have ended up a drunken sot like Sullivan after his wife died if he hadn't had Brian to take care of. At the time, grief-stricken over his loss, he'd certainly been tempted to abandon the boy, who'd been born with a crippled foot. He hadn't even known then that Brian was deaf. If he had, would that have made a difference? Would that have made the burden of caring for his son too much to bear? Frank was glad he didn't know the answer to that question. He headed uptown to the address he had for the Wooten family.

THE WOOTENS LIVED IN A COMFORTABLY LARGE HOUSE on the Upper West Side of Manhattan. The maid looked frightened when she saw who was at the door. Although Frank wore the same kind of dark suit every other businessman in the city wore and the same kind of derby hat that every other man wore, something about him always told people he was the police. He'd often thought it was his Irish face. For decades, the police force had been the only source of steady employment for the Irish. But deep down he knew it was probably the way years on the police force had hardened that Irish face.

Frank gave the maid his card. "I need to see Mrs. Wooten. It's about her husband."

Now the girl looked terrified. Her blue eyes widened, and she darted away, disappearing into the house and leaving the front door hanging open. She hadn't invited Frank inside, but he took the liberty of admitting himself, if only to close the front door and keep out the flies. He could have made himself at home, but he waited politely until the girl came scurrying back down the stairs and invited him to meet her mistress in the sitting room.

Mrs. Wooten was what Frank's mother would have called a fine-looking woman. Not beautiful or even pretty, but everything about her spoke of quality, from her carefully styled hair to the toes of her kid leather shoes. Her impressively buxom figure was encased in a dark blue gown. She was standing when he entered the room, barely waiting for the maid to announce him.

"That's all, Annie," Mrs. Wooten said. Her voice was low and oddly sensual. Frank felt the effect of it in the pit of his stomach. As the door clicked shut behind the girl, Mrs. Wooten visibly gathered herself, straightening ever so slightly, as if preparing to receive a blow. "What has happened to my husband?"

"You should sit down, Mrs. Wooten," Frank said.

"He's dead then," she replied flatly. To Frank's surprise, the stiffness relaxed, almost as if . . . Frank could hardly credit it, but she seemed almost *relieved*. "I should have known when he didn't come home. He said he'd be here by four." She sighed, but she didn't seem the least bit grief-stricken.

"Should I call your maid?"

"That idiot girl? Certainly not." Her hands were clasped at her waist, and Frank noticed the knuckles were white. At least she wasn't quite as unmoved as she appeared. "Tell me what happened. An accident, I suppose."

"Mrs. Wooten, you should sit down," Frank tried again.

Her eyes might have been attractive at another time. They were a startling shade of blue, but at the moment they were glacial. "Just tell me and get it over with."

"He was murdered," Frank said.

At least she had the grace to look surprised. If he could call the brief widening of her eyes true surprise. "Murdered?" she echoed as if the word left a bad taste in her mouth.

"Yes, murdered. Someone killed him."

Frank watched her carefully, but she betrayed nothing else.

"Who did it?" she asked after a moment, and once again she looked as if she were bracing herself for a blow.

This was very strange. Family members always wanted to know the details, how did it happen and all that. Mrs. Wooten was oddly uncurious. "We don't know yet."

And once again she looked almost relieved. She drew a breath. "This is all very . . . unpleasant, Mr. . . . What was your name again?"

"Malloy," Frank supplied. "Murder usually is, Mrs. Wooten. I'd like to ask you a few questions, if you don't mind."

"What could you possibly want to ask me?" Now she was alarmed, or almost. She'd been trained very well to hide her true feelings, so maybe Frank was just misreading her.

"Well, for one thing, do you know anyone who might've wanted to kill your husband?"

"Certainly not," she assured him. "Men like my husband simply do not get themselves murdered. It's unthinkable!"

"But not impossible," Frank pointed out. "And I'm sure you want us to find out who did it and see that he's punished."

Frank might have been sure, but Mrs. Wooten didn't look

sure at all. In fact, she looked extremely doubtful. "Perhaps I will sit down after all," she decided.

She moved over to one of the sofas and lowered herself onto it very carefully, as if afraid the slightest jar might shatter her. She did not invite Frank to be seated, however. She wouldn't want him to think he could stay.

Frank figured he'd better ask a few more questions while he had the chance. She could dismiss him at any moment, and he wouldn't dare refuse to leave. A complaint about him from someone like Mrs. Wooten could mean the end of his career. "Do you know who your husband was meeting with today?"

"I don't think that's any of your business, Mr. Malloy," she said coldly.

"It is if that person killed him," Frank said, hoping to shock her into cooperation. He'd never seen anyone react like this to news of a spouse's death.

She gave him a look that could have cut glass, but she said, "He was meeting with an official from our daughter's school, but he couldn't possibly be—"

"Mr. Higginbotham," Frank supplied. "Yes, I know. He's the one who found the . . . found your husband. But he didn't kill him. Do you know if he was planning to meet with anybody else?"

"No, I do not. My husband didn't bother me with details of his business affairs."

"And do you know if he was having any kind of trouble with anybody? Maybe somebody had threatened him."

"If so, he said nothing of it to me. I told you, I have no idea who might have done this terrible thing. I'm going to have to ask you to leave now, Mr. Malloy. I'm very upset by your news, as you can imagine."

She didn't exactly look upset to Frank, but he wasn't

going to argue with her. Even if she knew something, she wasn't going to tell him, at least not right now.

He was just about to take his leave when the door flew open. They both looked up in surprise to see a young woman burst into the room. Frank's first impression was of singular beauty—creamy, white skin and raven black hair and a face that looked as if it had been carved by the hand of a master. Her appearance was all the more stunning because her braided hair and her youthful clothes indicated she was a mere schoolgirl.

"Mother, what's happened?" she demanded in a startlingly odd voice, not at all the refined accent he had expected from Mrs. Wooten's daughter. The words were strained, the inflection uneven. "Annie is crying because the police are here." She gave Frank a scathing glance before turning back to her mother.

Mrs. Wooten had risen to her feet, and Frank saw that the girl's appearance had shattered her calm. Suddenly, she looked almost frightened. "Electra, go to your room. I'll explain later."

Electra. The deaf girl. That explained her odd-sounding voice.

"Annie said something happened to Father," she was saying. "Tell me!"

"Electra," Mrs. Wooten said, shaking her head in some kind of warning.

But the girl ignored it. She turned to Frank instead. "What happened to him?" she demanded.

Frank knew that the students at the Lexington Avenue School could speech-read. He wasn't sure how difficult it was for them to do, so he spoke slowly and distinctly, just in case. "Your father was murdered."

She frowned, her lovely brow wrinkling in confusion. She turned back to her mother. "Murdered?" she asked.

"Yes," Mrs. Wooten said with great reluctance. "Your father is dead."

Electra absorbed the news for a second. Frank waited, expecting an explosion of tears, but none of the emotions playing across her beautiful face was grief. The one she finally settled on looked very much like satisfaction, and then she lifted her pert little chin and said, "Good."

2

"Electra!" her mother tried, but the girl wasn't looking at her, so she did not know she'd been reprimanded.

"Why is it good?" Frank asked, curious.

"Because he won't torment me anymore," the girl said in the instant before her mother reached her.

Mrs. Wooten grabbed her arm and wrenched the girl around to face her. "Electra, go to your room!" she commanded when she had the girl's attention. Then Mrs. Wooten looked over at Frank. "She doesn't know what she's saying. She probably didn't even understand what you told her. She's deaf, you see, and—"

"I understood!" Electra cried, fury staining her porcelain cheeks crimson. "I'm deaf, not stupid!"

Frank silently cursed Mrs. Wooten. Without her there, he could probably learn some very interesting facts about the dead man from his ungrateful child. The mother wasn't going to let him find out anything, though.

"I know this is a shock," he said when the girl turned her angry gaze on him again. "I'm sorry about your father."

"*I'm* not!" the girl informed him defiantly.

For a second, Frank thought Mrs. Wooten would slap her, but she must have decided she didn't want Frank to see her lose control. She settled for giving Electra's arm another violent shake, drawing the girl's attention back to her face.

"Go to your room at once," she said, her own cheeks scarlet with fury.

Electra jerked her arm free of her mother's grasp, and with one last rebellious glare, she turned and strode out without bothering to close the door behind her. Being deaf, she probably didn't realize the dramatic effect of a loudly slammed door. Before Frank or Mrs. Wooten could think of what to do next, the red-eyed maid appeared in the doorway, looking terrified.

"Show Mr. . . ." Mrs. Wooten had forgotten Frank's name again. "Show this gentleman out, Annie."

"If you think of anyone who might have wished Mr. Wooten harm," Frank said, offering her his card, "let me know."

Mrs. Wooten ignored the card, and she ignored him, gazing at something only she could see as he followed the maid out. On a table by the front door sat a silver salver, and Frank tossed his card onto it, along with all the other cards from the society people who came to visit the Wootens.

"Is it true?" the maid whispered as she handed Frank his hat. "Is Mr. Wooten dead?"

"Yes, he is," Frank assured her. "Somebody bashed his skull in."

The blood drained from the girl's face, and for an awful

moment Frank thought she might faint. This was the reaction he'd expected from Electra Wooten. She crossed herself quickly, but she didn't faint, thank God.

"Did you like working for Mr. Wooten?" he asked kindly.

"I'm sure I couldn't say," the girl said tentatively.

Which meant she didn't, of course. "His daughter didn't like him much," he observed.

"Miss Electra has a hard life," the girl said. "She's deaf, you know."

"My son is deaf, too," Frank said, hating to use Brian this way, but knowing he needed to reach someone in this house if he had any hope of getting information.

Her eyes widened in outrage. "I don't believe it!"

"It's true. He was born that way. He's only four, but he goes to the New York Institution for the Deaf and Dumb."

"That's Mr. Oldham's school!" the girl said in surprise, then quickly covered her mouth.

"Mr. Oldham?" Frank echoed. "Is he a student there, too?"

"I'm sure I couldn't say," the girl said, frightened again. She knew she'd revealed too much, although Frank had no idea what she had revealed.

She might not be able to say, but Frank knew who he could ask about it. Meanwhile, he would work on the maid. "My son is learning sign language," Frank said. "Does Miss Electra know how to sign?"

Now she really was terrified. "Oh, no, sir, not at all. Mr. Wooten, he would never allow it, not for anything! Miss Electra, she can tell what you're saying by looking at your lips. I don't know how she does it, but she does. She went to school to learn it. Not Mr. Oldham's school, another school. And she can talk as good as anybody, too."

Electra did speak extremely clearly, Frank had to admit. "Yes, she can. It's amazing. She's real mad at her father, though. Did he mistreat her?"

The girl's eyes grew wide again, and this time he knew he'd gone too far. "You better leave now," she said, scurrying around him to open the front door. "Mrs. Wooten, she'll be mad if you don't."

Frank nodded as he passed her on the way out. "Thank you, Annie. You've been very helpful."

"Oh, no, sir, I never!" she cried in dismay and slammed the door behind him.

Frank took a moment to place his derby hat firmly on his head before making his way down the Wootens' front steps. He wondered if he had enough time to visit Wooten's partner before the man went out for the evening. He wanted to get to him before he heard about Wooten's death from someone else, so he'd better try. And then he'd go home, where he could find out everything he might want to know about the mysterious Mr. Oldham.

F RANK DOUBLE-CHECKED THE ADDRESS THAT SULLIVAN had scribbled down for him. Terrance Young lived in a respectable town house only a few blocks from the Wootens. The girl who answered his knock was more experienced than the Wootens' Annie. She glared at him.

"Tradesmen use the kitchen door," she said and would have slammed the door in his face if he hadn't braced his hand against it.

"I'm Detective Sergeant Frank Malloy with the New York City Police," he informed her, shoving his card at her through the opening. "I need to see Mr. Young about his partner."

"I don't know if Mr. Young is home," the girl hedged, eyeing his card as if it were a poisonous snake. When rich people didn't want to see someone, they just had their servants say they weren't home. Frank wasn't going to let the girl turn him away.

"Let him decide," Frank suggested. "Tell him what I said. He'll want to hear this news tonight."

She finally accepted the card, but she said, "You'll have to wait here," and forced the door shut in his face.

Frank waited, fuming, on the stoop until the door opened again. This time she stood back and let him enter. Her expression told him how much she hated escorting someone like him into her master's house, but she led him up the stairs and into a stuffy room that had been decorated to within an inch of its life with figurines and bric-a-brac and antimacassars on overstuffed furniture and doilies on every flat surface and heavy velvet draperies that kept the sun from fading everything. A large portrait of a young woman hung over the fireplace. The artist's skill had not been able to disguise the fact that she wasn't very attractive, and she certainly wasn't very happy.

A burly man, Terrance Young looked as if he'd been stuffed into his well-made clothing. A roll of fat bulged over his stiff collar, and his round face had flushed red with annoyance. "What's this about Wooten?" he demanded as soon as the maid had closed the door behind him. "And don't try asking me to donate to the police benevolent society. I know how you scalawags operate."

Frank could have taken offense, but then he'd never find

out anything from Terrance Young. "Is Nehemiah Wooten your business partner?"

"Of course he is," Young snapped. "You already know that or you wouldn't be here. Just tell me what you came here for and get out. I have an engagement this evening, and I don't want to be late."

"Mr. Wooten is dead."

Mr. Young looked confused. "Dead? What are you talking about?"

"Mr. Wooten is dead. He's been murdered."

"Murdered! That's impossible!" He glared at Frank the way his maid had, angry at him for being so unpleasant.

"I'm afraid it's very possible. He was attacked in his office this afternoon and killed. A Mr. Higginbotham found his body when he arrived for an appointment."

Young frowned, trying to take it all in. "Higginbotham? He's from that deaf school, isn't he? The one Electra goes to."

"That's right."

"Murdered, you say? That . . . That's unbelievable." He passed a hand over his face and reached a finger into his collar, as if trying to loosen it. "How did it happen? Who did it?"

He was asking the right questions. "We don't know yet. It looks like he got into an argument with someone who attacked him."

"Nehemiah?" Young scoffed. "He never got into arguments. He told you what he wanted, and you either liked it or you got out of his way. Smarter than everybody else, or so he thought. Always right about everything." Young sounded almost bitter. He walked over to a sideboard where a crystal decanter sat, surrounded by matching glasses. He pulled the stopper out of the decanter and poured himself a generous measure of whiskey. Then he lifted the glass to his lips and downed it in one gulp.

Frank waited patiently, knowing his silence would probably produce more information than a rush of questions.

Young stood still, staring at the wall above the sideboard for a long moment before suddenly remembering he wasn't alone. He turned back to Frank. "Is that what you came to tell me? That Nehemiah is dead?"

"I also need to ask you some questions," Frank said, reaching into his pocket for his notebook.

"Questions? I don't know anything about this. I never even go into the office on Saturday anymore. I haven't seen Wooten since . . ." He had to think, and whatever he was thinking made him scowl. "Since Thursday afternoon."

"Maybe you know someone who might have disliked Mr. Wooten," Frank tried.

Young gave a bark of bitter laughter. "Someone who disliked him? I don't know anybody who *didn't* dislike him! I told you, he was always right. People tend to take offense at that after a while."

"Someone in particular, then?" Frank suggested. "Maybe something that happened recently? A dissatisfied business associate, maybe?"

"People in business are always dissatisfied, but they don't go around killing each other over it," he said, angry now, although Frank couldn't figure out why. "If somebody killed him, it was probably a robbery or something."

"Nothing was stolen," Frank said.

Young liked to be right, too. His flush deepened at Frank's challenge. "A lunatic, then. Some crazy man who broke into the office."

Frank pretended to write that down. "But how would a lunatic know Mr. Wooten was alone in his office on a Saturday afternoon?"

"How should I know?" Young cried in exasperation. "That's your job to find out."

"I wonder if Mr. Wooten was having some family troubles," Frank mused, pretending to study something written in his notebook, and when he looked up, he was surprised by a look of alarm on Young's now-perspiring face.

"What do you mean?" he asked uneasily.

"Lots of people have family troubles," Frank pointed out. "Do you have children, Mr. Young?"

Oddly, he blanched at the question. "What does that have to do with anything?"

"Nothing," Frank allowed. "I was just thinking that if you have children of your own, then you know how it is when they grow up. They don't want to obey you anymore. Mr. Wooten has children, and he wasn't a very tolerant man."

"Nonsense! Are you suggesting Electra killed her father?" he demanded.

Apparently, Electra's opinion of her father was well known. "Did she want to?" Frank countered.

The color flooded back to Young's face. "I've had enough of this," he said. "Get out of my house."

Frank sighed. He'd have to stop questioning Young now. "I'll need to come to your office on Monday and question everybody who was there this morning."

"Is that really necessary?" he asked with distaste.

"Maybe one of them saw something that will help. A suspicious stranger, maybe," Frank added, knowing that idea would appeal to Young.

"I suppose there's no help for it," he said. "But don't try any of your third degree on my employees."

"I'm sure that won't be necessary," Frank said, holding his temper with difficulty. "I'll leave my card in case you need to contact me."

"I won't," Young assured him. "I told you, I don't have any idea who might have killed Wooten."

"Someone else might," Frank said. "And they might confide in you. I know you'll want to do everything you can to find out who killed your partner."

Young didn't even pretend to agree.

Frank closed his notebook and slipped it back into his coat pocket. "Oh, by the way, what happens to Mr. Wooten's share of your business?"

He'd surprised Young again. "I can't imagine that's any of your concern," he tried.

"It is if it gave somebody a reason to kill him. Does it go to you?"

"Absolutely not! It goes to his son, Leander."

Frank wondered if Leander shared his sister's opinion of their father. He'd make it a point to find out.

FRANK HEARD THE CLATTER OF RUNNING FEET ON THE stairs the moment he entered the familiar tenement building. His son, Brian, was running to meet him. He paused, savoring first the sound of his son running, something he wondered if he'd ever get used to, and then the sight of him. His small face was alight with happiness as he jumped the last three steps, straight into Frank's arms.

He hugged the boy fiercely, inhaling his scent and absorbing the feel of his sturdy body. He was growing so fast.

For years Frank had thought of him as a baby because he'd been forced to crawl, unable to walk on his clubfoot. But now he could walk and even run, thanks to Sarah Brandt's interference in his life. She'd sent Brian to the best surgeon in the city, who had repaired the damaged foot. She'd even been the one who recognized that the boy was deaf and not simpleminded, as Frank had always thought.

No, there was nothing simple about Brian's mind at all, Frank thought as the boy pushed away and began frantically signing something to him. He recognized the sign for "grandmother," but not much else. He set Brian on the steps and took one of his hands to indicate they should go upstairs together. Brian frowned. He knew Frank couldn't understand his new language, and he didn't like it one bit, but scrambled up the stairs beside his father, knowing their interpreter waited upstairs in their flat.

"It's about time you got here," his mother's voice called as they stepped into the immaculate front room. Mrs. Malloy came out of the kitchen, wiping her hands on her apron. She was a small, plump Irishwoman whom life had aged far beyond her years. "The boy's been asking for you every five minutes."

"I know, but I just couldn't tear myself away from all those hoochie-coochie dancers down at the theater," Frank said as seriously as he could manage.

His mother's eyes grew wide with shock for a few seconds before she realized he was teasing her. She did not like being teased. "What a thing to say! In front of the boy, too!" she huffed, outraged.

"He can't hear me," Frank reminded her, unrepentant. "Do you have anything for me to eat?"

"Of course I do," she snapped, and then noticed Brian

frantically signing. "He wants you to help him put a puzzle together. I'll call you when the food's ready."

Frank shrugged out of his suit coat and slipped off his shoes before allowing the boy to drag him over to where he had partially assembled a wooden puzzle. They had it completed by the time his mother informed him she'd made him a sandwich.

Brian tried to protest Frank's leaving, but he hoisted the boy onto his shoulder and carried him into the kitchen with him. Mrs. Malloy gave the boy a cookie, and he was content to sit and watch his father eat his makeshift supper.

Frank waited until he was finished eating before asking the question that had been on his mind for several hours now. "Do you know a teacher named Oldham at Brian's school?"

Because Brian was only four, Mrs. Malloy accompanied him on the long trip to school each day. She'd been determined to make sure they treated the boy well, so she'd stayed to watch for the first few days, until she'd been recruited as a volunteer. Now she helped out every day, and she had learned to use signs almost as well as Brian had.

"Mr. Oldham? Why are you asking about him of all people?"

"Because I am," Frank said. He could be as contrary as she. "I met a family with a deaf child today, and his name came up. I'm wondering what you know about him."

"He's not in trouble, is he?" she asked in alarm. "Did something happen to him?"

Frank looked at her in surprise. She'd never shown that much concern about *him*! Not to his face, at least. "No, nothing happened to him. I told you, his name came up. So you do know him, I take it."

"Of course I know him," she snapped, annoyed about something he could only guess at. "He teaches the older students. A fine young man."

"What does that mean?"

"What does what mean?" she asked, still annoyed. She was always annoyed by Frank.

"That he's a fine young man. Does it mean he doesn't smoke or drink or does it mean he's a good teacher or does it just mean he's handsome?"

"I don't know where you get these ideas!" she exclaimed, snatching up the empty plate in front of him and carrying it over to the sink to wash.

Frank bit back a smile. "I guess that means he's handsome."

She gave him a glare over her shoulder, and Frank noticed Brian was watching the conversation with great interest. He could only imagine the boy's interpretation of what was going on. "He's a nice-looking young man, if that's what you mean," she conceded, "but he's also very responsible, and he doesn't smoke or drink, at least that I know of."

"He's a good teacher, then?"

"I suppose so. They wouldn't keep him if he wasn't. He's deaf, you know."

"I did know," Frank said, recalling that was the reason he was an unsuitable husband for Electra Wooten.

"If you know so much, why are you asking me about him?"

Frank bit back his own irritation. "Did you know he wanted to marry a deaf girl?"

This surprised her, he was gratified to see. She frowned as she dried the dish he'd used and put it into the cabinet. "I never heard nothing about it," she decided. "All the female students . . . Well, like I said, he's handsome, and girls can be silly. Even some of the teachers . . . But the female teachers aren't deaf, at least not most of them."

"This girl isn't a student there. She goes to the Lexington Avenue School."

Now she was even more surprised. "What would he want with a girl from there? They don't teach signing. How would he even talk to her?"

Frank thought that two healthy, attractive young people could probably figure that out, but he said, "That's a good question. Does Mr. Oldham know how to talk at all?"

"Not that I know of. How did you know about the girl?"

Frank ignored the question. "Do you know anything about his family?"

"No, why would I?"

Frank persevered. "Does it seem like he comes from rich people or poor people?"

"How would I know that?"

"His clothes, for one thing," Frank said impatiently. "Are they shabby, like he lives off what they pay him at the school, or are they expensive, like somebody else buys them for him?"

"Shabby," she said in disgust, but he wasn't sure what she was disgusted about. "They don't pay the deaf men teachers as much as they pay the ones who can hear, and the women get even less than that."

"Why don't they pay the deaf men as much?" Frank asked curiously. He didn't have to ask why they paid the women less. Women always got paid less.

"Because they don't have to," his mother said, shaking her head at his stupidity. "A deaf man can't work just anywhere, like a man who hears can. He has to take what they give him, and be happy about it."

"Just like the Irish," Frank said.

His mother frowned. She didn't like being reminded that, to many, being Irish Catholic still meant you weren't as good as other people. "Worse than that," she said, surprising him.

"What do you mean, worse?"

"I mean even if you're Irish, you can talk to people and know what they're saying back. You can go into a shop and buy something without using a pencil and paper to make yourself understood. You can listen to music or go to a play. You can go to church, if you've a mind to, and know what they're talking about."

Frank was sending Brian to school so someday he'd be able to support himself, and Frank didn't like thinking how limited Brian's opportunities would still be. "But you have to take the jobs they'll give you, Irish or deaf."

"Mr. Oldham, he went to college and everything. There's a college just for deaf people in Washington."

"And they taught him how to be a teacher?"

She gave him a withering glare. "Of course not! They don't teach deaf people to be teachers, not even at that deaf college. They taught him something else, but he wanted to be a teacher, so he came here, and they hired him."

"Even though he's deaf?"

She sniffed. "Like I said, they don't have to pay him as much as a hearing teacher."

"So they hired him because he's cheap."

She shrugged, apparently unwilling to speak for the school administrators. "You never did say why you're so interested in Mr. Oldham," she reminded him.

"A man was murdered this afternoon, and his daughter is deaf."

Her eyes widened. "Is she the girl Mr. Oldham was supposed to marry?"

"According to Mr. Higginbotham, who works at the Lexington Avenue School, where she goes."

"She's a student? How old is she?"

"Sixteen."

She was frowning again.

"What's the matter?" he asked.

"Seems a little young for Mr. Oldham."

"How old is he?"

"No more than thirty, I'd guess, but still . . ."

"She's a looker," Frank said.

This time her frown was more like a glower. "That still don't explain how he met her. Those people at the Lexington School . . ."

"What about them?" he asked when she hesitated.

"They don't mix," she said.

"Mix? Who don't they mix with?"

"With the other deaf people, the ones who use signs. It's like . . ."

"Like what?" Frank asked, growing impatient again.

"Like they think they'll catch something. They don't want their students to know anything about signing at all for fear . . . Well, I don't know exactly what they're afraid of, but they don't want them anywhere near somebody who uses signs."

Frank had known about the differences of opinion between those who taught speechreading and those who taught signing, but he didn't know it ran quite so deep. "Who told you all this?"

"Nobody in particular," she said indignantly. "The teachers just talk. They think it's important for me to know things, so I can take better care of Brian."

Frank looked at his mother as if he'd never seen her before. He'd known her all his life, of course, but she'd always just been his mother, someone who cooked and cleaned and sewed and gossiped with the neighbors. When Kathleen had died, and he'd needed someone to take care of Brian, she'd stepped in, but she'd just kept on doing the same things she'd always done.

Until now.

Now she was someone who was advising him on a murder case.

"What are you looking at?" she snapped, annoyed at him again.

"Nothing," he said, rising from his chair and helping Brian scramble down from his. After a moment, he asked, "What do you think a father would do if he found out his daughter who can speech-read and talk was being courted by a deaf man who used signs?"

"He wouldn't like it one bit," she said without the slightest hesitation.

"Would he forbid them to marry?"

"He'd forbid them to even see each other again."

"And what about your Mr. Oldham? What would he do?"

"He's not *my* Mr. Oldham!" she informed him indignantly.

"What would he do?"

She sniffed. "The same thing you'd do. Don't think he's any different from any other man, just because he's deaf."

Frank sighed as he let Brian lead him back into the front room, where his toys awaited. "That's what I was afraid of."

* * *

SARAH BRANDT SAT ON HER BACK PORCH, WATCHING HER
daughter, Catherine, and Catherine's nursemaid, Maeve,
as they pulled weeds from the flower bed they had planted
in the spring. Maeve was carefully explaining to Catherine
which of the sprouts were weeds and which were flowers, so
she didn't pull the wrong ones.

Sarah smiled, savoring the warm Sunday afternoon sunshine and the sweet domesticity of the moment. They'd all
been to church that morning—a rare opportunity, since Sarah's job as a midwife often kept her away from home. Now
that Sunday dinner was over, they had nothing to do but
enjoy the beautiful day.

The back gate opened, and they all looked up to see
Sarah's neighbor Mrs. Ellsworth entering. She was carrying a napkin-covered plate, and the girls hurried to greet
her. Maeve took the plate from her and offered her some
lemonade, which she gratefully accepted. After a few minutes, when Mrs. Ellsworth had been served and everyone had
sampled the cookies she had brought, the girls went back to
their gardening, leaving the two women sitting in the shade
of the porch, sipping their lemonade.

"You spoil us, Mrs. Ellsworth," Sarah said, holding up
the cookie she was about to eat.

"Who else do I have to spoil?" her neighbor replied.
An elderly widow who kept house for her grown son,
Nelson, she used to spend her days sweeping her front
stoop in order to know what everyone on Bank Street was
doing. Now she spent her days helping Sarah and Maeve
take care of the child Sarah had found at the Prodigal
Son Mission. Mrs. Ellsworth's gaze drifted to where Cath-

erine was enthusiastically pulling weeds. "She's doing so well."

"Sometimes I can't believe it myself," Sarah confirmed. "When I first brought her home, I was afraid she might never speak again." When Catherine had been found abandoned on the doorstep of the Mission a year earlier, she had been mute and, with one exception, hadn't spoken a word until she'd been living with Sarah for several weeks.

"Does she ever say anything about her past?" Mrs. Ellsworth asked.

"Not to me, but I haven't really asked if she remembers anything. The doctors I consulted said that she'd probably stopped speaking because something had terrified her, and I've been afraid to bring up bad memories."

"I don't blame you for that, but I thought she might have said something, maybe even without realizing it."

"She probably spends more time with you than she does with me," Sarah reminded her with a smile, "so you would know better than I."

Mrs. Ellsworth smiled back. "I do enjoy being with them both. But you're her mother, Mrs. Brandt."

"You know I'm not really her mother," Sarah reminded her.

"Maybe not legally," Mrs. Ellsworth said with a dismissive wave of her hand, discounting the technicality that forbade unmarried women from adopting. "But you're her mother in every way that matters, and she'd say things to you that she'd never say to me."

"Maybe she will, in time. But the doctors also said that she just might not remember anything at all from her previous life. Whatever shocked her into silence may have blocked out those memories, too."

"Maybe it's for the best, then. I'd hate for her to remember something terrible."

"Me, too, but . . ." Sarah sighed. "I also can't help wondering if she has a family somewhere who's been looking for her. As much as I love her and would hate to lose her, if her real mother is out there someplace, grieving for her . . ."

"There, there, now don't upset yourself. If someone did separate her from her family, it's not your fault. I know you'd do anything you could to bring them back together again, but you can't feel guilty about it when we both know how impossible that would be."

Sarah watched Catherine for another moment, and then said, "I just keep thinking about that female Pinkerton detective who helped us last spring."

"Do you think she'd be able to find out what happened to Catherine's family?" Mrs. Ellsworth asked in surprise.

"Not really," Sarah admitted. "Even a trained detective would need someplace to start, and we don't know a single thing about Catherine's background. I guess it's just wishful thinking."

"Maybe someday Catherine will tell you something that will help."

"Maybe," Sarah conceded without much enthusiasm.

The two women sat in companionable silence for a while, watching the two girls.

Suddenly, Mrs. Ellsworth said, "I wonder how Mr. Malloy's son is doing in that school."

Sarah looked at her sharply, but the older woman's expression was a mask of innocence. "I don't know," she admitted.

Mrs. Ellsworth looked surprised. "Haven't you seen Mr. Malloy lately?"

"You know I haven't," Sarah said, not fooled. "And no, I don't have any plans to see him either."

Mrs. Ellsworth frowned her disapproval. "I don't know what's wrong with that man. First, he's here every day, and then he disappears for weeks at a time."

"He's never here every day," Sarah corrected her, "and he's only here when he's investigating a murder that someone close to me is involved with."

"I suppose no one you know has been murdered lately, then," she said with a sigh.

Sarah bit back a grin at Mrs. Ellsworth's misplaced disappointment. "No, I'm happy to say, they haven't. My mother hasn't gotten herself involved in anything strange, and Maeve has been minding her own business, and none of my friends or acquaintances have been dispatched in an unnatural way."

"I suppose that is good news," Mrs. Ellsworth allowed. "But I really do wonder how his little boy is. He'll be back in school by now after the summer break, won't he?"

"He probably is," Sarah said, trying not to encourage any further discussion.

"I'm sure Catherine would love to see him."

"You're talking to the wrong person," Sarah said. "Mr. Malloy will have to bring him here, if Catherine is to see him."

Mrs. Ellsworth looked over with a twinkle in her eye. "Are you *sure* none of your friends has been murdered?"

Sarah rolled her eyes and resolutely looked away, out to where the girls were finishing up their gardening. Maeve was using the shears to cut the last of the summer's flowers to form a final bouquet as Catherine watched her intently. Sarah couldn't see the child's face, but her little body was nearly rigid with attention. Then Maeve glanced at the girl's face and her expression changed in an instant to alarm.

"Catherine?" Maeve asked. "What's wrong?" Then more urgently, "Catherine!"

Sarah was already out of her chair when Catherine began to scream.

3

FRANK DIDN'T REALLY HAVE A GOOD REASON TO VISIT Mr. Oldham on this lovely Sunday afternoon, but he didn't have anything better to occupy his time either. He couldn't question any of the people from Mr. Wooten's office until they reported for work on Monday, and he didn't think he should bother the Wooten family or Mr. Young again so soon. Besides, he wanted to be the one to break the news of Wooten's death to Mr. Oldham so he could see his reaction. If he waited much longer, Oldham might hear about it from somebody else.

Frank's mother had been able to tell him where Oldham lived. He didn't ask her how she knew, but since the address was near the school, he figured everyone knew where the handsome young teacher lived. He found the building without any trouble, and some children playing outside directed him to the right flat. After he'd knocked on the door, he realized a deaf man wouldn't be able to hear it, but before he could figure out an alternate method of making his presence known, the door opened.

A woman stood there. If she'd been to church that morning, she'd changed into a housedress with an apron over it. Her hair had been neatly pinned up at some time, but the natural curls had worked themselves loose during the day, forming wisps around her face, and she hadn't bothered to pin them back up. She appeared to be in her forties but was still a fine-looking woman. Her brown eyes took him in with one wary glance.

"Are you lost?" she asked in a pleasingly soft voice.

"I'm looking for Adam Oldham. Is this his flat?"

Her eyes narrowed. "What do you want with him?"

"I'm Detective Sergeant Frank Malloy from the New York City Police. I need to speak to him."

Now she was frightened. "About what?"

"I'll have to talk to *him* about that, ma'am."

She glanced over her shoulder, then stepped out into the hallway and pulled the door shut behind her. "I'm his mother, and he can't talk with you at all. He's deaf, you see, and—"

"I know he's deaf. I still have to talk to him."

She lifted her chin in silent defiance. "Then you'll have to talk to me first, because I'm not going to let you in until you tell me why you need to see him."

Frank looked at her feminine frame, as if considering whether he could force his way past her, but to her credit, she didn't flinch.

"If you lay hands on me, I'll scream," she informed him.

"Your son won't be able to hear you," Frank reminded her.

Surprisingly, *that* made her flinch, but before she could

reply, someone jerked the door open behind her. Frank looked into a face even he could see was amazingly handsome. Adam Oldham had his mother's dark eyes and almost feminine eyelashes. Her dark curly hair was merely unruly on him, giving him a rakish air that must have been enormously appealing to young girls. He wasn't tall and was slight of build, almost delicate, but a latent masculinity kept him from being effeminate.

His piercing gaze went from Frank to his mother, asking a silent question. Her hands moved, telling him something in the secret language of the deaf. Frank realized he should have brought his own interpreter, although finding one he could trust on a Sunday afternoon would have been nearly impossible. He'd expected to find Oldham alone and to use paper and pencil to communicate.

Oldham's face registered surprise and something else, the kind of wariness that most people felt when the police showed up at their door. His hands moved, asking her a question.

"What's he saying?"

"He wants to know why the police are here," she told him angrily.

"Invite me in, and I'll tell him," Frank replied.

"I'm not going to invite you in," she snapped, fury sparkling in her fine eyes.

"Tell him I'm Brian Malloy's father," Frank suggested.

"I'll do no such thing!"

"Then I will." Frank reached into his coat pocket and pulled out his notebook and pencil, but before he could even open the notebook, she was signing again, defeated.

Oldham's face lighted with recognition, and he nodded fiercely, signing a reply to his mother.

"Your son is a student at the school?" she asked in surprise.

"That's right, and my mother is a volunteer. Now can I come in, or do you want your neighbors knowing all about your business?" Frank added, glancing meaningfully around at the other doors on the corridor, which were all open at least a crack so the occupants could overhear—and observe—their conversation.

With a weary sigh, she signed something to Oldham, and he stepped back, allowing his mother and Frank to enter the flat's windowless kitchen.

The place was small but neat as a pin. The light coming from the front room showed that the dishes from their Sunday meal had been washed and sat draining beside the sink. A well-scrubbed wooden table and two chairs sat against one wall. To the rear of the flat would be a tiny bedroom, Frank knew. Oldham led them into the front room. Overlooking the street, it had been furnished as a parlor, with a shabby upholstered chair and small sofa. A narrow bed along the far wall showed it doubled as a bedroom, probably for Oldham.

A light breeze stirred the cheap curtains at the window. A newspaper lay on the floor beside the chair. He'd interrupted Oldham's Sunday afternoon relaxation. Frank wondered idly if the story of Wooten's murder has been printed yet.

Oldham motioned for Frank to sit down in the chair, and the young man snatched up the scattered newspaper pages, folding them neatly and laying them on the floor again. He and his mother took the sofa. Before she was even sitting, he began signing to her again.

"What's he saying?" Frank asked.

"He wants to know why you're here. Is something wrong with your son?"

"No, he's fine." Frank watched as she informed Oldham. Then he said, "I came to tell him that Nehemiah Wooten is dead."

She froze, her shock obvious. "Wooten? What happened to him?"

"Just tell him," Frank said, sitting back against the cushion and folding his hands across his stomach in a parody of nonchalance.

Oldham had seen his mother's surprise, and he was signing frantically, trying to get her to tell him what Frank had said.

She ignored him. Her full attention was still on Frank. "You don't sign yourself?"

"No," he said, resisting the urge to make an excuse. "How did *you* learn?"

"Adam taught me," she said simply.

Adam was shaking her arm, desperate for her attention. Finally, she gave it to him, signing slowly and then doing something rapidly with just her fingers, which Frank recognized as finger spelling. Would she have to spell Wooten's name for him? Frank thought it likely.

When she was finished, she dropped her hands into her lap, as if the effort had exhausted her, and she watched her son's face carefully. Frank watched it, too.

He had an expressive face, but he showed no expression now. His lively eyes grew blank, and his gaze moved warily to Frank. Frank waited patiently for his reply, and when he made none, she asked, "How did he die?"

"Ask your son, Mrs. Oldham."

"Sechrest," she said.

"I beg your pardon?"

"My name is Alexandra Sechrest," she said, her anger still

an undertone in her voice. "Adam's father died when he was a baby, and I remarried."

"Ask your son, Mrs. Sechrest."

"How would he know?" her voice rose, almost shrill.

"Ask him," Frank repeated mildly.

She signed to Adam, the movements swift and sharp, as if she were shouting.

Adam's head snapped around to Frank, his eyes alive again, this time with outrage. His answer also looked as if he were shouting.

"He doesn't know!" she said. "How could he?"

But he hadn't been at all curious about it, Frank noted. "He was murdered."

"Murdered?" she echoed in astonishment.

Adam was shaking her arm again, wanting to know what Frank had said. She signed it to him almost absently. He made a strange sound in his throat that might have been shock, but she hardly noticed.

"Adam didn't have anything to do with it," she was saying to Frank. "He's been with me all morning!"

"Did he go to church with you?"

That stopped her. "I was only gone an hour," she amended. "He wouldn't have had time to . . . He couldn't have!"

"Mr. Wooten wasn't killed this morning," Frank said, ending her misery. "Where was your son yesterday, Mrs. Sechrest?"

"Here, at home with me, all day," she insisted.

Adam was demanding an interpretation, and she started signing for him again. What he saw made him even angrier.

"He didn't leave the house at all?"

"He went out last night, but he went to a friend's house.

One of the other teachers. He'll tell you. He was there all evening."

Frank pulled out his notebook again. "What's his name?"

She signed something to Adam, who replied.

"Uriah Rossiter."

"Is he deaf, too?"

"No, he's not. But he teaches at the school with Adam."

And is paid much better, Frank thought, but he said, "Do you know where he lives?"

She consulted Adam and gave him the address.

"And the rest of the day he was here with you?"

"Yes, yes, I told you he was," she said, but Frank was pretty sure she was lying. "You can't accuse an innocent boy of murder just because he's deaf!"

Frank knew the police could accuse pretty much anybody they wanted of murder, but he didn't think that information would make Mrs. Sechrest any more cooperative.

Adam was signing something to his mother. She didn't like it.

"What's he saying?"

"He . . ." She had to swallow down her anger. "He wants to know if Electra is all right."

"Did you know that your son was acquainted with Electra Wooten?" Frank asked curiously.

Her lips thinned down the way Frank's mother's did when she disapproved strongly of something. "Yes, I know. She was a private student of his."

"Do you know how they met?"

She signed the question for Adam, who took offense.

"He says it's none of your business," she said with some satisfaction.

"Everything is my business," Frank said. "And if Adam doesn't tell me what I want to know, I'll take him down to Police Headquarters and lock him up until he does."

Mrs. Sechrest blanched again, and this time she didn't have to be prompted to start signing. Her hands flew as she frantically tried to communicate something to her son.

"What are you saying to him?" Frank asked.

The look she gave him was venomous. "I'm telling him what will happen to him if you take him down to the station house."

Whatever she'd told him had the desired effect. Oldham was frightened now, frightened and wary.

"How does your son know Electra Wooten?" Frank asked again.

She hated asking the question. Every movement she made radiated her fury.

Adam responded, equally reluctant, and her eyes widened in surprise. Frank waited patiently, giving her time to absorb the truth and to see if she would convey it to him voluntarily.

"He says . . . he was teaching her to sign," she said in confusion. She asked another question and was even more confused by his answer. "He says she is a student at the Lexington Avenue School. They don't teach signing there," she added by way of explanation for her surprise.

"I know," Frank said, as astonished as she to learn this information. "And Mr. Wooten would never allow her to learn. Is that how they met? Because he wanted to teach her to sign?"

She asked Oldham a question, and he replied.

"He says he was asked to meet with her and teach her privately."

"Who asked him?"

"He won't say," she replied after an exchange of signs. "He doesn't want to get anyone in trouble."

"So you knew your son was seeing Miss Wooten, but you didn't know why?" Frank asked her.

"I knew he'd met her someplace and was tutoring her privately. He was . . . smitten," she decided, choosing a word that didn't convey much romanticism. "I understand she's very beautiful," she added with a trace of bitterness.

"She is," Frank said, goading her. "But she's only sixteen."

She hadn't known that, and she wasn't pleased to know it now. She had to interpret for her son, and his reply was indignant.

"She's almost seventeen, he says," she told Frank wearily. She rubbed her forehead as if it had begun to ache. "I didn't know he was teaching her to sign. I thought she was just a rich deaf girl he'd met and—"

"Let me get this straight. Somebody he won't name introduced him to Miss Wooten and asked him to teach her to sign. Did her father know about this?"

She asked Oldham, who shook his head vehemently and signed something furiously in reply.

"No, he wouldn't allow her to sign. He wanted her to be *normal*." She said the word as if it left a bad taste in her mouth.

"I know," Frank assured her. "He wanted her to be able to understand what people who can hear said to her and to make herself understood by them. I've met her. She seems to do pretty well at both those things."

"Is it easy to understand what she says?" Mrs. Sechrest asked with interest.

"If you listen carefully," Frank said.

Mrs. Sechrest nodded. "And how many people in the world will take the time to do that? And how many will speak clearly to her and remember to look directly at her when they talk so she can read their lips? Even then, lip-readers often can't tell what people are saying. It's a very difficult skill to master."

"I know. That's why I sent my son to learn sign language," Frank said. "So who decided Electra Wooten needed to learn it?"

She asked her son. His answer surprised her.

"She did! She asked a friend to help her find someone to teach her," Mrs. Sechrest reported.

Having met Electra Wooten, Frank had no trouble believing the girl had taken matters into her own hands. The question is, why had she made the decision in the first place? Not that it mattered. Frank doubted the daughter's desire to learn to sign had driven someone to murder the father. Her desire to marry a deaf man might have, however. "Did you know your son wanted to marry Electra Wooten?"

She hadn't, but she didn't seem too upset by the notion. "Young men can get odd fancies when a beautiful girl is involved, but her family is very wealthy. They would never have allowed it."

Frank smiled wolfishly. "Which may be why someone murdered Nehemiah Wooten."

SARAH PICKED UP HER SKIRTS AND RACED DOWN THE porch steps and across the narrow yard to where Catherine's small body had gone rigid with terror. Mrs. Ellsworth was right behind her. By the time Sarah reached the child, Maeve had snatched her up, burying Catherine's face in her shoulder to drown the sounds of her screams.

Maeve was calling the child's name in an effort to break through to her, but she didn't seem to hear. Her little body shook from the force of the shrieks. Sarah snatched Catherine from Maeve's arms and slapped her lightly on the cheeks. Startled, she stopped screaming, blinked a few times, then seemed to suddenly realize Sarah was holding her.

"Mama, make it stop!" she wailed pitifully.

Sarah enfolded her and carried her back to the porch. She heard Mrs. Ellsworth sending Maeve for a glass of water for the child. When Sarah reached the chair where she'd been sitting moments ago, she sat down again, cradling Catherine in her lap.

"What happened, darling?" she asked the child.

"I saw them," she said in a small voice that was so terrified, Sarah's heart nearly broke.

"Who did you see?"

"The bad people. They came back."

Sarah looked up and saw Mrs. Ellsworth hovering, her eyes reflecting the same fear that Sarah felt. "They didn't really come back," Sarah said. "See, there's no one here but us."

"I saw them," Catherine said simply.

"They're gone now," Sarah tried.

Maeve had returned with a glass of water. Sarah took it and offered it to Catherine, who gulped it down.

"What were the bad people doing?" Maeve asked when the child had finished drinking. Sarah gave her a silent reprimand, but Maeve said, "She was looking straight at me when she started screaming. She was watching me cut the flowers." Maeve knelt down so she was on eye level with Catherine. "Were the bad people with me?"

"No, they were with the pretty lady," Catherine said. "She was cutting flowers, and they came." She looked up at Sarah. "I want to go inside now."

"Of course, my darling. We'll all go inside."

By the time they had moved indoors, Catherine's fright had faded, and she seemed calmer, almost normal. She asked Maeve to go upstairs with her and play with her dollhouse. When the girls were gone, Sarah and Mrs. Ellsworth sat down at the kitchen table.

"What do you suppose all that was about?" Mrs. Ellsworth asked.

"I have no idea. It was almost like she had a bad dream, except she was wide awake."

"Has she ever done anything like that before?"

"Not that I know of," Sarah said, "but there's so much I don't know about her. She's only been with me a few months. I'm not even sure how she acted at the Mission before I met her."

"Maeve should know that," Mrs. Ellsworth reminded her. "She was there."

"I'll have to ask her after Catherine goes to bed tonight. What do you suppose set her off?"

"She was watching Maeve cutting flowers. It must have reminded her of the pretty lady she was talking about. She said the lady was cutting flowers."

"And the bad people came. I hate to think what that means." Sarah shivered.

"Maybe it doesn't mean anything," Mrs. Ellsworth tried, but neither of them believed it.

* * *

THE LOOK ALEXANDRA SECHREST GAVE FRANK COULD
have cut glass. "You are a horrible man," she informed him.
"I already told you, my son had nothing to do with Mr.
Wooten's murder."

"Young love can be a powerful force," Frank said. "He
wanted to marry the girl, and you said yourself that her father never would've allowed it."

"I also said that my son was home all day yesterday. I
must ask you to leave now, Mr. Malloy," she added, rising to
her feet. "We can be of no further help to you."

Frank rose, too, and Oldham jumped to his feet as well.
He didn't like them talking without interpretation, and he
let his mother know it. She made a few perfunctory signs.
Frank figured she was telling him she'd kicked him out.

"Thank you for your time, Mrs. Sechrest," he said.

She didn't reply, and she slammed the door a little too
loudly behind him.

Frank sighed as he made his way out of their building.
He was making enemies right and left in this investigation. He would probably be wise to wait until tomorrow,
so he could consult with the chief of detectives before questioning anyone else and find out if anybody in authority
was really interested in solving this crime. Most people
would assume that solving the murder of somebody as rich
and powerful as Nehemiah Wooten would be extremely
important. But not if solving it meant inconveniencing
somebody equally rich and important. Wooten was dead,
and he wouldn't be complaining to Frank's superiors about
anything. His killer still could. And if other living people

had secrets they didn't want Frank discovering, they'd cause trouble for him, too.

So he'd call it a day and head back home. Brian, at least, would be happy to see him.

BY THE TIME FRANK GOT TO POLICE HEADQUARTERS ON Mulberry Street the next morning, he'd collected seven newspapers proclaiming the details of the gruesome murder of Nehemiah Wooten. The newsboys hawking the papers on street corners with cries of "Rich man murdered in his office!" and "Businessman beaten to death!" had been doing a brisk business.

Frank was still glancing over the newspapers to see how much of the real story the reporters had been able to gather when he was summoned to Captain O'Brien's office. Stephen O'Brien was the acting chief of detectives, and like everyone in the police department since the departure of Police Commissioner Theodore Roosevelt, he was being very careful not to offend the wrong people. The problem, of course, was that no one was yet certain just who those people were. Everyone was still talking about reform, but nobody really believed that Roosevelt's policies would hold up now that he'd gone to Washington.

Frank gave his report, bringing O'Brien up to date on everything he knew about the Wooten murder so far.

"Must've been some lunatic who broke in," O'Brien said. "The door wasn't locked, was it?"

"Higginbotham said it wasn't when he got there. I'm going to the office today to talk to everybody who was working on Saturday. Whoever was the last to leave will remember if he locked the door behind him."

O'Brien frowned. He didn't like this. "And you said nothing was stolen?"

"It didn't look like it, but I won't know for sure until his partner gets in today and checks."

"Maybe it was a robbery then."

"Maybe," Frank said, willing to be agreeable.

"Try to find a thief, then. Or a lunatic." The message was clear. It would certainly be a lot more pleasant for everybody if Wooten had been killed by a stranger.

"I'll try," Frank said, hoping it would be that easy.

He arrived at Wooten's office building shortly after the staff had begun their workday. This morning, a nice-looking young fellow was sitting at the desk in the lobby. He was pale and somber in his stiff collar and cheap suit, and he jumped to his feet as Frank walked in.

"No reporters!" he cried almost desperately. Obviously, he'd already had to chase away some of those pesky fellows. "I must ask you to leave, or we'll have you thrown out."

Since he didn't look as if he could have forcibly ejected Frank's mother, Frank wondered who would have carried out this threat, but he said, "I'm Frank Malloy with the New York City Police Department. I'm investigating Mr. Wooten's death. Is Mr. Young in yet?"

The clerk swallowed and tried to regain his dignity. "I'll see if he's available to meet with you."

As he scurried away, Frank noticed a few curious employees leaning out of their offices to get a look at him. Frank couldn't help hoping one of them had lost his temper with a demanding employer and bashed his skull in with a college trophy. Unfortunately, none of them looked particularly guilty.

"Mr. Young will see you," the clerk reported when he returned, looking calmer.

All the curious heads had withdrawn as Frank made his way along the same corridor he'd walked down yesterday to find Wooten's body on the floor of his office. This morning the door of that office was closed, and the clerk led him to the office next to it.

Young was sitting behind his desk, looking like his bowels had been locked for a week. "I told the staff you'd need to speak with them," he said by way of greeting. "Peters here has a list of everyone who was working on Saturday." Then he turned his attention back to the papers on his desk, silently dismissing Frank.

The young clerk Peters escorted Frank to the same conference room where he'd questioned Higginbotham on Saturday, and he officiously introduced each member of the staff in turn as they endured Frank's patient interrogation. Frank learned that none of them had seen or heard anything unusual. None of them had ever seen the mechanical pencil that Frank had found in Wooten's office. They all had done their work that morning and left promptly at noon. The front door had been locked, according to those who left last, at Mr. Wooten's instructions. Mr. Wooten was a careful man who knew the dangers of the city and would not have felt safe in the building if the door had been left unlocked. Mr. Wooten had an appointment with Mr. Higginbotham and no one else that afternoon. And no, Mr. Wooten was not in the habit of entertaining strangers who did not have a scheduled appointment.

So now Frank knew that either Wooten had admitted someone he knew into the building prior to his appointment with Higginbotham or else the staff members were lying and they had forgotten to lock the door behind them, as Wooten always instructed them to do. So he'd wasted most of his morning and learned nothing useful. When the last person on Peters's list had gone, Peters himself came in.

"Will there be anything else?" he asked, plainly relieved that this unpleasant task was over.

"Are you sure that's everybody?" Frank said, knowing that it never hurt to check.

"All except for Mr. Young," Peters said and then caught himself. Plainly, he hadn't meant to reveal this information.

"Mr. Young was working on Saturday?" Frank asked, remembering he'd specifically asked him that question and he'd denied it.

"No, not *Mr. Young*," he said. "I mean, it was *young* Mr. Young . . . Mr. Young Junior, that is."

"Mr. Young has a son who works here?" Frank asked, recalling how Young had been somewhat alarmed when Frank asked if he had children.

"Yes, well, of course he works here. He'll inherit the business someday, so naturally . . . Well, he was here on Saturday, but he isn't in this morning."

"Do you know where he is?" Frank asked with interest.

Peters hesitated, probably debating with himself Frank's right to know. "I really don't know, but I image that since his father must be *here*, he's probably offering the Wooten family whatever assistance he can during this difficult time."

A perfect excuse to visit the Wooten house again. Frank managed not to smile.

FRANK STARTED THINKING ABOUT ALL THE PEOPLE AT THE Wooten house he needed to question. He'd like some time with the mysterious Electra, who made no secret she was happy her father was dead. He'd also like to meet Electra's brother. He hadn't even laid eyes on him yet. And if Young Jr. was on the premises, he'd have a go at him as well. Mrs. Wooten was another one he'd like to question more thoroughly, but he didn't imagine she'd stand for it again.

Someone had hung a black wreath on the front door of the Wooten house, and all the shades had been pulled. The same maid who had opened the door to him before opened it now. She looked positively terrified at the sight of him.

"The family is in mourning," she tried. "They aren't seeing any visitors."

"I'm not a visitor," he reminded her. Taking advantage of her timidity, he stepped closer to her, knowing she'd retreat. When she'd retreated far enough, he squeezed past her into the house.

"You can't come in here," she cried. "You've got no right!"

"I'm trying to find out who killed Mr. Wooten," Frank reminded her. "Don't you want his killer brought to justice?"

This question obviously confused her, so she didn't answer it. "Mrs. Wooten won't like you being here again."

"I didn't come to see Mrs. Wooten."

"Who did you want to see, then?"

"How about Mr. Young? I understand he's visiting the family."

Frank had been bluffing, to see if Young really was here, and the girl's mouth dropped open in surprise, telling him his information had been correct. "You can't see him either!"

"Annie, who's there?" a woman's voice called from the top of the stairs.

"It's that policeman, Mrs. Parmer," the girl replied. "The one who was here before. I told him he can't come in here."

Frank heard footsteps on the stairs, and in a moment,

a middle-aged woman appeared at the top. She wore the unrelieved black of full mourning, and the quality of her clothing and her bearing marked her as a member of the household, not a servant. Her blond hair was touched with gray, and her face bore the signs of recent strain. She wasn't as striking as Mrs. Wooten or beautiful like Electra, but her face held an intelligence that interested Frank. She was studying him intently as she made her way down to the bottom of the steps.

He nodded politely and introduced himself.

"I'm Betty Parmer, Mr. Wooten's sister," she informed him. "Why are you here?"

"I didn't get a chance to speak with all the family members when I was here on Saturday," he said as kindly as he could. "I'm trying to find out who killed your brother, and I need as much information as I can get."

"What sort of information do you need, Mr. Malloy?" she asked.

Frank knew she wouldn't be satisfied with anything except the whole truth. "I need to know if Mr. Wooten had any enemies, anyone who might be angry enough to kill him."

"Wouldn't his partner, Mr. Young, be in a better position to help you?" she asked.

Frank debated how honest to be in his reply, but something in her tone when she said Mr. Young's name made him take a chance. "Mr. Young says everyone disliked your brother."

The maid Annie made a small sound of outrage, but Mrs. Parmer's lips pursed as she held back a smile. "He would."

"I also would like to speak with Mr. Young Junior," Frank added. "He was at the office on Saturday, and I was told I might find him here."

Mrs. Parmer's fair eyebrows rose at this. She looked at Annie. "Is Terry Young here?"

Annie's gaze flickered to Frank and back, as if weighing the wisdom of revealing that information in front of Frank against the penalty for refusing to answer Mrs. Parmer. "Yes, ma'am."

"They'll be in Mrs. Wooten's sitting room, I assume," Mrs. Parmer said, but it wasn't a question, and Annie said nothing. She just looked terrified again. "Come with me, Mr. Malloy. I'll take you to him."

"She said no interruptions," Annie tried desperately, moving as if to follow them as Mrs. Parmer led Frank up the stairs.

"I'll take full responsibility," Mrs. Parmer assured her.

The promise didn't relieve Annie's anxiety in the slightest. She stood at the foot of the stairs, wringing her hands in impotent distress as she watched them climbing higher and higher.

"I'm sorry about your brother's death," Frank said as they reached the top.

"So am I," Mrs. Parmer replied. "He wasn't always like . . . Well, he wasn't always a man whom no one liked," she added. "And he was very kind to me after my husband died."

She led him past the room where Frank had met with Mrs. Wooten the other day and up another flight of stairs to the part of the house where the family would have their bedrooms. Ordinarily, a stranger would never be admitted to this floor of the house. Mrs. Parmer had guessed that Mrs. Wooten was entertaining Young in her private sitting room. The families must be very close, Frank thought, as Mrs. Parmer stopped in front of one of the doors that lined the upstairs corridor.

She half turned, looking at Frank over her shoulder, as if checking for something. He couldn't imagine what she'd be checking for, and then she threw open the door, and he realized what it was. She'd wanted to be sure he was in a position to see straight into the room, and she had stepped aside in one swift motion to make sure his line of sight was unimpeded.

At first he didn't comprehend what he was seeing, and then the two figures on the sofa pulled apart and jumped to their feet. The two figures were Mrs. Wooten and a man Frank guessed to be almost young enough to be her son. When the door had opened, they had been in an embrace. There was no other word for it. Frank didn't think it was a comforting embrace either.

"I told you, Annie—" Mrs. Wooten was fairly shouting, and then she saw who was there.

Mrs. Parmer stepped in front of Frank and preceded him into the room. "I'm sorry to disturb you, Valora," she was saying as if nothing untoward had happened, "but Mr. Malloy told me he needed to speak with Terry, so of course I brought him right up. It's about Nehemiah's death, so I know you'll both want to help him in any way you can."

Frank looked at Mrs. Parmer in amazement. She must have known what they would find here, and she had wanted to make sure he understood exactly what was going on between Mrs. Wooten and Terry Young.

Mrs. Wooten was glaring at Mrs. Parmer as if she'd like to rip her head right off her body, but Mrs. Parmer appeared to be blissfully unaware, although Frank knew that was impossible. Young was still too shocked to really comprehend any of it. He stood blinking in surprise, looking from one to the other of the women and then at Frank, trying to make sense of what they were saying. Then Mrs. Wooten wrapped her arms around herself and hunched over, as if suddenly in pain, and uttered a startled cry.

"Valora?" Mrs. Parmer said in apparent concern. "What is it?"

Then they all noticed that Mrs. Wooten was looking down in horror at where a puddle was rapidly forming around her on the beautiful carpet.

4

"THE BEST THING ABOUT THIS TIME OF YEAR IS THE fresh fruit," Mrs. Ellsworth was saying as she pulled a pie out of the oven.

"I never had peach pie before," Maeve said, inhaling the delicious aroma. "I never even saw enough peaches at once to even make a pie!"

"I love peaches," Catherine informed them all, looking up from the half-eaten one she was cradling in her hands.

"I do, too," Sarah said with a smile. They were all gathered in Sarah's kitchen, and Mrs. Ellsworth had spent the morning helping the girls peel and slice the fruit she'd gotten at the Gansevoort Market that morning and bake it into pies.

"Look how many pies we've got," Maeve said, looking at the collection they had cooling on every flat surface in the room. "Can you count them, Catherine, and tell me how many we have?" she added. She'd been teaching Catherine her numbers.

"Oh, no," Mrs. Ellsworth exclaimed in alarm. "You mustn't count them once they've come out of the oven. They'll go bad."

Sarah and Maeve exchanged a glance, but Sarah decided not to scold her neighbor for her superstitions.

"Well, however many we have, what are we going to do with all of them?" Maeve wondered.

"Maybe you can take some to Mr. Malloy and Brian," Mrs. Ellsworth suggested archly.

"I'm sure Mr. Malloy's mother would be insulted," Sarah reminded her.

"All the more reason," Mrs. Ellsworth replied with a twinkle, making Maeve laugh.

"Why do you want to insult Brian's granny?" Catherine asked with a frown.

"We don't, dear. Mrs. Ellsworth is just teasing," Sarah replied with a warning look at the older woman.

"That's right, I am," Mrs. Ellsworth assured her.

"It's not nice to tease people," Catherine informed them gravely.

"That's right, it's not," Maeve confirmed in her best nursemaid voice.

They heard the doorbell, and everyone looked up with varying degrees of disappointment. The doorbell usually meant Sarah was being summoned to work.

"I didn't tell you this morning, but I saw four crows on the fence when I came out my back door," Mrs. Ellsworth said apologetically. "That always means a birth."

Sarah managed not to wince. She didn't believe in Mrs. Ellsworth's superstitions, but she didn't like to hurt the older woman's feelings. "We should be happy," Sarah reminded them all. "Delivering babies is what keeps a roof over our heads and peaches in our stomachs!"

Catherine giggled.

"I'll get the door," Maeve said, hurrying off with Catherine at her heels.

Sarah got up and started removing her apron. "Thank you for this morning," she said to Mrs. Ellsworth.

"I get more pleasure out of being with the girls than they do from being with me, I'm sure," she replied, waving away Sarah's gratitude. "You better get your things together."

Sarah followed the girls out to the front room, which served as her office. A young man in a footman's uniform stood just inside the door. He seemed enchanted with Maeve, but the girl was more interested in a note he had handed her.

EVERYONE KEPT STARING, TRANSFIXED BY THE PUDDLE. Frank felt a rushing in his ears and everything grew fuzzy, as if a fog had formed around him. Suddenly, he was no longer in the Wooten house but in his own, in the flat he'd shared with Kathleen when they were first married, on the night when Brian was born, on the night when Kathleen had died. The pain of her loss was like a knife, as it always was, but his mind was racing past it, on to something else, something vitally important that he had to remember. That evening Kathleen had stood up and water had started running down her legs and forming a puddle on the floor around her. That's how she'd known her baby was coming.

"Valora, what on earth is wrong?" Mrs. Parmer was saying, genuinely confused and not a little horrified.

"Valora?" Terry Young said, equally confused and horrified.

What was wrong with them? Didn't they know what was happening? He hadn't suspected, but surely, they both knew about Mrs. Wooten's condition.

"It's the baby," Frank said when no one made a move to do anything to help her.

They looked at him as if he'd lost his mind. Except for Mrs. Wooten, of course. She simply looked terrified.

"She's going to have her baby," he told them, mortified to be mentioning such a subject in mixed company but knowing it had to be done.

"Baby?" Mrs. Parmer echoed, her horror increasing tenfold. "What are you talking about?" And then she must have realized the answer to her own question and turned to Mrs. Wooten. "Are you with child, Valora?"

Terry Young made a strangled sound in his throat, but no one seemed to notice.

Valora Wooten's eyes narrowed with pure hatred as she glared at Frank. "You're insane," she informed him. "Get out of my house!"

But Mrs. Parmer had realized the truth of it.

"You *are* with child!" she cried in outrage, looking the woman up and down. "That explains . . . Did Nehemiah know?" She looked at Young, who had paled visibly. "Of course he didn't know," she realized. "Nobody knew because it wasn't Nehemiah's child!"

"Don't be ridiculous!" Mrs. Wooten hissed. "You don't know what you're saying!"

"Shouldn't someone get a doctor?" Young said, glancing reluctantly at the puddle again. He looked as if he might faint.

"No!" cried Mrs. Wooten, terrified again. "No doctors!

I don't need a doctor. I just need for all of you to get out of here and leave me alone!"

"Of course," Young said and made a break for the door.

Frank caught his arm before he could escape. "Don't leave the house," he warned the young man. "I need to talk to you, and I'll be very annoyed if I have to go looking for you."

Young blanched, but he nodded frantically before wrenching free and fleeing the room.

"Don't be a fool, Valora," Mrs. Parmer was saying, her disgust evident in her voice as she studied the moisture staining the carpet. "You're going to have a baby. You need someone to help you. I'll send for Dr. Smith."

"Not that old busybody! He'll tell everyone in the city!"

"It's not a secret you can keep much longer," Mrs. Parmer pointed out reasonably.

"Not Smith! Not anyone who knows us!"

"I know a midwife," Frank said.

The two women looked up in surprise. They'd completely forgotten he was there.

"I know a midwife," he repeated. "She's Felix Decker's daughter," he added, in case his own recommendation wasn't enough.

"Felix Decker?" Mrs. Parmer echoed.

"Felix Decker's daughter can't be a midwife," Mrs. Wooten said with disdain.

"Well, she is," Frank said impatiently. "I'll send one of your servants for her, and you can see for yourself."

"Who's Felix Decker?" Mrs. Parmer asked.

"The *Deckers*," Mrs. Wooten snapped. "One of the oldest families in the city."

"That's right, and I'm going to send for her. You can send her away if you decide you want your doctor, but somebody has to do something," Frank said, turning away from them in exasperation.

Frank found Terry Young pacing the hallway at the bottom of the first flight of stairs. "What's wrong with her?" he demanded, but Frank ignored him.

"Annie!" he called, leaning over the railing to the hallway below.

The girl came racing up the stairs, holding her skirts in both hands, her eyes wide and her face pale with fright.

"I need to send for someone. Give me some paper and a pencil, and I'll write down the address."

She hesitated, looking up the stairs to see if someone in authority would appear to tell her if she needed to obey his request, but no one did.

"Give him whatever he needs," Young snapped, and that apparently was all she required.

She took Frank into a small room that had a desk and rummaged for the writing implements. He jotted down the directions to Bank Street and then wrote a short note. He folded it and gave it to the girl. "Have one of the servants take this to Mrs. Brandt at this address and tell her I need to see her here at once."

The girl took the paper gingerly. "Should I send the carriage?" she asked uncertainly.

"No, it'll be faster to go on foot." It was often faster to go on foot than to maneuver a carriage through the traffic that clogged the city's streets. He just hoped they'd find Sarah at home. He wasn't sure what he would do if she wasn't available.

The maid nodded and hurried off. When Frank returned to the hallway, Mrs. Parmer was coming down from the floor above.

"I sent for the midwife," he told her.

"I can't believe this," she said, looking slightly dazed. Then she saw Young lurking and she turned on him. "You . . . you *cad*!" she cried. "How could you do such a thing!"

Frank didn't think she really wanted to know the answer to that question, and he was sure Young didn't want to answer it, so he tried to distract her. "Shouldn't someone stay with Mrs. Wooten?"

"I called for her maid. She's getting her settled," she said distractedly. "I can't believe this is happening!"

"Where are the children?" Frank asked, thinking he could use his time productively while he waited for Sarah by questioning them in addition to Young.

"I have no idea," she said, giving Young another glare.

"I should go," he said and started sidling toward the stairs.

"I told you, I need to talk to you," Frank reminded him. "If you'll excuse us, Mrs. Parmer," he added, "I need to ask Young some questions about your brother's murder."

"Ask him some questions about my brother's widow's seduction while you're about it," she said through gritted teeth.

Frank clapped a hand on Young's shoulder and directed him to the parlor where Mrs. Wooten had received him on his first visit.

"It's from Mr. Malloy," she told Sarah, passing it to her.

Sarah ignored the small flutter in her stomach at the mention of Malloy's name. He'd sent her plenty of messages in the months she had known him. This one shouldn't cause her any special excitement. And of course, it wasn't exactly a personal message. His familiar scrawl informed her that someone needed her professional services immediately and would she please come?

The young footman didn't appear to be as excited as the normal male who was sent to fetch a midwife. Usually, the messenger who came to summon her was nearly panicked by the time he reached her door. "I'll just be a few minutes. I have to gather my medical supplies," she told him.

This distracted him from admiring Maeve, and he looked up in surprise. "Medical? Are you some kind of doctor?" he asked. "I never saw a woman doctor."

To his chagrin, Maeve and Catherine giggled at his ignorance. "She's a midwife," Maeve informed him.

"What's a midwife?" he asked, making them giggle again.

"She delivers babies," Maeve informed him.

This surprised him, and his surprise dismayed Sarah. She glanced at Malloy's message again and saw that it clearly said he needed her professional services. Was it possible this boy didn't know someone in the house where he worked was expecting? Yes, she realized, that was indeed possible.

She pulled out her medical bag and began to check her supplies to make sure she would have everything she needed.

TERRANCE YOUNG WASN'T YET THIRTY YEARS OLD. HE was his father's son, stocky but not yet fat, and not particularly handsome. His mousy brown hair was already thinning and had been carefully pomaded into place to cover the bare spots.

Sweat had beaded on Young's upper lip, and he licked

it off nervously. "I can't imagine why you want to question me," he protested unconvincingly.

"Well, let's start with what you and Mrs. Wooten were doing when I came into her room just now."

"We were talking," he informed Frank defensively. He wasn't very good at outrage, and Frank managed not to roll his eyes.

"Are you hard of hearing?" Frank asked blandly.

"Hard of hearing? No, of course not!"

"Then why did you have to sit so close to her? She was practically in your lap."

The color bloomed in Young's face, turning it crimson. "I don't know what you mean."

"Then you're even stupider than I thought," Frank replied.

Young decided to take offense at that. "You have no right to keep me here," he tried.

"You're right, I don't. Maybe I should take you down to Police Headquarters and lock you up instead."

The crimson stain drained from his face. "I haven't done anything wrong!"

"Most people would think that seducing another man's wife was wrong," Frank countered.

"You don't know what you're talking about!"

"Don't I? Well, then, why don't you explain it to me."

"It's none of your business!" he tried desperately.

"Of course it's my business. If you and Mrs. Wooten are lovers and she's carrying a child and Mr. Wooten would have known it couldn't be his, then both of you have a good reason to want him dead."

"I never! How dare you even suggest such a thing! I could never . . . Mr. Wooten was like a father to me!"

"And was Mrs. Wooten like a mother to you?" Frank asked curiously.

His face grew scarlet again. "You can't speak about her that way!"

"What way?" Frank asked. "I didn't intend to insult her, although it's hard not to, knowing what I know about her. Answer my question, was she like a mother to you?"

"My mother died when I was two," Young told him, every word sounding as if it were being pulled from him like a bad tooth. "When my father and Mr. Wooten became partners, Mrs. Wooten was very kind to me, welcoming me into her home."

"Welcoming you into her bedroom," Frank added.

"None of this concerns you," Young insisted impatiently. "Wooten is dead and I had nothing to do with it. That's all you need to know."

"Then you won't mind telling me where you were on Saturday."

His expression tightened as he realized that was the day Wooten was murdered. "I was at the office that morning, as usual. I left at noon, like everyone else."

"Everyone?"

"Well, Mr. Wooten stayed. He often did."

"Who was the last one out of the building?"

"I don't know. It wasn't me."

"Do you have a key to the building?"

"No, I don't."

"But your father does."

"Of course he does. He owns it."

"And you're his son. Why don't you have one?"

"I don't need one. The clerk has one, and he opens the door for everyone first thing and locks up at the end of the day."

"And you can always borrow your father's key if you need it."

"I suppose I could . . . Wait a minute! I don't like your implication!"

"I don't have an implication. I was just stating a fact, and you agreed. Did you borrow your father's key and go back to the office on Saturday?"

"Certainly not!"

"Why not?"

"I didn't need it. I had no intention of going back to that godforsaken office again until Monday. Why should I?"

"Don't you like your work?"

He sputtered at that, loath to admit he didn't and unable to deny it.

"All right," Frank said, relieving him of the burden of replying. "What did you need to talk to Wooten about that afternoon?"

Young's eyes grew wide. "Nothing!" he lied, too forcefully.

Frank had taken a shot in the dark and hit a bull's-eye. "Were you going to confess your love for Mrs. Wooten and ask him to divorce her so you could live happily ever after?"

"Of course not!" he cried, although Frank wasn't sure if he was telling the truth or not. Even though that would have been a foolish thing to do, people had been doing foolish things that ended in murder ever since Cain killed Abel.

"Then what *were* you going to talk to him about?"

"I wasn't, not really. I just . . . Well, uh . . . I was going to speak to him about Electra."

"What about her?" Frank said, his interest piqued.

"She . . . It had just come to my attention that she has

been conducting herself in a manner completely inappropriate for a girl in her position."

"What position is that?"

"As Nehemiah Wooten's daughter," he clarified indignantly. "What else could it be?"

"I thought you might have meant her being deaf. Was she acting inappropriately for a deaf girl?"

"I don't think a deaf girl is held to a different standard than a normal girl," he said haughtily.

Frank wondered if Electra Wooten would appreciate being considered different from a "normal" girl. He'd have to ask her. "How was she being *inappropriate*?"

Young's lips thinned down into a stubborn line.

Frank shrugged. "I can wait all night for your answer, Mr. Young, but it will be much more convenient for me if we're at Police Headquarters because I can lock you up down there."

"You wouldn't dare lock me up," Young said, having recovered some of his common sense as the shock of Valora Wooten's pregnancy began to wear off. "My father would have your job."

He certainly would, Frank knew. "But you would still have been locked up in a cell with every drunk and crook and murderer in the city overnight. So why don't you just explain what you wanted to tell Mr. Wooten on Saturday."

Young heaved a weary sigh. "It has come to my attention that Electra is . . . Well, she's been secretly seeing a young man who is totally unsuitable for her. I was going to inform him of that."

"But you didn't?"

"No, I did not."

"Why not?"

"Because I learned that Mr. Wooten had already learned this information and Mr. Higginbotham from the school Electra attends was meeting with him that afternoon to discuss the matter."

"So you're saying you didn't meet with Mr. Wooten that afternoon?"

"No, I did not."

"And what did you do instead?"

"I went for a long walk in Central Park."

"Did anyone see you?"

"Hundreds of people saw me."

"Would anyone *remember* seeing you?" Frank tried.

Young's expression was bleak. "Probably not, but since I didn't kill Mr. Wooten, it doesn't matter. I'd like to leave now."

Frank studied him. He wasn't going to get anything else out of him today. Still, he couldn't resist a parting shot. "Don't you even want to know if your child is a boy or a girl?"

Young's gaze darted upward as he recalled Mrs. Wooten's condition and what it meant. "I had no idea!" he told Frank. He actually sounded aggrieved. "She never said a word to me."

"Didn't you notice that she got fat?" Surely somebody had noticed that, but Mrs. Parmer had seemed as surprised as Young.

"Valora . . . I mean, Mrs. Wooten has always been a voluptuous woman. She has seemed a bit more so of late, but I never thought . . . Did *you* think she was with child?"

Frank had to admit it had never crossed his mind. She certainly didn't have the usual profile of a pregnant female, and her age also made it unlikely, especially considering how

old her children were and how long it had been since she'd
last given birth.

"Why would Wooten have been so certain the baby
wasn't his?" Frank asked.

"The obvious reason," Young said, mortified by the
question.

"You mean Wooten no longer shared his wife's bed?"
Frank guessed. "Why not?"

"That's something you will have to discuss with Mrs.
Wooten," Young said, and from the satisfied gleam in his
eye, Young knew Frank would never dare do such a thing.

He could, however, ask Sarah Brandt to.

SARAH WAS GLAD THEY HADN'T SENT A CARRIAGE FOR HER.
Traffic in the city and the jams at every intersection made
traveling by carriage slow and nerve-wracking, which was
why Sarah usually refused to be transported unless the case
was especially far away. The young footman, whose name,
Sarah had learned on their brisk walk and their ride on the
Sixth Avenue Elevated Train, was Jack, had carried her bag
all the way to the Wootens' front door. On the way, she had
learned where she was going, although Jack knew nothing that could enlighten her as to why a midwife's services
might be needed at his employer's house. The master had
been murdered a few days ago—maybe she'd heard about
it. Sarah hadn't been out since Friday and hadn't seen any
newspapers or even had the opportunity to hear the corner
newsboys shouting the details of the latest crimes in order to
sell their wares. So she hadn't heard about the murder.

Jack was only too happy to tell her all the ugly details
of how Mr. Wooten had had his head smashed in by some-

one who had broken into his office. She couldn't help wondering how much of the story was true and how much had been exaggerated in the servants' quarters from rumors and eavesdropping and from the sensationalized version in the newspapers. Sarah comforted herself in the knowledge that Malloy would never have sent for her unless he was in desperate need of her assistance. A woman in labor had inspired many men to a desperate need for her assistance.

A frantic-looking maid admitted them, and to Sarah's amusement, she instantly began berating Jack for taking so long in fetching her.

"I ran nearly all the way there," he protested, "but I couldn't make her run back, now could I? She says she's a midwife, but I told her nobody here was having a baby," he added, aggrieved that he'd been sent on a wild-goose chase.

The maid sighed in exasperation. "Go back to the stables, and forget anybody ever spoke to you today."

Jack made his farewells to Sarah and gave her back her bag. She thanked him for his assistance, and he disappeared into the bowels of the house.

"This way, please," the maid said to Sarah when he was gone. "Mrs. Wooten is in her room, but that Mr. Malloy wants to see you first."

She led Sarah up a flight of stairs to what would be the main living area of the town house. Malloy met them at the top of the stairs. He didn't smile at her. That would have been inappropriate, especially with the maid watching, but she could see the warmth in his dark eyes. Maybe it was just relief, but she doubted it. She didn't smile either, but she knew he could read the expression in her own eyes.

"Malloy," she said by way of greeting.

"Thank you for coming, Mrs. Brandt," he said formally. "Would you step into the parlor for a moment, please?"

Malloy conducted her to a room that opened off the hallway while the maid stood watching, anxiously wringing her hands, as if afraid of what she might be asked to do next.

"That's all, Annie," Malloy told her when it became apparent she wasn't going anywhere.

She turned reluctantly and retreated back down the stairs.

Malloy closed the door behind them. "I was afraid she'd eavesdrop," he explained.

"What on earth is going on here?" Sarah asked, setting the heavy medical bag down on the floor and taking a quick look around the room. It was fashionably furnished with overstuffed furniture and every sort of knickknack available for purchase. More money than taste had been expended in its decoration, but that could be said of most of the parlors in the city.

"A rich businessman named Wooten got himself murdered on Saturday," he began.

"The boy who fetched me said he'd had his head beaten in by somebody who tried to rob him at his office."

"I wish that was what happened," Malloy said with a sigh.

"What did happen?"

"We don't know, but it wasn't a robbery, and it's starting to look like lots of his friends and relations might have had good reasons for wanting him dead. One of those reasons is why you're here."

"Mrs. Wooten is with child, I gather."

"Yes," he said grimly, color creeping up his neck. Childbirth was a subject rarely mentioned in polite company, and she knew Malloy especially hated discussing it because his wife had died in childbirth.

"Is the birth imminent?" she asked, choosing her words carefully so as not to embarrass him further.

"Yes, she . . ." He sighed again, hating this whole conversation. "There was a puddle on the floor," he said, his voice strained.

"Oh, dear, you mean her waters broke?" Sarah said, somehow managing to sound shocked instead of amused at his chagrin. "In front of you?"

Malloy seemed to be gritting his teeth. "In front of me and her sister-in-law and her lover."

"Her *lover*?" Sarah echoed. Not exactly a word she had expected to hear.

"Yes, her lover, who is also apparently the father of the child."

"Oh, my, I'm beginning to understand what you mean about people having reasons to murder Mr. Wooten."

"And to make it even more complicated, neither he nor Mrs. Parmer seemed to know she was expecting. Mrs. Parmer is the sister-in-law."

"They couldn't tell?" Sarah asked in surprise. "*You* couldn't tell?"

"No, Mrs. Wooten is a . . . a large woman," he explained. "They were both very surprised when I told them they needed to send for a doctor."

"Oh, my," was all Sarah could think to say.

"And from what I gathered, Wooten couldn't possibly be the father of the baby, so it has to be the lover."

"Oh, *my*," Sarah repeated, feeling stupid but unable to form a more coherent response in the face of such a situation.

"So I need for you to find out if that's the truth, because

it would give Young—that's the lover—a good reason to kill Wooten."

"It would give Mrs. Wooten an even better reason," Sarah pointed out. "Is this Mr. Young still here?" She glanced around, almost expecting to find him crouching behind the sofa.

"No, he left as soon as I was finished with him."

"That was pretty brazen of him to be visiting her at her house with her husband barely cold."

"He's a family friend, the son of Wooten's business partner," Malloy said with some disgust. "He's also at least ten years younger than she is."

Sarah raised her eyebrows. She was getting very anxious to meet this Mrs. Wooten. "Is that all?"

"No, but that's all you need to know right now."

"Are you planning to wait for the baby to come?"

"God, no!" he said, making her smile. "I mean, well, I *would* like to question her children while she's . . . indisposed."

"Her children?" Sarah asked. "Surely, little children won't know anything about their father's death or their mother's indiscretions."

"They aren't *little* children," he said. "The girl is sixteen and her brother is older, and the girl, at least, had a reason of her own for wanting her father dead."

"Good heavens, she's not with child, too, is she?"

"I hope not," he said fervently. "But you don't need to worry about anything right now except Mrs. Wooten. By the way, I told her you're Felix Decker's daughter."

"Why did you do that?" she asked with a frown. Revealing her family heritage could make people uncomfortable around her, not the best situation when she was working.

"Mrs. Wooten didn't want them to call in a doctor. I think she was afraid of gossip, so I suggested you."

"I see," Sarah said, seeing perfectly. If the woman had kept her pregnancy a secret even from her family, she certainly didn't want the news spread by a family physician. "But she wasn't willing to have a stranger help her either."

"No, she wasn't, so I tried to impress her by telling her who your father is, but no harm done. She didn't believe me."

"I'm sure she didn't. But she did agree to allow me to come?"

"She didn't have much choice."

"Which means she didn't actually agree," Sarah guessed. "No matter. I'm here now, and if she really is going to have a baby, she should be glad. I guess I better go find out."

Malloy picked up her medical bag and opened the door for her. They found a middle-aged woman dressed in mourning, standing in the hallway a discreet distance from the door to ensure they understood she hadn't been trying to overhear their conversation.

"Is this the midwife?" the woman asked Malloy.

"Mrs. Parmer, this is Mrs. Brandt, the midwife I sent for. Mrs. Parmer is Mr. Wooten's sister."

"He said you're Felix Decker's daughter," she said doubtfully, looking Sarah over for any signs she might be the offspring of one of the wealthiest and most powerful men in the city.

Sarah knew she would find none. "Yes, I am, but more importantly, I'm a trained midwife. Would you take me to see Mrs. Wooten, please?"

Mrs. Parmer sighed in resignation. "Of course. This way, please."

Malloy handed Sarah her bag, and she followed Mrs. Parmer down the hall to another set of stairs, leading up to the third floor.

"I must assure you," she told Sarah when they were out of Malloy's earshot, "I knew nothing about Valora's condition. If I had, I most certainly would have . . . Well, I'm not certain exactly what I would have done, but I would have done something."

Sarah didn't think she was expected to reply, so she simply nodded and followed Mrs. Parmer up the stairs.

"I can't imagine what Electra and Leander will think about all this," Mrs. Parmer murmured.

Sarah blinked at the unusual names. Obviously, someone in the family had been enamored with the Greeks. But she assumed these must be Mrs. Wooten's children, the ones Malloy wanted to question. "Are they here?" Sarah asked as innocently as she could. "Perhaps someone should explain the circumstances to them."

"They're out this afternoon, I'm happy to say, but as soon as they return, I'll break the news to them as gently as I can."

Sarah wondered where two young people whose father had just died could possibly have gone, but a noise below distracted her. A beautiful girl was running up the stairs from the first floor and making quite a racket. Mrs. Parmer's breath caught, and she pushed Sarah unceremoniously aside to hurry back down the stairs to meet her.

The girl was calling something, but she couldn't make out the words. Mrs. Parmer met her in the hallway below and took her by the shoulders, thrusting her face close to the girl's, and began to say something.

The girl recoiled. "A baby?" she cried, shaking her head as if such an idea were incomprehensible.

But Mrs. Parmer was nodding, confirming the unthinkable.

The girl made an odd sound, almost like she was strangling, and she pushed past Mrs. Parmer and ran toward the stairs, where Sarah still stood, frozen with indecision.

"Electra!" Mrs. Parmer called, but the girl ignored her.

Sarah stood aside to allow her to pass, but Mrs. Parmer called, "Stop her! Don't let her pass!" She was running after her in a futile attempt to catch her.

Not wanting to lay hands on the girl and uncertain that she could hold her in any case, Sarah put out her black medical bag at the last possible moment. It struck the girl in the chest, or rather she ran right into it and it stopped her cold and sent her bouncing backward, right into Mrs. Parmer, who also lost her balance and the two of them went careening backward to certain disaster.

5

F<small>RANK WATCHED</small> E<small>LECTRA RACING UP THE STAIRS WITH</small> Mrs. Parmer close on her heels. He wasn't sure what would happen when she caught the girl, but he knew he wanted to be there to take control of the situation. Luckily, he was close enough to stop the two women when they started falling backward. Actually, stopping Mrs. Parmer was enough. She'd already caught the girl. The two of them would have gone down in a heap, but Frank was able to set them back on their feet on the steps with a minimum of manhandling.

"Are you all right?" Mrs. Brandt was asking them solicitously, as if she wasn't the one who'd caused them to fall in the first place. Well, in all honesty, it was really Mrs. Parmer who'd told her to stop the girl, but still, she could've just grabbed her by the pigtails or something.

The girl was struggling against Mrs. Parmer's grip, trying to get away, to get to her mother.

"Electra, be still!" Mrs. Parmer was saying, trying to turn the girl's face to hers so she could read her lips.

Electra refused to look at her, however. She was staring at Sarah, having suddenly realized she had no idea who she was. "Who are you?" she demanded.

"I'm Mrs. Brandt," she said. "I'm the midwife."

The girl frowned and turned impatiently to Mrs. Parmer. "Who is she?"

Frank realized she hadn't understood what Sarah said.

Mrs. Parmer did some finger spelling, probably giving the girl Sarah's name.

Sarah was watching them with a puzzled frown.

"She's deaf," Frank told her, knowing the girl wouldn't hear him.

Mrs. Parmer did, however, and she gave him a black look.

"Why is he here?" the girl asked Mrs. Parmer, nodding at Frank.

"He's causing trouble," Mrs. Parmer said angrily.

"I'm so sorry," Frank said sarcastically, backing down the steps. "Next time I'll just let you fall down the stairs."

"Where is Mama?" the girl asked, looking from one of them to the other desperately.

"She won't be satisfied until she knows her mother is all right," Sarah said to Mrs. Parmer.

"She's right," Frank confirmed. "Let her go up and see her."

Mrs. Parmer sighed in defeat. "Come with me," she told the girl, and she started up the stairs. "You'd better come along, too, Mrs. Brandt," she added. "I'm sure you'll be needed soon enough."

Sarah allowed Mrs. Parmer and Electra to pass her. Then

she made a face that expressed her astonishment at this whole situation, for Frank's benefit, and followed them up the stairs.

Biting back a smile, Frank withdrew, determined not to leave the house now until he'd had an opportunity to speak with Electra. In preparation, he returned to the small room where the maid had found writing materials for him and began to compose a message for the girl.

MRS. PARMER LED THEM TO ONE OF THE DOORS THAT opened off the upstairs corridor. They entered a lavishly furnished lady's bedchamber. The shades had been drawn, so they all stopped just inside the doorway to allow their eyes to adjust to the dimness. Then Electra pushed past her aunt and ran to the other side of the room, where a woman reclined on a brocade settee. She wore a silky Chinese robe in shades of blue, which draped her ample figure in generous folds of fabric.

"Mama!" the girl cried as she flung herself at the woman, falling to her knees. "Are you sick?"

Now that Sarah knew the girl was deaf, she was astonished at her ability to speak. The words were oddly pronounced, but Sarah could understand her fairly well.

Mrs. Wooten leaned toward the girl. "I'm not sick. I'm fine," she said. "You don't need to worry about me."

"Aunt Betty said you have a baby!" the girl wailed, then looked around frantically, as if searching for it.

Mrs. Wooten gave her sister-in-law a murderous glare, but Mrs. Parmer glared right back. "Annie already told her something was wrong with you," she explained. "I just told her what it was."

"Where is it?" Electra demanded, turning back to see her mother's answer. "Where is the baby?"

"It hasn't arrived yet," she said. "You must go to your room and wait there until I send for you."

"I want to see it!" Electra cried.

"You will, when it gets here," her mother said gently. "Betty, take her out of here," she added, less gently.

Mrs. Parmer went over and took Electra's arm, encouraging her to rise. She shook off her aunt's hand and scrambled to her feet. "Why do you want a baby?" she demanded of her mother.

Mrs. Wooten closed her eyes, and Sarah suspected she was having a contraction.

"Mrs. Parmer, please take Miss Wooten out," Sarah said. "This is no place for her right now."

"Electra," Mrs. Parmer said, turning the girl's face toward hers. "I'll explain everything to you. Come along now. Your mother needs to rest."

"Mama?" the girl tried, but Mrs. Wooten shook her head.

"Go with Aunt Betty," she said.

Mrs. Parmer fairly dragged the girl out of the room. A maid Sarah hadn't noticed before closed the door behind them. Finally, Mrs. Wooten opened her eyes and looked at Sarah, taking her in from head to toe.

"You must be the midwife," she said, her voice flat.

"Yes, I'm Sarah Brandt," she said, putting down her bag and going to Mrs. Wooten's side. The maid carried over a slipper chair so she could sit down beside her. "I understand your water broke."

"Yes," she said, her voice reflecting all the embarrassment she must have felt at the time.

"Do you know how far along you are?"

"The baby isn't coming early, if that's what you're asking."

"This is your third child?"

"Fourth. I lost a child after Electra. He was stillborn."

Sarah nodded. "Are you having labor pains?"

Mrs. Wooten sighed wearily. "I guess I am. I've probably been having them all day. I just didn't want to believe it."

"Do you know how far apart they are?"

"Minnie?" she said, addressing the maid.

"About ten minutes, miss," the woman told Sarah.

"Well, then, we've got plenty of time to get everything ready," Sarah said and started giving the maid instructions.

When the maid had gone to fetch some of the necessary items, Mrs. Wooten said, "Are you really Felix Decker's daughter?"

"Yes, I am," Sarah admitted.

Mrs. Wooten raised her eyes to heaven. "What is this world coming to?" she asked of no one in particular.

FRANK HEARD THE DOOR OPEN UPSTAIRS, AND HE WAITED impatiently at the bottom of the steps. He could hear Mrs. Parmer and Electra arguing, although Mrs. Parmer was speaking too softly for him to make out her words. Electra, it seemed, was outraged that her mother would want another child.

Plainly, Electra had no idea where babies came from or how they were delivered. She seemed to think her mother could just send it back wherever it was coming from. This wasn't particularly surprising. Few girls of her age and class knew about such things until they were married and it was far too late.

Mrs. Parmer was trying to convince Electra to retire to her bedroom, but she didn't want to do that. Frank wondered how he could get her to come back downstairs. Calling wouldn't help. She couldn't hear him. But Mrs. Parmer could.

"Mrs. Parmer?" he tried.

He couldn't see her, but she must have heard him because Electra said, "What is it?"

Mrs. Parmer said something he couldn't hear, and then Electra said, "Who is it? Who's there?"

As Frank had hoped, she came running to the top of the stairs. She wasn't pleased to see him. Mrs. Parmer was close behind her.

"Go to your room, Electra," she tried again, but Electra wouldn't even look at her. She was staring down at Frank.

Frank held up the paper on which he had written the message he wanted to convey to the girl, the message she wouldn't want anyone else to know. As he had hoped, curiosity drew her down the stairs.

"Electra!" Mrs. Parmer tried, but Electra couldn't hear her.

The girl didn't like him one bit. She didn't like him being there either, but she had to know what he was trying to show her. She snatched the paper from him and read it, quickly scanning the scrawled words in the seconds before her aunt caught up with her.

"What's that? What have you given her?" Mrs. Parmer demanded.

But Electra had seen the message. Her face went white, and she crumpled the paper in her hands and clutched it to her chest so Mrs. Parmer couldn't see it.

"Give it to me," Mrs. Parmer tried, but Electra shook her head violently, her eyes wide with fright.

"No, no," she said. "I must speak to him."

"You most certainly will not! I won't allow it! Your mother would never—"

"I must!" the girl cried, her eyes welling with tears. "Take me to jail!" she told Frank, startling him with her vehemence. He'd certainly convinced her of her need to cooperate with him.

"You aren't going to take her anywhere!" Mrs. Parmer said, her voice rising hysterically.

"No, I'm not," he assured her. Frank got the girl's attention. "We can write," he said, making a motion of a pencil on paper. "Your aunt can sit in the room with us, but she won't see what you write." He turned to Mrs. Parmer. "I need to ask her some questions. I'll write them down, and she can write her answers."

"I'll need to see what you're writing," Mrs. Parmer said stubbornly.

"No!" Electra said.

"If Electra wants you to know what we talk about, she can show you afterward," Frank said.

"This is outrageous!" Mrs. Parmer exclaimed. "I can't permit it."

Electra set her chin stubbornly. "Take me to jail," she told Frank again, grabbing his arm and pulling him toward the stairs that led to the lower floor.

"No, wait!" Mrs. Parmer cried, finally defeated. "All right, but you can't be alone with her, not for a moment!"

"You can sit right there with us the whole time," he said.

"Come," Electra said and led them to the small room with the desk and writing materials.

After some more negotiations, Mrs. Parmer sat herself in a small upholstered chair as far from them as possible, at an angle where she could not see what they were writing. Electra sat in the desk chair, and Frank drew up a straight-backed chair from the hall so they could share the desk.

The message he'd written out for Electra had informed her that he knew about her romance with Adam Oldham and her plans to marry him. He hadn't been sure who already knew her secret, so to frighten her enough to get her cooperation, he'd added that he needed to ask her some questions to make certain Adam wasn't the one who killed her father. Obviously, he'd succeeded.

"How did you meet Adam?" he wrote.

The girl might be young, but she possessed all the ability she would ever need to make a man feel like the dirt beneath her feet. Her very body radiated her disdain for him and her resentment at answering his questions. Still, she wrote her reply in a precise, schoolgirl hand. "Mr. Rossiter introduced us."

Rossiter. That was the man Adam Oldham was supposedly visiting on Saturday evening. He also taught at Brian's school.

"Why did he introduce you?" Frank asked.

The girl looked up to make sure her aunt still couldn't see what they were writing. Then she wrote, "I wanted to learn to sign."

Even though Oldham had told him that, he was still surprised to hear it from her. She had set her jaw defensively, and Frank could imagine why. Her father had made certain that she could speak and lip-read so she would never have to rely on signing to communicate. He had been determined that she would be able to live among hearing people and have no need of the language that deaf people used. "Why?"

She hated him now. He could see it in her lovely eyes. They filled with tears that she angrily blinked away, and when she wrote, she used such force that she nearly broke the pencil point. "So I can talk to other deaf people."

Well, well, well, wasn't this interesting? Her father would have hated this reason.

Frank reached for the pencil to write another question, but she started writing again, the words forming like magic beneath the pencil, her careful handwriting disintegrating into a scrawl as the story poured out of her.

She'd started studying lipreading and learning how to speak almost as soon as her parents realized she was deaf, when she was three years old. She'd spent years mastering the difficult skills, but even still, she knew her speech was different from hearing people and hard to understand. She knew people could tell as soon as they heard her voice that something was wrong with her, that she was different. And even though she could lip-read better than anyone at the Lexington Avenue School, it wasn't the same as hearing, not at all. She could understand only a bit of what people said in the best of times, and sometimes with some people, she couldn't understand anything at all. She usually had to guess at least some of what people were talking about and sometimes she just pretended to understand so people wouldn't lose patience with her.

"What is she writing?" Mrs. Parmer demanded, alarmed at Electra's frantic scribbling. "What is she telling you?"

She half rose from her chair, but Electra snatched up the pages and clutched them to her chest as she had before. "No! You promised!"

"She hasn't confessed to killing her father," Frank told

her, earning a scathing glare from both of them. Mrs. Parmer sank back into her chair, although she continued to watch Frank as she would have watched a snake she was afraid would strike.

Electra laid the papers down again and continued to write, her knuckles white as she gripped the pencil. She hated being different. She hated not understanding. She hated not being understood. She wanted to be with people like her. She wanted to be able to talk to someone!

"Aren't the students at your school like you?" Frank wrote.

"Yes!" she scribbled. "It's hard for us to understand each other, too, except when we finger-spell."

Frank knew that there was a sign for every letter in the alphabet and deaf people could spell words with their hands. It was a laborious process, however, useful for only limited communication. Sort of like this writing he was doing with Electra.

"Did Adam teach you to sign?" Frank wrote.

"Yes."

Frank raised his eyebrows at the short answer. "How long have you been meeting with him?"

"Six months."

"Where do you meet him?" Frank asked, wondering if Adam had seduced the girl as well as winning her affections.

"Different places. Why does it matter? He didn't kill Father."

Frank wasn't so sure of that yet. "How did your father find out about him?"

"Miss Dunham told him. She's a teacher at my school. *I hate her*," she added in bold, dark letters.

"When did this happen?"

"Last Thursday."

"What did your father do when he found out?"

"He locked me in my room. Mother let me out when he went to work."

"Did your mother approve of you learning to sign?"

"She didn't know about it."

"She knows about it now," he reminded her.

Her lip curled in disgust. "She doesn't care what I do."

That was an interesting answer, Frank thought. "How did your teacher find out about Adam teaching you to sign?"

"She caught us."

"Doing what?" Frank asked, feeling a frisson of alarm.

"Signing," she told him in disgust.

"Was your father angry?"

"Of course!"

"So he locked you in your room?"

"Only after I told him Adam wanted to marry me."

"Why didn't he want you and Adam to get married?" Frank asked. "Too poor?"

"Too deaf," she wrote in renewed disgust.

Had Nehemiah Wooten explained his theory of eugenics to his daughter? And if he had, would she have understood any of it? Probably not. She would have only been interested in one thing: the fact that he was forbidding her to marry Adam.

"Does your mother know Adam proposed to you?"

"Yes."

"Does she approve?"

"No. She says I'm too young to marry. She was seventeen when she married Father!" she added in outrage.

Which was probably why she didn't want her daughter to marry so young, but he didn't bother to write that. "What does she think of Adam?"

"She never met him."

Which didn't answer his question, Frank noted. "Did Adam ever meet your father?"

Electra stiffened in her seat and stared at him for a long moment.

"What did you ask her?" Mrs. Parmer asked in alarm.

"Nothing improper," Frank assured her. "Did he?" he wrote more firmly.

She touched her pencil to the paper and drew the letters with exaggerated care.

"No."

Frank knew she was lying, but before he could challenge her, he was distracted by the sound of running feet on the stairs from the floor below.

"Mother!" a male voice was shouting. "Where are you?"

This, Frank thought with satisfaction, must be the son.

"I DIDN'T TELL MY CHILDREN ABOUT THE BABY," MRS. Wooten told Sarah.

This wasn't unusual, of course. Children were often completely surprised to wake up one morning and find they had a new baby brother or sister that the doctor had brought in his black bag the evening before. Children as old as Electra might notice their mother's changing figure and inquire about the reason, of course, but even now, Sarah could see that Mrs. Wooten was such a large woman that her condition wouldn't necessarily have been noticed.

"I gathered she didn't know about the baby," Sarah said. She didn't mention that Malloy had told her that Mrs. Parmer and Mrs. Wooten's lover hadn't suspected either. "I understand your husband recently passed away," she added after a moment. "I'm very sorry."

"He didn't *pass away*," Mrs. Wooten said brusquely. "He was murdered, as I'm sure you already know, so don't bother trying to spare my feelings."

"I just didn't want to upset you unnecessarily," Sarah said. "You'll need all your strength to focus on the birth, and I was trying to judge your frame of mind."

"My frame of mind is no concern of yours. I just need for you to get this baby delivered and then get out of my house."

"Very well," Sarah said, not letting her annoyance show. She was used to dealing with ill-tempered women in labor. "I need to ask you some questions and examine you, if you don't mind, to make sure everything is as it should be."

"Nothing is as it should be," Mrs. Wooten said bitterly.

Sarah chose to ignore that remark. No use provoking her patient any further. She sat down and began asking her questions about her general health and any symptoms she might have experienced recently that would indicate problems with the baby. Then she listened to the mother's and the baby's hearts with her stethoscope, and laid her hand on Mrs. Wooten's stomach as she experienced a contraction.

"Is everything all right?" Mrs. Wooten asked when she was finished.

"I don't see anything unusual. The baby's heartbeat is good and strong," Sarah added encouragingly. She couldn't tell if Mrs. Wooten was relieved or disappointed. Oddly, she just seemed angry.

"I had very short labors with my other children," Mrs. Wooten said after a few moments. Sarah sensed that she was beginning to surrender herself to Sarah's care, however grudgingly. "Six hours was the longest, and only three the last time."

"That was a long time ago, and you're much older now,"

Sarah reminded her. "But we can hope." She didn't mention that a woman who was almost forty also had a risk of many complications that a woman in her twenties wouldn't.

Before Mrs. Wooten could reply, the maid returned with armloads of linens. When Sarah and the maid had remade Mrs. Wooten's lavish, four-poster bed with a rubberized sheet and clean bedding and the maid had gathered everything else that Sarah would need, Sarah turned her attention back to her patient.

"If you feel up to it, walking can help things move along faster," she said.

"I don't feel up to it," Mrs. Wooten said wearily, "but I do want to get this over with." She swung her slippered feet to the floor and struggled to rise, accepting Sarah's help with obvious reluctance. Sarah offered her arm for support, and the two began slowly circling the room, pausing occasionally for a contraction.

"I know what you must be going through, losing your husband so suddenly," Sarah said after they'd made several circuits of the room in strained silence.

"I'm sure you have no idea what I'm going through," Mrs. Wooten snapped. "Was *your* husband murdered?"

"As a matter of fact, he was."

Mrs. Wooten jerked to a stop, her eyes wide with shock as she stared at Sarah, trying to judge the truthfulness of her claim. "I . . . I'm terribly sorry," she stammered, her inbred manners overcoming her bad temper. "I had no idea."

"Of course you didn't," Sarah said graciously. "My husband was a doctor. He was murdered one night when he was out on a call."

"How long ago?"

"Four years."

"Did they ever . . . Do you know who did it?"

"Yes," Sarah said. "Mr. Malloy found the killer."

Her eyes grew wide again at this, then narrowed as she considered the information. "So that's how he knows you."

The truth was much more complicated than this, but she said, "Yes. Mr. Malloy is very good at his job."

For some reason, this news didn't seem to comfort Mrs. Wooten at all. Before she could reply, if indeed she'd intended to reply, a contraction came and captured her entire attention for several moments. When it passed, she straightened slowly and began to walk again, making no further reference to Malloy's talents.

After a while, she said, "I couldn't believe I was going to have a baby."

"I'm sure it was a surprise after all that time."

"I thought . . . I thought it was the change coming on. I thought I was too old."

Sarah remembered her assignment from Malloy, to find out if her husband could have fathered this child. "I'm sure your husband was surprised as well."

Her gaze cut sharply to Sarah, as if trying to judge her depth of knowledge. Sarah stared back, hoping she looked as innocent as she was trying to.

"Yes, well, I suppose so," was all Mrs. Wooten said.

Sarah let the matter rest for now.

AT THE SOUND OF LEANDER'S VOICE, MRS. PARMER JUMPED to her feet and hurried out to meet him. Although Electra couldn't hear her brother's voice, she knew something was happening from her aunt's reaction. She looked to Frank for an explanation.

"Your brother is home," he said to her.

She jumped up to follow her aunt, but stopped when she remembered the papers on which she'd written some of her deepest fears and all of her secrets. She snatched them up, making sure to get all of them, and quickly folded them up and stuffed them into her pocket. Then she looked at Frank and said, "Adam did not kill Father."

Before he could reply, she turned and hurried out to meet her brother. Frank followed, hanging back discreetly so he would have a better chance of overhearing something.

Mrs. Parmer had met the young man at the top of the stairs. She was speaking to him urgently but keeping her voice too low to be overheard. Leander Wooten was large boned and solidly built, like his mother, and as handsome as Electra was beautiful. His dark hair waved on his well-shaped head. Every girl who met him must have fallen instantly in love.

"That's impossible!" he was saying, apparently outraged by the news that his mother was in the process of giving birth. "I want to see her."

"You can't," Mrs. Parmer said, trying to grab his arm as he moved past her, but he easily shook her off.

By now Electra had reached him.

"Where's Mother?" he asked her.

"In her room," Electra replied. "But you can't go there!" she called after him as he pushed by her.

Then he saw Frank and stopped in his tracks. "Who are you?" he demanded.

"Detective Sergeant Frank Malloy of the New York City Police," he told him in his most commanding voice.

But rich boys weren't trained to fear the cops the way

poor boys were. In fact, rich boys weren't trained to fear anything much at all. "What are you doing in our house?"

"I'm trying to find out who killed your father."

He didn't even blink. "Then you're wasting your time here. No one in this house killed him."

"Something you know might help me find out who did, though," Frank countered.

That got his attention.

"He's been asking Electra questions," Mrs. Parmer informed him.

That got him angry. "Electra? What could she know that would help you?"

"Did you know she's been seeing a deaf man secretly?"

He was surprised, but only at finding out Frank knew about Adam Oldham. "He's been teaching her to sign," Leander said, instantly defensive of his younger sister.

"What's this?" Mrs. Parmer cried. "Who are you talking about?"

"It's nothing, Aunt Betty," Leander said. "Nothing for you to be concerned about."

"How can you say that? Everything about you and Electra concerns me!" She turned on Frank. "Is that what Electra was telling you? All that writing? Was that what she said?"

"What writing?" Leander asked, furious now. He turned to Electra. "What have you been saying to him about Father?"

But Frank could see that Electra had lost the thread of the conversation. She didn't know why Leander was angry. "You can't go see Mama. She's getting a baby, and she doesn't want us to see her!"

Leander ran his hand through his hair in frustration.

"What is going on here? Will somebody please say something that makes sense?"

"Your mother is having a baby," Frank said, figuring he might as well answer the young man's questions, since no one else seemed willing to do so. "A midwife is upstairs with her."

"That's impossible!" Leander said.

"I'm afraid it's not," Frank said quite firmly. "And I'm here trying to find out who might have wanted to kill your father. I was talking to your mother and Mr. Young when the baby started to come, so I sent for a midwife—"

"*You* sent for a midwife?" He turned to where Mrs. Parmer was standing, wringing her hands in dismay. "Why didn't *you* send for the *doctor*?"

"Your mother didn't want the doctor. You know what a gossip he is and—"

"Gossip? Who cares about gossip?" Leander demanded, but no one had an answer for him. Stymied, he tried another tack. "Did you know about this baby?" he asked his aunt.

She stiffened at once, her lips tightening to a thin, bloodless line. "I most certainly did not." She glanced at Frank and apparently decided the damage was already done, so she needn't hold back. "I don't believe your father did either."

"What are you saying?" Electra cried, completely lost and nearly in tears. "Tell me!"

Leander controlled his own shock and turned to her, instantly tender. "Nothing important," he assured her. "Don't worry. Everything will be all right."

"No, it won't!" she cried. "Father is dead, and Mother is getting a baby, and this man won't leave us alone!"

"Mr. Wooten," Frank tried, "if you answer some questions for me, I'll be glad to leave you alone. I'll also be glad to answer all of *your* questions," he added when Leander looked like he was going to explode from frustration.

"All right," he snapped, then turned back to Electra, instantly gentle again. "I need to speak with this man. Please go with Aunt Betty. She'll explain everything to you."

"I most certainly will not!" Mrs. Parmer said.

"Then tell her as much as you can," Leander said impatiently. "And for God's sake, don't upset her any more than she already is."

"I don't know how I'll manage to do both," Mrs. Parmer grumbled, but she took Electra by the arm and started speaking to her as she led her away, back to the small room where Frank had been questioning her.

Leander turned back to Frank and for an instant he looked as if he would like to throw him out the window. Then his good manners overtook his temper, and he said, "Let's go in there," and indicated the parlor where Frank had questioned Terrance Young earlier.

As soon as he'd closed the door behind them, Leander asked, "What's this about my mother having a baby?"

"I'm afraid it's true. I don't know how much you know about the process . . ."

"I know how they're made," he said with a trace of irony, "but not much after that."

"I arrived here this afternoon to ask your mother some more questions, and Mrs. Parmer took me up to her room."

"Her *room*?" he echoed in outrage. "Why would she do a thing like that?" A man would never be allowed to enter a lady's bedroom unless he was married to her.

"I think Mrs. Parmer wanted me to understand your mother's relationship to Mr. Young."

"How would going to her room do that?"

"He was in there with her. Alone."

"Uncle Terrance?" he scoffed. "I don't believe it!"

"If by 'Uncle Terrance,' you mean your father's partner, then no, you shouldn't believe it. It was Mr. Young Junior who was with her."

Leander opened his mouth to protest again, but the words seemed to die in his throat. The blood draining from his face, he made a strangled sound and started to keel over.

6

Frank lunged and caught Leander before he completely collapsed. Then after managing to walk him over to a chair and sitting him down, Frank slapped the young man's face a few times, until he came to enough to sputter in protest.

"What the . . . ? What happened?"

"You fainted," Frank told him.

"The hell I did!"

"Then you passed out, or nearly did. I saved you from cracking your head on the floor, so show a little gratitude."

"Why would I . . . ? Oh," he said, answering his own question as the memory came back. "You said Terry Young was in Mother's room," he remembered, trying to dredge up some anger but managing only a little outrage.

"Did you know about his . . . *interest* in your mother?" Frank asked as diplomatically as he could.

Leander sighed in disgust. "His own mother died years ago, when he was a child. Mother always paid a lot of attention to him. I just thought she felt sorry for him."

"And what did he feel about her?"

The color rose in Leander's face. "I thought he idolized her. He was always so . . . so *thoughtful*," he said, making the word sound like a curse.

"How was he *thoughtful*?" Frank asked.

"He always had a special gift for her on her birthday and at Christmas, something she'd say was her favorite present, something she'd say she'd always treasure. And when he was visiting, they'd be off sitting in a corner, talking for hours." He looked up at Frank, outrage shining in his fine eyes. "I can't believe he took advantage of her!"

"What makes you think he did?" Frank asked mildly.

Leander's lip curled in a sneer. "She's having a baby that my sister and I knew nothing about, and Aunt Betty said Father knew nothing about."

"Your aunt might be wrong," Frank pointed out, thinking Mrs. Wooten might be the one who had taken advantage.

"She wouldn't lie about something like that, not about family," Leander said with certainty. He rubbed a hand over his face, as if trying to wipe this whole unpleasantness away.

"What made you pass out?" Frank asked.

Leander looked up, angry again. "I didn't pass out."

"Something shocked you," Frank reminded him. "What was it?"

"I think I've already answered all the questions I'm going to answer," Leander said, starting to push himself to his feet.

"It's just that I was thinking," Frank mused, or pretended

to. "If this Terry Young was taking advantage of your mother, he certainly had a good reason to want your father dead."

As Frank had suspected, this got Leander's attention. "Do you think he killed my father?"

"He was at the office on Saturday. He has a key, or at least he has access to his father's key, so he could have come back after everyone left and let himself in. If your father had found out about his . . . his *interest* in your mother, he would have been very angry. Maybe he threatened him somehow."

"What do you mean?" Leander asked with some concern. "How would Father have threatened him?"

"I don't know, but he would've wanted to punish him somehow. Would Terry's father have been upset by this news? Would he have been worried about the scandal if word got out? Would he have cut off his son's inheritance or something?"

Leander thought about this. "I don't know what Uncle Terrance would do. What do you do to a son who seduced your partner's wife?" he asked bitterly.

Frank doubted there was much seduction involved. Mrs. Wooten didn't seem like the type of woman who would be wooed into adultery by silly romantic gestures or even "thoughtful" gifts. He didn't think it would be a good idea to mention this to Leander, though. "Maybe we're thinking about this all wrong," he said instead. "Maybe your father didn't know anything about it. Maybe Terry just decided he was tired of sneaking around to see his lady love and it was time to take some action. With your father out of the way . . ." Frank let that sink in for a moment.

"He didn't waste any time either," Leander recalled angrily. "We haven't even buried my father, and he was in my mother's room today!"

"He must have been feeling desperate," Frank said, watching Leander's face as the idea of Terry Young as his father's killer took root. "With the baby coming soon, he must have known . . . Well, maybe not."

"He must have known what?" Leander demanded, jumping to his feet. "What must he have known?"

"I was thinking that with the baby coming soon, your father would know . . . but of course, he might have thought the baby was his. And we don't really know if he knew about it or not—"

"He didn't know," Leander said with certainty.

"How can you be sure?"

"Because . . ." He stopped, hating telling all this to someone like Frank.

"Terry Young might have killed your father," Frank reminded him. "He definitely seduced your mother."

Leander ran a hand over his face again. "Mother was expecting a child when they found out Electra is deaf. It was a boy. He was stillborn. Father said . . ." He swallowed down the pain of the memories. "Father said there would never be any more babies. He didn't want to take the chance of bringing any more damaged children into the world."

"What do you think he meant by that?"

Leander gave him a disdainful glare, as if he thought Frank wasn't quite bright. "It meant that he and Mother never slept in the same room again. It meant that they could hardly stand to be in the same room together. Aunt Betty says that Father . . ."

"What does she say about your father?" Frank asked when Leander hesitated.

He sighed in disgust. "She says he changed after that. I don't remember him being any other way except the way he was, but she says he was kinder and happier before that. The news about Electra turned him into a different man, someone who was angry and bitter."

"Maybe Terry Young thought he was doing your mother a favor by killing her angry, bitter husband," Frank suggested.

Leander leaped to his feet. "How dare he——?"

Frank laid a hand on Leander's shoulder and collapsed him back into his chair again. "Easy now, son," he said. "We don't know for sure that he had anything to do with it."

"But you just said——"

"I said he might have. I can't arrest a man for that, because there's other people who might've wanted your father dead, too."

"Like who?" Leander scoffed, thoroughly angry now.

"Like Adam Oldham."

Leander's eyes widened in surprise. "Electra's teacher? Why would he want to kill Father?"

"Because your father didn't want Electra to marry a deaf man."

"Marry? What are you talking about? Electra isn't going to marry anyone. She's too young!"

"She's almost as old as your mother was when she married your father," Frank said.

"What does that have to do with anything? Electra's still a child!"

"Adam Oldham doesn't think so."

"What does that mean?"

"It means he asked her to marry him."

Leander lunged to his feet again, ready to do battle. "That son of a——"

Frank pushed him back down into his chair again. For

someone so large, he was surprisingly easy to push around. "What did you think would happen when your sister started sneaking out to meet him?"

"He was supposed to teach her to sign!" Leander insisted. "And he's old enough to be her father!"

"He's not *that* old," Frank said.

"Well, he's a lot older than *she* is, old enough to know better than to . . . Oh, my God, did he seduce her? If he did, I'll—"

"You'd better wait until you know for sure," Frank cautioned him, and this time Leander sank back down of his own accord.

"How did all of this happen?" he asked of no one in particular, putting both hands to his head as if afraid it might fly into pieces if he didn't hold it together.

"So it seems that Mr. Oldham wanted to marry your sister, and your father didn't approve," Frank said.

"Of course he didn't. He would have been furious!" Leander assured him. "He would have sent this Oldham packing and made sure he never got another teaching job anywhere in the country."

"Could he really have done that?" Frank asked curiously.

"Of course he could. My father is a very powerful man. If he told the faculty at the deaf schools not to hire him, they wouldn't have."

Which made a very good motive for murder, Frank thought. "How did you find out your sister was meeting with Oldham?"

Leander winced. "I . . . I helped her."

"How did you help her?"

"I found him for her. When she told me . . . You have no

idea what it's like for her," he said, his young face twisting with the pain he felt over his sister's plight.

"My son is deaf," Frank said.

Leander's face registered his surprise. At least he didn't think Frank was lying about it. "He is? Does he go to the Lexington Avenue School?"

"No, he goes to the New York Institution for the Deaf and Dumb."

This surprised him even more. "That's where Oldham teaches."

"I know. So why did you get Oldham to teach your sister?"

Leander sighed. "She told me how miserable she was, how hard it was for her to read lips and figure out what people were saying. She was always on guard, always watching in case someone spoke to her. And sometimes she couldn't make herself understood. She speaks really well, for being deaf, but sometimes she can't say a word clearly, and we don't know what she means. She gets so angry and frustrated . . ." He shook his head.

"So you decided to help her."

"Yes, after she asked me to. She knew that some deaf people learn to sign. She'd seen someone doing it somewhere, I guess. She wanted to be able to do it, too. She thought it would be easier to talk to other deaf people."

"How did you find Oldham?"

"I went to the school, the one where your son goes. I met one of the teachers there, a Mr. Rossiter. He's not deaf, so I was able to explain to him about Electra. I offered to hire him to teach her, but he suggested Oldham. He said it would be better for a deaf person to teach her."

"Who was going to pay him?"

Leander shifted uncomfortably in his chair. "He didn't charge very much. I paid him out of my allowance. I wanted to help my sister," he added defensively.

So it was Rossiter who had put Oldham and Electra together. Surely he'd known what would happen when a handsome young teacher was alone with a beautiful young girl. She'd certainly fall in love with him, the man who was going to open a whole new world of communication for her. And what about Oldham? Even if he hadn't developed real feelings for her, how could he resist the temptation to marry the daughter of a wealthy man? He'd never have to struggle to get by on the meager salary a deaf teacher earned. And from what Frank had seen of Oldham, he really did have feelings for the girl, young as she was.

Had Electra known her father's determination that she not marry a deaf man before she met Oldham? Had Oldham known? Frank would have to find that out.

"Did you know that your father found out about Electra learning to sign?"

"I was away at school," he hedged. "I go to Princeton University."

"Where's that?" Frank asked.

"In New Jersey. It used to be the College of New Jersey. They changed the name last year."

Frank either hadn't heard or had forgotten. It didn't matter. "So you were away at school. Does that mean you didn't know your father found out?"

"I didn't know until Father . . . Until I got home on Sunday," he admitted reluctantly. "They telephoned to tell me about Father and said that I had to come home right away. When I got here, Electra told me her teacher had caught her signing."

"Electra said the teacher had caught her with Oldham."

"She saw Electra practicing, and she confronted her. Electra admitted she was learning, but she said she was doing it on her own. Miss Dunham didn't believe her, so she followed Electra when she left school and caught her meeting Oldham."

"Where did they meet?" Frank asked, wondering just how compromising the situation was.

"Different places, I understand, but that day they were at the Astor Library."

Frank frowned. Not exactly the location a young man would choose for a seduction. Maybe Electra's virtue was safe, at least for the time being. "Electra said Miss Dunham told your father."

"Yes. She didn't really have any choice. Electra was secretly meeting a strange man, which was bad enough, but he was teaching her to sign, and that was unforgivable."

"Why was it unforgivable?"

"Because it went against everything Father believed. He wanted Electra to be able to talk to people and understand what they were saying. Hearing people, that is. She didn't need to use signs with people who can hear. They wouldn't know what she was saying with signs anyway. They're only good for talking to other deaf people, and Father never wanted her to associate with other deaf people."

"But she went to school with them," Frank pointed out.

"That couldn't be helped, but she'd never associate with them again after she left the school."

Frank considered what he'd learned so far from Leander Wooten. The young man was amazingly forthcoming. Frank figured he'd regret this conversation later, but that was too bad. Frank was going to find out as much as he could before Leander realized he shouldn't be talking to Frank at all. "What do you know about eugenics?"

"Who told you about that?" Leander wanted to know. He didn't look happy.

"Mr. Higginbotham."

"My father . . . He was totally unreasonable. After he heard Mr. Bell lecture on the subject, he made up his mind, and nothing would change it."

"Does Electra know your father didn't want her to marry a deaf man?"

Leander opened his mouth to reply but caught himself. He seemed to suddenly have realized that Frank's questions might have a purpose, and he wasn't sure he liked that idea. "I don't know what she knows," he hedged. "I've been away at school."

He would have been away only a few weeks, Frank thought. Not long enough to really lose track of what was going on with his sister. "If she told Oldham that your father wouldn't ever allow them to marry, Oldham had a good reason for getting rid of him."

Leander rubbed a hand over his handsome face. "I told you, I don't know what she might have told him. Haven't you asked enough questions? You're really wasting your time here. None of us knows anything about who killed my father."

Frank had already proved him wrong about that, but he said, "Thank you for your help, Mr. Wooten. If you think of anything else that might identify your father's killer, please let me know." He handed Leander his card, and Leander took it automatically.

"I'm sure I won't," he said.

Frank figured he wouldn't either, and even if he did, he wasn't likely to tell Frank.

M RS. WOOTEN HAD BEEN RIGHT. HER LABOR WAS PRO- gressing rapidly. Sarah and the maid had helped her into bed, where she now sat, propped up with pillows. The con- tractions were coming closer together, and she was feeling the urge to push.

Sarah had delivered hundreds of babies, and this was the time when the mother's true feelings always made them- selves known. She'd heard women scream and curse their husbands. She'd had women beg her to make it stop, to cut the infant from their bodies and leave them to die. Or beg her to crush the infant and take it away where they'd never have to see it again. She'd heard just about everything pos- sible. The younger the mother, the more vocal she usually was, and since Mrs. Wooten was much older than her usual patient and much more refined, Sarah really wasn't expect- ing much in the way of swearing or screaming.

Still, she hoped for some indiscreet utterances, but the most she heard was the occasional *damn*, uttered on a gasp as a contraction came on. Mrs. Wooten labored doggedly, her face growing red with the effort of expelling her child, the sweat soaking through her nightdress and darkening the sheets. The maid made a valiant effort to keep her mistress comfortable, sponging her face and limbs with cool water in between contractions, but nothing could cool the room as the heat of the early autumn day turned it into an oven.

"We should've stayed in White Plains," Mrs. Wooten said to Minnie as the maid wiped her brow, her tone accusing, as if it was the maid's fault they hadn't. "It's so much cooler there."

"Miss Electra wanted to come home," Minnie reminded her patiently. "They've got a summer cottage there," she added to Sarah with a shrug. "But they always come home when school starts up."

Sarah had fashioned cloth loops and attached them to the headboard for Mrs. Wooten to hang on to when she needed the support. She was holding them constantly now. The contractions were coming so closely, she didn't have time to work her hands out and back in again between them. Panting, she went limp against the pillows as the latest contraction faded.

"I could die, couldn't I?" she asked breathlessly.

"You aren't going to die," Sarah assured her. "You're doing fine."

"I was a fool, a stupid fool. He said he loved me!"

Sarah knew better than to reply to such a statement. She took the damp cloth from the maid's hand and gently patted Mrs. Wooten's face with it.

Then Mrs. Wooten groaned as another contraction tightened around her. "I can't stand this!" she cried. "I'm going to die!"

"No, you're not," Sarah said patiently. "You're going to have a baby, and then you're going to be fine. It won't be much longer now."

"How do you know?" Mrs. Wooten demanded furiously. "You don't know anything! You're just a stupid midwife. I should have gotten the doctor. Minnie, call the doctor!"

"You didn't want him, ma'am," Minnie reminded her, giving Sarah a desperate look. "You told Mrs. Parmer you didn't."

"We can call him if you want," Sarah said reasonably. "But the baby will be here before he is."

"No, it won't! It's never coming," she cried. "I'm going to die! Don't let me die!"

"You aren't going to die," Sarah said, lifting her nightdress to check on the baby's progress. "I promise you won't. The baby's crowning. I can see his head. When the next contraction comes, I want you to push as hard as you can."

"Oh, God, oh, God, I can't, I can't," she moaned. "I can't do it. I can't!"

"Yes, you can," Sarah said. "Just once more. Now push."

"That son of a bitch! He said he loved me, but he won't want me now! Not after this!" She made a sound like a growl in her throat as she hunched into the push and bore down with all her strength.

As Sarah had hoped, the baby's head emerged, all wet and streaked. "Just once more," Sarah said. "He's almost out. Just once more!"

"I can't, I can't," she sobbed as the maid wiped the rivulets of sweat and tears from her face.

"Don't you want to see your baby?" Sarah asked.

"No!" she cried, surprising Sarah. "I never want to see him!" And then she groaned as another contraction clamped down. She bared her teeth and made the growling sound again and this time the little body slipped free.

Sarah caught him—it was a boy—and started wiping the mucus from his mouth.

"It's a boy," Sarah told her.

"Is it dead?" Mrs. Wooten asked, her voice shrill. "It isn't crying. Is it dead?"

"No, it's just—"

"Then kill it! Smother it! Do something!" she cried.

In all her experience, Sarah had never heard such a request. When she looked at Mrs. Wooten, the eyes staring back at her held cold determination. Before she could think of what to say, the baby in her hands took a breath and released it on a wail. Sarah had always thought that was the most beautiful sound in the world, but Mrs. Wooten winced and fell back against her pillows again, this time in despair.

"Damn, damn, damn," she murmured as the baby's wail grew louder.

Sarah worked mechanically, tying off the umbilical cord and cutting it, then wrapping the baby in the clean blanket Minnie handed her. When her gaze met Minnie's, she saw her own horror reflected there, but Sarah knew better than to say anything and invite a reply from the maid that Mrs. Wooten could hear. Tomorrow, Minnie would still have to work in this house, and Sarah would do nothing to make that more difficult for her. Mrs. Wooten would forget what she herself had said here today, but she would never forget anything she heard from servants.

Minnie held the baby gingerly, as if afraid to offer it too much of a welcome into the world, and she kept watching Sarah for instruction. But Sarah was busy with the afterbirth and getting Mrs. Wooten cleaned up again. When she'd sponged her off and helped her change into a clean nightdress, she assisted her over to the settee so they could change the sheets.

"If you nurse the baby, even for a day or two, it will help you recover more quickly," Sarah told her.

"Absolutely not," Mrs. Wooten said with a shudder of revulsion.

Sarah had encountered reluctant mothers before. She also knew the power of a newborn to charm. "Then perhaps you'd just like to hold the baby while we make up the bed," she tried.

"No!" Mrs. Wooten said. "I don't want to hold it. I don't want to see it. I don't want it here at all."

Minnie's eyes widened in horror, but Sarah had to remain calm. "Minnie, would you take the baby into the other room and ring for one of the other maids to help me with the bed?"

"Yes, ma'am, I will," Minnie said gratefully, and carried the mewling infant into the other room of Mrs. Wooten's bedroom suite.

Sarah began to strip the sheets from the bed, giving Mrs. Wooten a few minutes to collect herself.

Another maid appeared, her eyes wide as she glanced around, taking in the scene before her so she could give a full accounting when she returned below stairs to the other servants. All she saw was her mistress, reclining on the settee, and Sarah waiting for her help in remaking the bed with fresh linens. The two worked in silence, and Sarah dismissed her with an armload of soiled sheets when they were finished.

Sarah helped Mrs. Wooten back to her bed. When the woman was comfortable, lying back against the pillows, half-asleep, Sarah said, "Would you like me to find a wet nurse for you?"

Mrs. Wooten's eyes popped open. "Can't you take it away? To an orphanage or something? I can pay you whatever you want. No one would ever know."

Sarah schooled her expression to conceal her true emotions. "Mrs. Wooten, too many people already know about it."

The woman looked desperate. "Then I could say it died. Babies die all the time. My last baby did!"

"Minnie knows he's alive. By now, so do the rest of the servants. And your other children, and Mrs. Parmer."

"Oh, yes, Betty," Mrs. Wooten said in dismay. Obviously, she had no faith that her sister-in-law would keep her terrible secret.

"There's no disgrace in a married woman having a baby," Sarah pointed out. "If anyone asks why you kept your condition a secret, well, that's easily explained. You were worried, perhaps even superstitious about it, after your last child died and considering your age." She could see Mrs. Wooten understood what she was saying, but just in case she had missed the underlying message, she added, "And no matter what anyone else might think, only you and your husband would know for sure if he wasn't the baby's father."

And of course that husband was now dead and long past raising any objections.

"Yes, yes," Mrs. Wooten murmured, closing her eyes again as she contemplated the situation and considered what Sarah had said. It would work. She knew it would.

"He's a fine boy," Sarah added idly, smoothing the sheet that covered Mrs. Wooten. "He'll be getting hungry soon."

"I suppose I should see him," Mrs. Wooten said with a sigh. "No use giving the servants any more gossip to spread."

Sarah gave her an approving nod and went to fetch the baby from Minnie.

"You're not going to take it away, are you?" the girl asked in alarm when Sarah reached for him.

"Sometimes women say silly things when they're having a baby, things they don't really mean," Sarah said, hoping Minnie would believe her, or at least pretend she did. "Mrs. Wooten would like to see her son now."

Minnie sighed with relief as she handed the baby over.

"Does the house still have a nursery?" Sarah asked.

"Yes, but it's been all shut up these ten years or more."

"Have the servants open it up then, and find some clothes and diapers. Buy some if you have to. We'll need some right away."

"What about a wet nurse, ma'am?"

"I'll take care of it."

Minnie scurried off to do her bidding.

The child looked up at Sarah with the wide blue eyes of total innocence only the newly born possessed. Did he have any idea how close he had come to rejection? Hopefully, not.

Sarah was smiling when she brought the baby back to his mother. Nothing in her expression or manner would betray her disgust for a mother whose initial reaction had been to murder her infant.

"I sent Minnie to get some diapers and clothes," Sarah said. "In the meantime, here is your son."

She placed the baby into Mrs. Wooten's arms and was gratified to see the woman's expression turn instantly tender. "He looks just like Leander did at that age," she marveled.

A few minutes later, Sarah had convinced her to nurse the child for her own benefit, after promising to arrange for a wet nurse as soon as possible. His belly full, the baby fell asleep, and Sarah tucked him in beside his mother for the moment.

"I'm glad he's a boy," Mrs. Wooten remarked, glancing down fondly at the child she'd wished dead only a short hour ago. "Females have a difficult lot in this world."

Sarah had to agree. "Beginning with the weakness of our own bodies," she said, thinking of how men's physical strength alone gave them such an advantage.

"Yes," Mrs. Wooten agreed eagerly. "A man can take his pleasure, and what are the consequences? Nothing for him and everything for the woman." She placed a hand over her belly, probably recalling her recent ordeal. "How fortunate that my husband . . ." She caught herself just in time, and her face registered the shock she felt at realizing she had almost said how fortunate that her husband had been murdered so he couldn't expose her adultery.

"Yes," Sarah said helpfully, deliberately misunderstanding. "How *unfortunate* your husband never got to see his new son. Have you thought what you will name him?" she added to distract them both from the woman's awkward slip.

"I haven't allowed myself to," she said. "I was so afraid he wouldn't survive, I haven't thought of anything beyond his birth."

Managing not to smile at how easily Mrs. Wooten had adopted her suggested lie, Sarah said, "I believe you can safely begin to think about it now. Will you choose another reference to Greek mythology?"

"Heavens, no," Mrs. Wooten exclaimed in disgust. "That was my husband's idea. I always thought it was ridiculously pompous. No, I'll choose something more sensible this time."

"Perhaps you could name him after his father," Sarah suggested, unable to resist.

Mrs. Wooten's head jerked up, her eyes glittering with fury. "What do you mean?"

"I mean it would be a nice tribute to your late husband to have the child named for him," she said innocently.

Her eyes narrowed shrewdly. "Yes, it would indeed."

* * *

FRANK WAS ONLY TOO GLAD TO ESCAPE THE WOOTEN home before Mrs. Brandt was finished with her assigned task. The idea of being nearby when a baby was born had turned his blood cold ever since he'd lost Kathleen after Brian's birth. He truly hoped he'd never have to return to the Wootens', too, although he knew that was unlikely. Someone in that house could lead him to Nehemiah Wooten's killer. So far the only person there who didn't seem glad—or at least relieved—that he was dead was his sister, Mrs. Parmer, and even she had information that might help him.

Of course, he'd never be allowed to arrest any of them, even if they were guilty. Rich people were never tried for murder in New York City. The best he could do was to privately identify the killer and proclaim the case unsolved. But more importantly, he could make sure an innocent person didn't hang because it would be easier to accuse somebody poor and powerless of the crime.

Energized by that thought, he went to Brian's school, grabbing a meat pie from a street vendor for a hasty lunch along the way. The next person he needed to confront was Uriah Rossiter. His name had been mentioned by three different people so far in the investigation, and Frank had a few questions for him.

Mr. Rossiter was teaching when Frank arrived, but because Frank's son was a student at the school, he agreed to allow someone else to monitor his class while he spoke with Frank. At least that was the story he gave when he got the summons, and his manner was pleasant and accommodating when he met Frank in the empty classroom to which Frank had been conducted so they could speak privately.

"I'm very happy to meet you, Mr. Malloy," Rossiter said,

shaking Frank's hand firmly with his bone-dry palm. Rossiter was a stump of a man, short and stocky and running to fat in his middle years. He didn't seem at all concerned about being summoned by a police detective. "We're very happy you chose to send Brian here to school. He's a delightful lad and quite bright for his age."

"I didn't come here to talk about my son, Mr. Rossiter," Frank said. "I'm investigating a murder."

"A murder?" Rossiter echoed in apparent surprise. "No one here at the school, I hope."

"No. Actually, it's Mr. Nehemiah Wooten." Frank watched carefully and saw a small flicker of recognition at the name. "Maybe you know him?"

"I can't say that I do," Rossiter said.

"But you know his son, Leander Wooten," Frank said. It wasn't a question.

"I don't believe I recall the name," he lied.

Frank was having none of it. "Leander already told me he approached you about teaching his deaf sister to sign."

Caught out, Rossiter suddenly remembered. "Oh, yes, of course. Now I recall. Such an earnest young man. He was very worried about his sister."

"What did he want from you?"

"Oh, he wanted me to teach the girl to sign, just as you said."

"Why didn't you?"

Rossiter considered his answer carefully. "I felt she would do better learning from a teacher who was deaf."

"Did you?" Frank asked with interest. "Why is that?"

"Because . . . because they would have more in common," he decided.

"But wouldn't it be difficult for them to communicate,

at least in the beginning? She couldn't read signs, and he couldn't read lips."

"Which would make it all the more necessary for her to learn to sign," he said, pleased to have come up with such a reasonable explanation.

Frank nodded, as if carefully considering his reasoning. "And having such a handsome young teacher would make her even more eager to communicate with him," he said.

Instantly wary, Rossiter said, "I don't know what you mean."

"Oh, I think you do, Mr. Rossiter," Frank said in the voice he used to cow hardened criminals. "There were no good reasons to give the girl a deaf teacher and a lot of reasons not to. And anybody with sense would know the girl would fall in love with Oldham. You put them together on purpose so that would happen. The only thing I don't understand is why."

"Really, Mr. Malloy, you're quite wrong—"

"No, I'm not, and I'll be glad to take you down to Police Headquarters, where we can talk about this some more. All night, in fact, if you're going to be stubborn about it. So tell me now, or I'll send for a Black Maria and have you hauled away like a common criminal."

"You wouldn't dare!" he exclaimed in outrage.

Frank never batted an eye. "Yes, I would."

Rossiter searched Frank's face and apparently saw the truth there. "All right. You're right, I did hope that Miss Wooten would be taken with Oldham, but I was only doing it for the good of the deaf community."

"What are you talking about?"

"I'm talking about her father," Rossiter said, the color rising in his face. "Mr. Wooten and his ridiculous theory about eugenics. I realized this was my opportunity to throw it into a cocked hat."

"By giving Electra Wooten the chance to fall in love with a deaf man?"

"Exactly! I couldn't be sure that Adam—Mr. Oldham, that is—would fall in love with the girl, too, but I made sure he understood the advantages of marrying into such a wealthy and influential family. When he developed feelings for her, that just made it easier to convince him to propose to her."

"So it was *your* idea for him to propose to her?"

"Let's just say that I suggested it to him. He needed no real convincing."

"And what did you expect to happen?" Frank asked with a frown.

Rossiter looked at him as if he couldn't believe Frank hadn't figured it out. "Adam and Electra would marry—elope if necessary to escape her father's disapproval—and their children would not be deaf! That would prove to Wooten that his theory of eugenics was wrong!"

7

SARAH WAS STILL PACKING AWAY HER EQUIPMENT WHEN someone knocked on Mrs. Wooten's bedroom door. Sarah moved to answer it, but the door opened before she could. Mrs. Parmer entered, her face set in determination, just in case someone tried to turn her away.

"I hope you're all right, Valora," she said, although her tone sounded more angry than concerned.

"I'm perfectly fine," Mrs. Wooten assured her, as if the concern had been real. "And so is the baby."

Mrs. Parmer stiffened at the mention of the child.

"Would you like to see him?" Mrs. Wooten asked, playing the role of proud mother perfectly now that she had decided to accept it.

"I most certainly do not," Mrs. Parmer said.

Mrs. Wooten pretended to be surprised. "I'd think you'd

want to see your poor dead brother's child," she said, making Mrs. Parmer gasp.

"How dare you say a thing like that? My brother had nothing to do with that child," Mrs. Parmer exclaimed.

"How dare *you* say a thing like *that*?" Mrs. Wooten replied.

"Because Nehemiah knew nothing about it, and all of us knew he was determined not to breed any more children with you."

"Nehemiah knew all about this child, but we were both afraid I wouldn't be able to carry him to term, because of my age." She seemed to be trying out the story for size, to see if it felt comfortable to her. Plainly, it did. "He and I had decided not to tell anyone else, just in case," she added with more confidence.

"You witch!" Mrs. Parmer said, quietly furious, as ladies were trained to be. "You can tell all the lies you want about my brother and what he knew or didn't know, but I know the truth, and I'll never accept your bastard as Nehemiah's child."

"I'm shocked at you, Betty," Mrs. Wooten said righteously.

"And I'm shocked at your behavior, Valora. Taking a boy young enough to be your son as a lover! What were you thinking?"

"He's not young enough to be my son! He's only ten years younger than I!" Mrs. Wooten protested, seemingly unaware that her vanity had made her admit to having taken a lover.

Mrs. Parmer smiled smugly, having won the battle of words. "And will you marry him now?" she challenged. "And make yourself the laughingstock of New York?"

"I'll do what I like now," Mrs. Wooten replied, stung by her sister-in-law's words but too proud to show it.

"Then you're even more depraved than I thought," Mrs. Parmer said. "Have you forgotten you've got two other children to think of? What about Electra and Leander? What will happen to them if they have a mother who's known to be a common trollop?"

Mrs. Wooten's face grew crimson, but before she could answer, the bedroom door flew open and Electra came rushing in, looking around frantically. "The baby?" she cried, and Mrs. Parmer reached out to her, as if trying to protect her from something. But Electra wasn't interested in being protected. "Baby?" she cried again, pushing past Mrs. Parmer.

"Here he is," her mother said, reaching down and picking up the tiny bundle lying beside her on the bed and holding him up for Electra's inspection.

The girl froze, staring at the bundle as if unsure of what it might contain. Then her mother turned back the edge of the blanket, revealing the baby's entire head, which was covered with dark fuzz. Electra's eyes grew wide.

"A girl?" she asked hopefully.

"A boy," her mother replied with a shrug.

Electra frowned and took a few steps closer to the bed, eyeing the baby suspiciously. "He's ugly," she announced.

As if in protest, the baby yawned hugely, making Electra start. His eyes opened to little slits, as if he were peeking out to see if there was something interesting enough out there to capture his attention. Then, apparently seeing nothing worthy of his notice, he closed his eyes and went sound asleep again.

Electra wasn't charmed. She frowned and said, "Why did you want a baby?"

"Sometimes babies just come, whether we want them to

or not," Mrs. Wooten said, earning a rude snort from Mrs. Parmer. Fortunately, Electra couldn't hear it.

"What is his name?" Electra asked.

Mrs. Wooten glanced at Mrs. Parmer, probably trying to judge just how far she could push the woman. She must have decided that naming her lover's child after her dead husband would be too far. "I haven't decided. What do you think we should name him?" she asked the girl.

"Orestes," Mrs. Parmer said behind Electra's back.

Even Sarah gasped at this reference to the brother of Electra in the ancient Greek tragedy. Orestes killed his mother and her lover, who had murdered Orestes' and Electra's father. A very interesting choice, Sarah couldn't help thinking.

Electra turned to see why her mother was glaring so angrily at her aunt, but Mrs. Parmer simply smiled benignly and said, "Yes, Electra, what should we name the baby?"

"Something easy to say," Electra suggested.

Sarah imagined that the girl had had a difficult time learning to say her own and her brother's unusual names.

Minnie came in the still open door, pausing just inside the room, as if sensing the anger radiating from Mrs. Wooten and her sister-in-law. She held a bundle wrapped in brown paper and tied with string.

"Is that for the baby?" Sarah asked, stepping forward to take it.

"Yes, ma'am," Minnie said, her eyes still watching the others warily. "Some diapers and sacques. Mary's looking through the attic to see what we have left from when Miss Electra was a baby."

"Nonsense," Mrs. Wooten said. "We'll want all new things for the baby. You can go back out and get whatever we'll need."

"Homer," Electra said, oblivious to the discussion around her. She'd been staring at the baby sleeping in her mother's arms.

Mrs. Wooten looked up in surprise. "What, dear?"

"Homer. For the baby. Papa would have liked that, and I can say it."

No one seemed to know how to respond to that. Sarah doubted that Mrs. Wooten was interested in pleasing her dead husband, though.

Sarah took the package from Minnie and began to tear away the paper. She took a diaper from the small pile inside and found some pins tucked in with them. Then she took the baby from Mrs. Wooten's unresisting arms, laid him on the bed, and unwrapped him. The blanket was already damp, and she asked Minnie to fetch another one.

"What's that?" Electra asked in surprise, pointing to the baby's penis.

While Mrs. Wooten stammered through an explanation, Sarah concentrated on folding the large square of fabric into a triangle small enough to fit and securing it to the baby's bottom. Then she pulled one of the sacques over the baby's head, slipped his tiny arms into the sleeves, and drew the drawstring tight at the bottom.

At least Electra's question indicated she was still an innocent. That was something.

When the baby was swaddled again, she returned him to Mrs. Wooten, who accepted the tidy bundle absently. She was still answering Electra's anatomical questions.

"Can he hear?" Electra asked when she'd been satisfied on the previous subject.

Mrs. Wooten's face fell, and she looked at Mrs. Parmer, who seemed equally stricken by the question.

Sarah got Electra's attention and said, "It's too soon to know."

"When will you know?" the girl asked.

"Maybe not for a long time."

Electra frowned and looked at the baby, still sleeping peacefully, in spite of all the turmoil around him. "I hope he's deaf," she said.

FRANK STARED AT ROSSITER, TRYING TO MAKE SENSE OF his reasoning.

"You planned all this just to prove some theory wrong?"

"It's more than just a theory. Do you know what Alexander Graham Bell is trying to do?"

"I know he doesn't think deaf people should marry each other."

"Oh, it's more than that. He also wants to forbid the deaf from learning to sign."

"What?" Frank asked in surprise. He hadn't heard about that before.

"That's right. Signing makes deaf people more inclined to associate with other deaf people. It just stands to reason, of course. Very few people who can hear understand signing, so if that's how you communicate, you're going to spend most of your time with other deaf people."

Frank was starting to understand it now. "So if you spend all your time with other deaf people and they're the only ones you can talk to, naturally you'll marry a deaf person."

"Yes, yes," Rossiter said, excited now that Frank understood. "And Bell is convinced that deaf people who marry are more likely to produce deaf children, and he wants to prevent more deaf children from being born."

"But Mr. Higginbotham told me that very few of the students in his school have two deaf parents."

"Higginbotham? From the Lexington Avenue School?"

"That's right."

"How do you know him?"

"I visited his school when I was trying to decide where to send Brian."

Rossiter frowned for a moment, and then he realized what that meant. "But you sent him here instead. Why?"

"Because when I met some of the former students from the Lexington Avenue School, I found out that even though they can talk and read lips, they still mostly associate with other deaf people. And when I found out that Brian probably wouldn't ever learn to speak clearly because he was born deaf, I decided he ought to at least be able to communicate with somebody. And when I met some deaf people who could sign, they seemed pretty satisfied with their lot in life."

Rossiter was nodding his approval of Frank's decision. "And those deaf people you met, did they have children?"

"Yes, they did, and their children could hear."

"My observation has been that deaf parents have about the same chance of having a deaf child as parents who can hear. Most of the parents of the students here can hear, and right now we don't have a single student with two deaf parents."

"Hasn't anybody pointed this out to Mr. Bell?" Frank asked.

"Mr. Bell isn't interested in hearing anything that disproves his theories. He is determined to do things his own way."

Well, that was one thing that Rossiter and Higginbotham could agree on. Frank had to remind himself he was investigating a murder. "Mr. Wooten liked to do things his own way, too."

Rossiter sighed. "He was using all his power and influence to convince the city that they should prohibit schools to teach signing to the deaf."

"What about the children who can't learn to speak or read lips?"

"Oh, they'd keep a few classes in signing, for the hopeless cases, but only as a last resort."

Frank considered Rossiter. He seemed like a completely rational man except for the gleam of the fanatic in his eyes. Had Wooten had that same fanatic's gleam? "So you decided it was your duty to use two innocent young people for your own purposes."

"I wasn't using them!" Rossiter sputtered.

"Yes, you were," Frank said blandly. "But don't worry. That might be immoral, but it's not illegal, so I'm not going to arrest you for it. Causing a man's death *is* illegal, though."

"I didn't cause anyone's death!" he protested.

"You gave several people a good reason to want Mr. Wooten dead, though."

"What are you talking about?" Rossiter's reasonable demeanor had evaporated, and now he was sweating and squirming uncomfortably in his seat.

"I'm talking about arranging for Wooten's young daughter to meet up with Oldham so the two of them would fall in love. You admitted that you knew Oldham and the girl would be attracted to each other."

"Oldham's a grown man," Rossiter argued. "He's responsible for his own actions."

"Oldham's a grown *deaf* man," Frank said. "There can't

be many females who'd consider him a good catch, even as handsome as he is. He'll never even be able to earn a respectable living."

"We teach our students a trade," Rossiter said defensively. "They can all earn a living, and Adam himself has a college education."

"Maybe he does, but the school doesn't pay him as much as they pay you, do they?"

Rossiter stiffened defensively, but he said, "I don't know how much they pay him."

Frank figured that if his own mother knew, Rossiter knew, too, but he wasn't going to waste time arguing. "Where were you last Saturday?" he asked instead.

"What?" Rossiter asked, confused.

"You heard me? What were you doing last Saturday?"

"I . . . I don't remember. Why does it matter?"

"Because Adam Oldham said he was with you."

"Adam?" he echoed in surprise. "Oh, yes, now I remember. I had some friends over for dinner, some fellow teachers."

"What time did Oldham arrive?"

"I have no idea. I didn't pay particular attention to when everyone got there."

"Roughly," Frank said impatiently.

"Well, I believe I told them to come around seven o'clock. I'm sure he was there by seven thirty at the latest."

"But he wasn't with you earlier in the day?"

"No, why . . . ? Oh, I see. That's when Mr. Wooten was killed, I suppose."

"And where were *you* that afternoon?"

"Me? What does that matter?" he asked, affronted.

"Because it does. Where were you?"

"At my home, preparing dinner."

"Alone?"

"Yes, alone," he snapped, growing impatient himself now.

"That's unusual, isn't it? A man who cooks?"

"The greatest chefs in the world are men," he said, affronted again. "And I'm a bachelor, so I've had to learn or eat in restaurants or from street vendors all the time. I value my digestion too much to do that."

"I see," Frank said, meaning it. If he didn't have his mother to do it for him, he'd be in the same situation. "Do you have any idea who might've killed Mr. Wooten?"

"Certainly not! I didn't even know the man."

"You never even met him?"

He thought about that for a few seconds. "No, why should I? And why should I even want to? I hate everything he stood for."

"Well, you don't have to worry about him anymore, do you?"

"No, I suppose I don't, although Mr. Bell has many more supporters who are just as ardent and just as influential." He sighed.

"How did you come to be a deaf teacher?"

"I'm not a deaf teacher," Rossiter corrected him with more than a little annoyance. "I'm a teacher of the deaf."

"A teacher of the deaf, then," Frank said, managing not to roll his eyes.

"My mother was deaf. I learned to sign before I learned to talk. Are you finished with me? I really should get back to my class."

"That's all for now," Frank said. "I may have some more questions for you later."

"I'm sure I've already told you everything I know," Rossiter said, rising from his chair. "I'm very sorry Mr. Wooten was murdered, but it couldn't possibly have been Adam who killed him."

"Why not?" Frank challenged, rising also.

"Because . . ." He had to think about this. "Because he's not the type of man who commits murder."

"And just what type of man commits murder?" Frank asked with interest.

Plainly, Rossiter had no idea. He said, "You would know that better than I."

Frank hoped he was right.

"How long will you stay?" Mrs. Wooten asked Sarah when Mrs. Parmer and Electra had finally gone.

"I think I should stay with you overnight," Sarah said, even while she wished to leave this house as soon as possible. "Or at least until the wet nurse arrives." She'd sent a message to the agency that she recommended to the few clients she encountered who could afford such a luxury. "You seem to be doing fine, but there's still a chance that you might need medical attention."

"Why? What could happen now?" she asked, alarmed.

"Excessive bleeding, for one thing," Sarah said, not wanting to give her the whole list of horrifying things that could go wrong with even a young, healthy mother.

"And what would you do if that happened?"

"I'd stop it," Sarah said with the confidence that had reassured countless new mothers. "But there's no need to worry. As I said, you seem fine, and I'm sure you are. You should really try to get some rest now, while the baby's asleep. I'll go and see how they're coming with the nursery. We should at least get a cradle in here for him to sleep in."

"And see that someone has gone to get more baby clothes. I'm sure everything I have left from Electra is moth-eaten by now."

Sarah nodded and let herself out of Mrs. Wooten's room. She sighed with relief to be away from that woman. Mrs. Wooten certainly didn't deserve the good fortune she'd had in losing her husband mere days before her guilty secret would have probably caused him to divorce her and put her out in the street without a penny. Men had done that with far less provocation than Mr. Wooten would have had.

Would her lover have taken her then? Since her lover was from a good family who wouldn't have wanted the scandal, Sarah had her doubts. And who would have taken the child? Wooten would have had the legal right to him, but would he have exercised it or disowned the baby as well? Not a very pleasant situation to imagine.

Sarah found the nursery at the end of the hall. The door stood open, and two maids, one of them the one who had helped Sarah change the bed earlier, were scrubbing every possible surface of the room. She saw that the cradle had already been washed, and she instructed them to take it down to Mrs. Wooten's room as soon as it was good and dry. When she turned to go, she found Mrs. Parmer waiting for her in the hallway.

"May I speak with you, Mrs. Brandt?" she asked anxiously.

"Certainly."

Mrs. Parmer indicated Sarah should follow her, and Mrs. Parmer took her into a room that was obviously her own bedroom. The room was modestly decorated compared to Mrs. Wooten's, the furniture more functional than fashionable and the bedclothes plain. When Mrs. Parmer had closed the door behind them, she turned to Sarah.

"Is my sister-in-law in any danger?"

"You mean from having the baby?" Sarah asked, not certain if Mrs. Parmer was worried about someone else being murdered.

"Yes, of course that's what I mean," she said impatiently.

"I don't think so, but there's always a possibility of complications, especially when the mother is older."

"What kind of complications?"

"The usual things," Sarah said, still unwilling to begin listing the various types of maladies that could befall a new mother. "I'm not overly concerned, since Mrs. Wooten is in good health and will be well taken care of." Mrs. Wooten certainly didn't have to worry about having to cook or clean or do laundry for her family before she was fully recovered from childbirth—or at any other time, for that matter.

"What about the baby?"

"He seems perfectly healthy." Sarah didn't mention that many seemingly healthy babies still died every day, but Mrs. Parmer would certainly know that. This baby had many advantages, however: a luxurious home with ample food and reliable care.

"He's not my brother's child, you know," she said.

"That's really none of my business, Mrs. Parmer," Sarah tried.

"She killed him, you know."

Sarah blinked in surprise. "Excuse me?"

"You heard me. Valora killed my brother. Oh, I don't think she struck the blow herself, but she's responsible for his death."

"What makes you say that?" Sarah asked carefully, not

wanting to seem too interested but also not willing to let an opportunity pass to find out something that might help Malloy solve the case.

"It's jealousy, pure and simple. Terry Young killed him, because Valora corrupted his mind."

"Do you have any proof of this?" Sarah asked.

"I don't need any proof. Any fool can see it. She ruined that poor boy. And he *was* a boy when she first met him. Just eight years old and motherless when his father and my brother became partners. Of course Terry adored her. She made sure of that, with her sweet smiles and her tender affections. Everyone said how good she was with him. He'd sit with her for hours, talking or reading or playing games. Even after she had her own children, she always favored him."

Sarah didn't know what to say. "That . . . that does seem unusual," she managed.

"Unusual? Oh, yes, very unusual, especially later, when he grew up, and he had no interest in girls his own age or in finding a wife. What did he need a wife for? He had Valora. And when she found out she was carrying Terry's child, she must have been terrified that her perversion would be discovered."

Sarah remembered her assignment from Malloy. "But how would her husband know the child wasn't his?"

"Because it couldn't have been his," she said with certainty. "Nehemiah hadn't touched Valora in almost thirteen years, not since they found out Electra is deaf and the baby Valora was carrying then was stillborn. Nehemiah was sure that baby would have been deaf, too, or at least damaged in some way. He said more than once that it was a blessing he didn't live."

"Is being deaf such a horrible thing?" Sarah asked, thinking of Malloy's son, Brian, and of Electra Wooten and knowing that it wasn't.

Mrs. Parmer stared back at her in surprise. "I . . . I love Electra dearly," she said, her voice husky with emotion. "But I would never want any child to be . . ."

"Less than perfect?" Sarah offered when she hesitated.

"Yes," she agreed readily. "Electra has suffered, and she'll suffer the rest of her life. Who will marry her? Who besides that deaf fellow whom she was seeing, that is?"

"She was seeing a deaf man?" Sarah asked in surprise. "She seems so young."

Mrs. Parmer's expression darkened. "She *is* young, far too young for a suitor, and of course her father knew nothing about it until a few days ago. Just before he died, as a matter of fact."

"I suppose he didn't approve," Sarah said.

"Of course not. He would never allow Electra to marry a deaf man, and certainly not some adventurer who was meeting her secretly in hopes of winning himself a place in this family."

Now wasn't this interesting? Malloy had only hinted at this part of the story. Sarah hardly knew which of her burning questions to ask first. She'd have to be careful not to seem too avidly interested. "How dreadful," she said. "What kind of a man would take advantage of an innocent young girl like that?"

"A man with no better prospects than catching himself a rich bride," she said, waving away this bounder's aspirations with a flick of her hand. "But that's neither here nor there. The important thing is that you understand how Valora deceived my brother."

Sarah was almost relieved to get back to the original

subject. "So you're sure Mr. Wooten would have known the baby wasn't his?"

"No matter what Valora says, Nehemiah was adamant he would not father any more children with her. And he would never have forgiven Valora for being unfaithful, and he certainly wouldn't have allowed her baby in his house. I want you to understand that."

"Why?" Sarah asked.

"So you'll tell that policeman. I want him to know that Terry Young killed my brother and why. I don't want him to get away with it. I don't want either of them to get away with it. You'll tell him, won't you?"

"Yes," Sarah promised her. "I will."

SARAH WAS MAKING HER WAY BACK TO MRS. WOOTEN'S room when a young man stepped out of one of the other rooms and stopped her.

"Are you the midwife?" he asked.

"Yes," Sarah said. "I'm Mrs. Brandt."

"How is my mother? No one will tell me anything, and they won't let me see her."

So this was Leander Wooten. "She's doing very well. She's tired, of course, and she's resting now. I'll tell her you'd like to see her when she wakes up."

He nodded, but he didn't move out of the way, so Sarah waited for the question he wasn't sure he wanted to ask. Finally, he said, "And the . . . the baby?"

"He's doing well," Sarah said. "I know it was a surprise, but babies can be a nice surprise."

Leander didn't look like he agreed with her. "It's a boy," he said. It wasn't a question.

"Your sister wants to name him Homer," she said.

"Homer?" he repeated in surprise. "Why did she pick that?"

"Because she can say it."

His lips tightened. "She still can't say Leander very clearly. Or Electra either, for that matter."

"She speaks amazingly well," Sarah said quite sincerely.

"She hates it," Leander said.

"She hates speaking?" Sarah asked in surprise.

"No, she hates it when people can't understand what she's saying. She hates it when she can't understand what they're saying, too. She gets so angry . . ." He sighed.

"I'm sure that's why she wanted to marry a deaf man," Sarah said.

"What did you say?" Leander asked in surprise. "Who told you that?"

"I . . . Mrs. Parmer mentioned it," Sarah remembered.

"She shouldn't have," Leander said, angry now, although Sarah couldn't tell if he was angry at her or his aunt. "Electra just had a schoolgirl infatuation. She has no intention of marrying anyone. She's just a girl."

"I see," Sarah said, although she didn't really. Mrs. Parmer had said Electra was "seeing" a deaf man. Not a deaf *boy*, she realized, which would have indicated someone her own age. She would have to find out more about this unsuitable suitor. "She does seem young to be seriously considering marriage."

"She *wasn't* seriously considering it," Leander assured her. "And she won't be seeing him again, I can promise you that."

Sarah wasn't sure why he should promise her anything, but she nodded encouragingly. Sometimes silence was the best way to promote conversation.

"I didn't intend for anything like that to happen when I hired Mr. Oldham," he continued. "If I had even suspected . . . But I didn't, of course. Who would? She's just sixteen."

"Sixteen can be a very dangerous age for a girl," Sarah said, recalling her own youth. "She feels like she's very grown up, but she's still very inexperienced."

"Exactly," Leander said, happy to find someone to agree with him. "I blame Mr. Oldham. He never should have encouraged her. I would have expected a teacher to be more . . . more *responsible*."

"A teacher?" Sarah said, surprised. This wasn't what she'd expected. "You're absolutely right. He *should* have been more responsible." Sarah's mind was racing, trying to make sense of this. "Did you say that *you'd* hired him?"

Leander's face flooded with color. "I . . . I don't believe I did," he hedged, although Sarah had heard him say exactly that.

"You couldn't have known his true character, though," Sarah said to excuse him. She didn't want him to flee out of humiliation before she'd had an opportunity to question him further. "You would never have entrusted your sister to anyone you didn't believe to be honorable."

"Of course not!" Leander said, mollified. "He teaches in a deaf school. I expected him to be completely trustworthy."

"I suppose you'll have to take Electra out of the school now," she said.

"Oh, he doesn't teach at her school. He teaches . . . Well, he teaches at a different school, but Electra wanted to learn something new, something they don't teach at the Lexington Avenue School, so . . . Well, I don't suppose you really care about all of this, and you probably need to get back to my mother."

Sarah was going to deny it in hopes of learning more from Leander, but then she heard the baby start to cry. She really did need to get back to Mrs. Wooten. "I'll tell her you would like to see her when she feels up to it," Sarah promised and hurried away.

Malloy had a lot to answer for, she thought to herself, turning her loose in this house without a proper explanation. Yes, he'd been worried about Mrs. Wooten giving birth at any moment, but really, there was no excuse for not taking a few more minutes to explain the rest of it. She'd have something to say to him when next they met.

8

FRANK FIGURED HE MIGHT AS WELL TRY TO FIND THE teacher at the Lexington Avenue School who had discovered Electra's involvement with Adam Oldham. He doubted she knew anything about the murder, but he liked to be thorough. And maybe Mr. Higginbotham had thought of something new by now that would help. Maybe he'd remembered that he did see the killer after all, running out of the building just as he arrived, with blood on his hands and a crazed expression on his face. Frank wasn't holding out much hope, but stranger things had happened. Just not lately.

Miss Helen Dunham turned out to be a respectable middle-aged lady, modestly dressed as became a female who had to make her own way in the world. Her pale blond hair had streaks of silver and was arranged in a neat bun on the back of her neck. Her brown eyes took him in with one practiced glance. In school, his teachers had all been nuns, but they'd used the same method of instantly sizing up a student. Frank could see that she'd already pegged him as a troublemaker. He decided not to disappoint her.

"Miss Dunham, I'm Detective Sergeant Frank Malloy and—"

"I know who you are, and I don't appreciate being taken away from my students like this. Can't you come back after school is over?" Plainly, she expected an apology and a promise not to bother her again.

"No, I can't," Frank said, absurdly pleased to see the flash of irritation in her eyes. "Please, have a seat," he added, offering her one of the two straight-backed chairs in Mr. Higginbotham's office. Higginbotham was out and the receptionist had allowed Frank to use it.

Miss Dunham took a seat, letting Frank know with a look that it was against her better judgment.

"I understand that you recently found one of your students in a compromising position," Frank said when he had seated himself.

"Who told you that?" she asked, horrified.

Frank had been taking a shot in the dark, but he hadn't really expected such a strong reaction. "Several people. Electra Wooten for one."

"I'm sure she didn't tell you I found her in a *compromising position*," Miss Dunham said with a frown. "She considered it all very innocent, but there was nothing innocent at all in the way that young man was looking at her."

"Where did you find them?"

"At the Astor Library," she said, confirming what he'd already learned, "but just because they were in a public place doesn't excuse their conduct. The fact that they were together at all was scandalous. Electra is only sixteen. She could have been ruined if anyone found out she'd been secretly meeting this . . . this person."

"How did you happen to be at the Astor Library at the same time they were?" Frank asked.

Miss Dunham had the grace to look embarrassed. "I had followed Electra."

"Was that something you normally did?" he asked as mildly as he could.

"Of course not!" she said, mortified at the suggestion she was in the habit of sneaking around after her students. "I suspected she was up to something when I saw her walking in the wrong direction when she left school that day, and as it turned out, she was. She was meeting that man."

"I understand he's a teacher at the New York Institution for the Deaf and Dumb."

"So he said," Miss Dunham said. "I can't confirm that. I only know that he was alone with Electra when I found them, and she admitted they had been secretly meeting for several months."

"If she's a student here, why did she need another teacher?" Frank asked with as much innocence as he could muster. He didn't think he was fooling her, though. She just glared at him.

"She had some ridiculous notion that she needed to learn to . . . to sign." She said the word as if it caused her pain.

"Don't you teach that here?" Frank asked, feigning ignorance.

"Only to the students who aren't able to master speech and speechreading, and we give the students every opportunity to do so before we allow them to learn to sign."

"Why is that?"

She really hated talking about this. He could see it practically radiating from her. "Because students who only know how to sign aren't able to communicate with the rest of the world."

"By 'the rest of the world,' I assume you mean people who can hear."

"Exactly."

"Have you been Electra's teacher for very long?"

"For five years," she said with a measure of pride.

"What subject do you teach?" he asked in surprise.

"I teach speaking and speechreading. It's very difficult, as you can imagine, and takes years and years of close individual attention. I only have four students at a time. Electra is my most accomplished," she added.

"After all your hard work, you must have been disappointed to find her with Mr. Oldham."

"I'm not sure I would say I was *disappointed*," she said, although she plainly was.

"After all the years you spent teaching her to talk?" he asked doubtfully. "Anybody would have been. You must've been angry, too. After all you did for her, and then she sneaks out with this fellow and learns to sign like . . . like . . ."

But Miss Dunham wasn't going to admit to being angry. "I was hurt, I'll admit. I simply can't imagine why she'd want to learn to sign."

"Did you ask her?"

"Of course I did!"

"And what did she say?"

"A lot of nonsense," Miss Dunham said, angry whether she wanted to admit it or not. "Why would she want to . . . to *limit* herself when she'd spent years and years learning to speak?"

Frank didn't think she really wanted him to explain that

to her. "What did you do when you found Electra with Mr. Oldham?"

"I took her away, of course, back here to the school. Then I told Mr. Higginbotham. I felt it was his place to deal with the situation."

"Then you didn't tell her parents?"

"No, of course not. That was Mr. Higginbotham's duty."

"Did you tell anyone else?"

"I . . . I suppose I may have mentioned it to some of the other teachers. I was upset, you see, and they wanted to know what was wrong."

"That would be understandable," Frank said. "Do you remember who else you told?"

"No, I don't. What does it matter? After what happened to Mr. Wooten, I'm sure everyone at the school knows by now anyway."

She was probably right. Frank wasn't even sure why he'd asked her that, but something was nagging at him. Someone had known about Electra and Oldham who shouldn't have, but he couldn't remember who it was. "Someone killed Electra's father," Frank reminded her. "I'm just trying to figure out who might have had a reason."

"That Mr. Oldham certainly did. I'm sure Mr. Wooten would have had him horsewhipped, if he could."

"And why is that?" Frank asked with interest.

"What do you mean?" she asked warily. His interest had alarmed her, for some reason.

"Just what I said. Why would Mr. Wooten have wanted to horsewhip Mr. Oldham? What do you think he did to deserve it?"

"He . . . He . . . Many things," she finally decided.

"Like what?"

"Like meeting Electra in secret," she said. "She's only a child."

"Do you think Mr. Oldham seduced her?"

Color flooded her face at such a frank question. "I have no idea, but the mere fact that they were meeting was enough to ruin her reputation."

This was true. "What else had he done?"

She pressed her lips together, as if trying to hold back what she really wanted to say.

Frank said it for her. "He taught her to sign."

"Yes," she said.

"And Mr. Wooten wouldn't have liked that."

"Of course not! It went against everything he believed in. He wanted her to speak and to understand the spoken word so she would never have to be isolated or shunned by people who can hear."

"In your opinion, which would have been the worst crime in Mr. Wooten's eyes—seducing his daughter or teaching her to sign?"

Miss Dunham stiffened in silent resistance. "I could not possibly speak for Mr. Wooten."

"Can you speak for yourself then?" he asked. "Which was worse in your eyes?"

To Frank's surprise, Miss Dunham's eyes filled with tears. She wasn't going to answer him, but she didn't need to. Frank knew. She would have considered Electra's learning to sign a personal betrayal of all Miss Dunham had taught her.

When Frank finally dismissed Miss Dunham back to her students, he found Mr. Higginbotham had returned and was waiting patiently for Frank to be finished using his office.

"Have you found out who killed Mr. Wooten?" Higginbotham asked when they were alone.

"Not yet," Frank said. "I don't suppose you've remembered anything else from the day you found Mr. Wooten's body."

"Not a thing I haven't already told you. I try not to think about it at all, quite honestly. I don't think I'll ever forget that scene, seeing him lying there . . ." Mr. Higginbotham shuddered.

"When did you find out that Electra was seeing Mr. Oldham?" Frank asked.

He considered the question. "Last Thursday, I believe. Yes, that's right. Miss Dunham brought Electra to me."

"What time was that?"

"I'm not sure, not exactly. But it was late in the afternoon. School was out for the day. Most of our students board with us because they live too far away to go home, but Electra went home each night. She'd left the school, as she usually did, but Miss Dunham had followed her that day."

Frank felt stupid. He hadn't asked Miss Dunham why she'd chosen to follow Electra that particular night. "Do you know why she did that?"

"Yes, she told me later. She said she'd seen Electra signing to one of the other students, and when she asked Electra about it, she lied and said it hadn't happened."

"I thought your students didn't learn to sign," Frank said.

"Only a few of them do," Higginbotham said. "The ones who can't master speaking and speechreading. It's very difficult, you see, and a few of them just aren't able. So we teach them what we can, and we teach them a trade."

"So Electra was signing to one of these students, and then she lied about it," Frank said.

"That's right. Miss Dunham said she acted very strangely, and so Miss Dunham watched her when she left the school and was alarmed to see her going in the wrong direction, so naturally, she followed her."

"Naturally," Frank said, although it wasn't natural at all. Miss Dunham would have had to be very alarmed to do something so drastic. And following someone in the city wasn't as easy as it sounded. The Astor Library was a long walk from the Lexington Avenue School. She could have easily lost her in the crowd unless she'd known ahead of time where Electra was going. But who could have told her? And why? More questions for Miss Dunham, who would probably lie or at least refuse to answer. "What did Electra have to say for herself when Miss Dunham brought her back here?"

"She begged me not to tell her parents, of course. She knew how angry her father would be about her learning to sign, although I would have expected him to be much more concerned about his daughter meeting with a strange man. She didn't seem concerned about that, however. She seemed to think they'd be getting married and everything would be fine."

"If you weren't going to see Mr. Wooten until Saturday, how did he find out what had happened?"

"I wrote him a letter and had a student deliver it to him that evening. His reply asked me to meet him at his office on Saturday afternoon."

"Who else did you tell about this?"

"No one! I was naturally concerned for Electra's reputation."

"But Miss Dunham told people."

"If she did, I have no knowledge of it."

Frank sighed. He wasn't getting anywhere with this. He had so much information, but none of it seemed to fit together. He was missing something. Maybe Sarah Brandt had learned something helpful by now. He wondered if he could call on her at the Wooten house without causing too much of an uproar.

"WHEN WILL THE WET NURSE BE HERE?" MRS. WOOTEN asked irritably.

"I'm sure they'll try to find someone as soon as possible, but it may take a day or two," Sarah replied, taking the sleeping baby from her arms. At least Mrs. Wooten hadn't refused to nurse him, so far.

"A day or two?" Mrs. Wooten echoed in dismay. "What am I supposed to do in the meantime? I'm already exhausted. I need my rest."

Sarah bit back the reply she really wanted to make. "You have to understand that they don't have wet nurses just sitting in their office, waiting for someone to request their services. If you'd given them some notice, they could have already arranged for someone, but under the circumstances . . ." Sarah shrugged eloquently before checking to make sure the baby was truly sleeping before placing him into the newly prepared cradle that the maids had brought in a few minutes ago.

Mrs. Wooten sighed dramatically. "Couldn't we feed him with a bottle until they send someone? I know that's possible."

"If there's no other alternative, a bottle is better than nothing," Sarah said, trying to sound patient and understanding, "but babies who are fed with bottles aren't as healthy as those who are breastfed."

"But they have those new, scientific formulas," Mrs. Wooten argued.

"And babies who drink them get sick more often, and they can get rickets and other diseases."

Mrs. Wooten sighed again. "But it would just be for a few days. I can't think what my friends will say if they find out I'm nursing a baby."

"Don't tell them," Sarah suggested. "Would you like to see your son now?"

She looked up, her dismay even greater now. "Oh, dear, I'd almost forgotten. Can't you tell him I'm too tired or something?"

"I could, but he's very concerned about you. I'm sure he just wants to see for himself that you're all right. I'll tell him he can only stay for a few minutes."

"Oh, all right, but *just* for a few minutes. Wait, give me my mirror first. And ring for Minnie. I want her to do something with my hair. It's a rat's nest."

Sarah pulled the bell rope, and a few minutes later, Minnie came in. She worked her magic with a comb and brush and some hairpins, and soon Mrs. Wooten looked more presentable, at least in her own mind. Then she sent Minnie to fetch Leander.

His knock was tentative, but perhaps he was afraid of waking the baby, Sarah told herself. She opened the door for him, and stepped back as he entered.

"Your mother is very tired, so you shouldn't stay very long," she said softly.

He gave a small sniff that told her he didn't believe that

for a moment, but he said, "Mother, how are you feeling?" and walked over to stand beside her bed.

She moaned softly, as if even opening her eyes was an effort. "Not very well, but I'm sure I'll be myself again in a few weeks," she allowed.

"This was quite a surprise," he said, unmoved. "Why didn't you tell us we were going to have a new brother?"

Sarah decided her presence could only be an embarrassment. "I'll wait in the other room," she said, moving toward the door to Mrs. Wooten's sitting room.

"Oh, no, please stay," Mrs. Wooten said. "I . . . I might need you," she added faintly.

Mrs. Wooten probably thought Leander wouldn't speak of anything unpleasant with a stranger in the room, Sarah decided, and moved discretely to the far corner and sat down to wait.

Leander had noticed the cradle, and he went over and looked down at the sleeping infant. "So that's him," he said to no one in particular. "He's awfully small."

"Babies usually are," Mrs. Wooten said, showing a trace of her true spirit before remembering she was pretending to be ill.

"What are you going to call him?"

"I haven't decided yet."

Leander turned back to her. "Surely, you and Father discussed names. He certainly had very strong opinions about what his other children should be called."

"I'm afraid I don't like your tone, Leander."

"What's wrong with it?" the young man asked, feigning innocence.

"It's . . . disrespectful," she decided.

"Oh, pardon me, Mother. I'm not exactly sure what tone I should be using with a woman who betrayed her husband with a man half her age and bore her bastard child in his very house."

Mrs. Wooten gasped. So much for her hope that he wouldn't say anything unpleasant in front of Sarah! "Leander! How dare you say such a thing to your mother!"

"How dare you *do* such a thing, Mother!" he replied. "And don't think that just because Father died so conveniently that your secret won't be found out."

"I have no secret," Mrs. Wooten insisted. "I have nothing to be ashamed of."

"But you have a very good reason for wanting Father dead," he said. "And so does Terry Young."

"How can you say such a thing to me! I have no idea what you're talking about."

"Aunt Betty does, though," Leander said. "And she has no reason to keep your secrets for you, especially not if Terry killed Father."

"Terry did no such thing, and please remember that any scandal that touches this family will ruin whatever chances Electra might have to make a suitable marriage. Heaven knows, she had little enough chance as it was, so before you decide to take some kind of petty revenge on me, think what it will mean to your sister."

Leander stiffened, fury radiating through him as the truth of her warning sank in. "I'll take care of Electra," he said.

"Do you think that's what she wants? To be someone's poor maiden aunt and live on your charity for the rest of her life?"

"And what makes you think that *you* know what she wants?" he demanded.

"Oh, I know what she *thinks* she wants," Mrs. Wooten said, abandoning all pretense of weakness. "She thinks she wants to marry that deaf teacher and live happily ever after! She has no idea what it's really like to live in this city without money or connections and to be deaf on top of it."

"Oh, no, far better that she marry someone she doesn't love who can take care of her, like you did," Leander snapped.

"That's enough!" Mrs. Wooten said. "Get out of here. I'm ill, and I need my rest."

"I just want you to know that Terry Young will never set foot in this house again," he said.

"That's not for you to say," Mrs. Wooten reminded him.

"Isn't it?" he replied confidently. "Let's wait and see what Father's will says, shall we?"

"What do you mean?" she asked in alarm.

"I mean Father had a talk with me several months ago. He told me that since I'm a man now, he was writing a new will leaving everything to me and charging me with taking care of you and Electra as I see fit."

"That's outrageous!" Mrs. Wooten cried, sitting bolt upright in bed. "You aren't even of age yet!"

Sarah knew this had gone too far, and she jumped up and hurried over to the bed. "Mrs. Wooten, you shouldn't be upset. Please, lie back down." She helped the other woman do just that, then turned to Leander. "I must ask you to leave. Your mother needs her rest. Really, it's not safe for her to be so upset."

"She should have thought of that before she took Terry Young to her bed," he said bitterly. "Her whole life is going to be upset now." He turned and started toward the door, then paused just as he reached it. "Oh, by the way, the funeral is tomorrow."

"Tomorrow! It can't be. I haven't made any of the arrangements," Mrs. Wooten protested.

"Don't worry, Aunt Betty took care of everything."

"Betty! What does she know about what I want!"

"Probably nothing," Leander said with a smirk and stepped out of the room, closing the door with a rude slam.

"I don't know what has gotten into that boy," Mrs. Wooten said, outraged. "Saying such horrible things to his own mother!"

"I'm sure he's not himself," Sarah said helpfully. "He did just lose his father."

"Which is no excuse to insult his mother. I hope I can trust your discretion, Mrs. Brandt. As I reminded Leander, any rumors about me will hurt Electra far more than anyone else."

Sarah knew that only too well.

THIS TIME FRANK USED THE TRADESMAN'S ENTRANCE. He didn't want anybody in the Wooten family to know he had returned, and even if they found out, they'd know he hadn't bothered any of them this time.

He'd been sent to the servants' dining room to wait, and a maid soon ushered Sarah Brandt in.

"Malloy," she said with the smile she always gave him.

"Mrs. Brandt," he replied with a smile of his own. He was ridiculously glad to see her.

He pulled out a chair for her at the table, and when she was seated, he pulled out the one next to it, turning it at an angle so they could speak more easily.

"How is your patient doing?" he asked.

"She's doing very well, although I'm going to stay at least

another day to make sure. Lots of things can still go wrong, especially when the mother is as old as Mrs. Wooten. And the funeral is tomorrow, so someone will need to stay with Mrs. Wooten while the family goes to the service."

"I hadn't heard that. Thanks for telling me. I'll need to go to the service."

"Why?" she asked in surprise.

"To pay my respects," he said with a grin, "and to see if anybody acts strangely."

"All these people act strangely," she said, not grinning at all.

"Could you manage to mingle with the guests that come back here after the funeral and eavesdrop to see if anybody says anything interesting?"

"I certainly cannot! I've got a patient to take care of."

"Just for a little while," he said. "You could tell Mrs. Wooten you were keeping an eye on Electra or something."

She glared at him, or pretended to. He didn't think she really meant it, but he decided to change the subject just in case.

"Have you found out anything about where that baby came from yet?" he asked.

"I found out where Leander Wooten thinks it came from. He thinks Terry Young is the father."

"So I gathered. Has Mrs. Wooten given you any reason to think so, too?"

"Yes, she has," she said. "She was quite apprehensive about the baby at first. She actually asked me to . . ."

"To what?" Frank prodded when she hesitated.

"To kill it," she admitted reluctantly.

"Good God."

"Exactly. I was horrified, and so was her poor maid, but

I managed to convince the girl that women often say crazy things during labor."

"Did she believe you?"

"I don't know. She pretended to, at least. And when Mrs. Wooten realized I wasn't going to do the baby any harm, she asked me to take it away to an orphanage or something."

"What kind of a woman would ask a thing like that?" Frank asked, horrified himself.

"A desperate woman," she said. "I'm not excusing her, but you have no idea how terrifying it is to be carrying an unwanted child."

Frank frowned. He didn't want to feel sorry for Mrs. Wooten. "She's not some shirt factory girl who's going to lose her job and be thrown out by her family to starve in the streets," he reminded her.

"No, but if her husband had realized the baby wasn't his, he could have divorced her and left her without a penny to her name. She also wouldn't have been allowed to see her children again. Her husband could even have kept the baby if he wanted to punish her more. She would have been just as desperate as the shirt factory girl, except she wouldn't know the first thing of how to take care of herself. I doubt she can comb her own hair."

Frank still didn't want to feel sorry for Mrs. Wooten. "She brought it all on herself," he reminded Sarah.

"I did say that I wasn't trying to excuse her," she reminded him. "I'm just explaining to you why she wanted to get rid of the baby."

"What changed her mind? That is, *if* she changed her mind."

"Yes, she did, after I pointed out that no one could

know for sure who the baby's father was except her and her husband."

"And since her husband is dead," Frank finished, "no one is left to accuse her."

"She saw that right away. The fact that she hadn't told anyone about the baby is also easily explained. I suggested that she might have been worried she couldn't carry it to term or that it would be stillborn, because of her age. So they decided to keep it a secret, just in case."

"You're very clever, Mrs. Brandt," Frank said with an appreciative grin. "Good thing you didn't decide on a life of crime. Heaven help the poor police."

"Heaven help them, indeed," she replied, returning his grin. "Have you made any progress at all in finding the killer?"

"No," he admitted with a sigh. "I just keep finding more people who wanted Mr. Wooten dead."

"Who?" she asked eagerly. "Besides Mrs. Wooten and her lover, that is."

"Electra Wooten," he said. "She was—"

"Seeing some deaf man she wanted to marry," she finished for him. "Leander let that slip. Honestly, Malloy, if you'd told me about that, I might have been able to get some more information out of him, but it caught me by surprise."

"Are you scolding me for not telling you all the details of the case?" he asked with some amusement.

She wasn't amused at all. "Yes, I am. You did ask me to find out as much as I could about who fathered Mrs. Wooten's baby, so why not tell me everything?"

"There wasn't time," he said, hoping she would accept that. "A baby was coming, remember?"

She didn't look pleased. "There's no baby coming right now. Tell me what you know about Electra and *her* lover."

"He's a teacher at Brian's school."

"Really?" she asked in surprise. "Oh, of course. Leander said he taught at a different school than the one Electra attends. I should have figured that out. Do you know him?"

"I just met him. My mother knows him, though. She says he's highly respectable, but that might just mean that all the females at the school are in love with him. He's young and handsome."

Her eyes lit with delight. "Is your mother in love with him?"

"I'm afraid so," he admitted, delighting her even more.

"Leander told me he'd hired this man to teach Electra. Why would he do that?"

"She wanted to learn to sign."

"You mean like Brian does?"

Frank nodded.

"Couldn't she learn that at her own school?"

"No, they don't teach signing there, and her father was determined that she not learn how."

"Why?"

Frank briefly explained Mr. Wooten's devotion to Alexander Graham Bell's theories of eugenics.

"But Electra still wanted to learn to sign," she marveled. "And she convinced her brother to help her."

"Yes, and he went to another teacher at Brian's school, an older man who probably wouldn't have caused any problems at all because Electra wouldn't have fallen in love with him. But when he realized who her father was, he recommended Mr. Oldham instead."

"You mean he purposely sent a handsome young man to teach her?"

"Yes, he wanted them to fall in love and get married and have children who weren't deaf so they would prove Bell's theory wrong."

"And prove *Mr. Wooten's* theory wrong," she realized. "But how could he even imagine it would all work out like that, just the way he planned?"

"He's an idiot," Frank said in disgust.

"Not completely an idiot," she pointed out. "Electra and this Mr. Oldham did fall in love, and Electra did want to marry him. That part of his plan worked perfectly."

"Her father never would've allowed it, though," Frank reminded her.

But she was thinking. "Remember what I said about an unwanted baby making a woman desperate?"

"Yes, but—"

"Wanted babies can make other people just as desperate," she said. "Of course, Electra and this teacher could just have simply eloped, but she's not of age and her father might have had it annulled or something. But if she was expecting a child, her father might have been convinced to approve of the marriage or at least to allow it."

"Is she expecting a child?" he asked in surprise.

"Not that I know of," she said. "And I don't think she and Mr. Oldham are lovers yet. She was very surprised to see the mark of a man on her new brother when I changed his diaper, which makes me think she's still innocent. But someone would have thought of it sooner or later, I'm sure."

"But Oldham wanted to marry the girl. Maybe he was in love with her or maybe he just liked the idea of a rich wife, but you can see that he had a good reason for wanting Mr. Wooten dead. And Electra . . ."

"Surely, you don't think she had anything to do with her own father's death!" she exclaimed.

"The first time I saw her, she told me she was glad he was dead."

"Oh, dear. That certainly doesn't look good for her and Mr. Oldham." She shook her head in dismay. "Haven't you found anyone outside the family who might have wanted him dead?"

"Not yet. I didn't like his partner much, but he doesn't stand to gain anything that I can see. The son inherits Wooten's share of the business, according to him. Oh, and he's the father of Mrs. Wooten's lover."

"Oh, I almost forgot, Mrs. Parmer told me some very interesting things about Terry Young and Mrs. Wooten, things she especially wanted me to tell you. I gather Young is only about ten years younger than Mrs. Wooten, but she's known him since he was a little boy, from when she first married Wooten, I guess. She wouldn't have been much older than Electra is now."

"How long ago would that be?" Frank asked, trying to do the arithmetic in his head.

"Twenty years or so, I would imagine . . . Oh, dear," she said again. "That really makes you wonder, doesn't it?"

"You mean wonder when they became lovers?"

"Yes." She gave a little shudder. "I don't even want to know."

Frank didn't either. This whole case was already disgusting enough.

"Do you think the man who recommended Mr. Oldham

could have been involved with the murder?" she asked after a moment.

"I don't see why he would want Mr. Wooten dead," Frank had to admit. "His plan was going just fine."

"But Mr. Wooten was killed at his office," she remembered. "Maybe it had something to with his business. I suppose you already thought of that, though."

"I talked to everyone who works there. If anybody knew anything, they didn't tell me."

"Maybe it's something they don't know," she mused. "Maybe something Mr. Wooten only just found out. Someone was stealing money from the company . . ."

"Where do you get these ideas?" he asked, amused again.

"I read the newspapers," she replied. "These things happen all the time."

"But people don't usually get killed," he reminded her. "They usually get caught and go to jail."

"But if they didn't want to go to jail and only one person knew about it . . ."

"Not very likely."

She sighed. "You're probably right. I just hope whatever it is won't cause a scandal."

"Why not?"

"Because, as Mrs. Wooten pointed out to Leander when he was threatening to expose her affair with Mr. Young, any scandal will ruin Electra's chances of making a good marriage."

"Then she can marry the deaf teacher," Frank said. "He won't care about a scandal, especially if he caused it."

She smiled. "Thank you for easing my mind, Malloy."

9

SARAH SPENT THE NIGHT ON A COT THAT HAD BEEN SET up in Mrs. Wooten's room. Both mother and baby passed the night with a minimum of disturbance, and Sarah slept soundly for several hours at a time.

When Minnie brought up the breakfast tray, she looked frazzled.

"I'm sorry, ma'am," she said, setting the tray down at the end of the bed. "This is the best cook could do. She's run off her feet getting everything ready for the funeral dinner today."

The tray seemed fine to Sarah. It held a selection of rolls and butter and jam, two plates with fried eggs and bacon, and a pot of coffee.

"What are they serving?" Mrs. Wooten asked with a worried frown. "What linens are they using? What is Electra going to wear? Who's helping her get ready? Who's coming to the dinner?"

"I'm sure I don't know, Mrs. Wooten. Nobody tells me anything."

"Then ask Mrs. Parmer to come to me," Mrs. Wooten said.

Minnie's eyes widened in alarm. "I couldn't do that, ma'am. She said she'd be busy and not to disturb her until it was time to go to the church."

"The church? Aren't they having the funeral here?" Mrs. Wooten asked, her voice rising shrilly.

"Oh, no, ma'am, Mrs. Parmer, she said it would disturb you too much. It's enough they have to have the dinner here after."

"But I won't get to see my husband! I won't get to say good-bye!" she cried.

Sarah wondered just how concerned she really was about seeing her husband one last time.

"But Mrs. Parmer said you couldn't come downstairs anyway, not in your condition, so there was no reason to cause a commotion in the household for nothing."

"Nothing! Does she think my husband's funeral is nothing!"

"Mrs. Wooten, you mustn't upset yourself," Sarah said, shooing Minnie away with a wave of her hand. The beleaguered maid gratefully made her escape.

"I can't believe it! Betty Parmer has taken over my household," Mrs. Wooten moaned. "Heaven knows what she'll do to embarrass me. And what about Electra and Leander? Who will look after them and make sure they're properly dressed and that they behave themselves?"

"I'm sure they're both well trained," Sarah soothed her.

"I can't stand it! I have to know what she's doing." She laid an arm across her eyes and moaned again. "Oh, wait, I know!" she said suddenly, removing the arm and looking at Sarah shrewdly. "You can go and tell me everything that happens!"

"I can't go to the funeral," Sarah said reasonably. "Someone has to stay here and take care of you."

"Minnie can stay with me for a few hours. I want you to go. You're the only one I can trust to tell me the truth!"

"Mrs. Wooten, you hardly know me," Sarah reminded her.

"But I know I can trust you. You're Felix Decker's daughter."

This seemed to make perfect sense to her, but Sarah had no idea why. "Mrs. Wooten, I can't go to a funeral. I don't even have any clothes with me." There, the perfect excuse that any lady of fashion could understand.

"But surely you own a decent suit you could wear to a funeral," she said, eyeing Sarah's serviceable skirt and shirtwaist.

"Yes, of course I do, but—"

"Then we'll send someone for it. Ring for Minnie. Is there someone at your house who can pack for you?"

"I suppose—"

"Then write them a note and tell them what to pack. You must be ready to go in the carriage with Mrs. Parmer and the children."

"I can't go in the carriage with them," Sarah protested.

"Of course you can. I'm still the mistress of this house, no matter what Betty Parmer thinks. Ring for Minnie. She can do your hair while you're waiting for your clothing to arrive."

* * *

Sᴀʀᴀʜ ᴄᴏᴜʟᴅɴ'ᴛ ʙᴇʟɪᴇᴠᴇ ꜱʜᴇ ᴡᴀꜱ ʀɪᴅɪɴɢ ɪɴ ᴛʜᴇ ᴄᴀʀ-
riage with Mrs. Parmer and Leander and Electra Wooten.
None of them was particularly pleased about the situation,
but even Leander's shouted protests hadn't changed his
mother's mind. Finally, Mrs. Parmer had decided to stop
objecting and go along with her sister-in-law's ridiculous
demands.

"I'm sorry if you felt unwelcome, Mrs. Brandt," Mrs.
Parmer said as the carriage rattled its way through the city
streets to the church where Mr. Nehemiah Wooten would be
mourned and eulogized.

"My feelings don't matter in the slightest," Sarah said
graciously. "I really don't want to be here any more than
you want me here. I'm only humoring Mrs. Wooten so she
doesn't get more upset than she already was."

"As we all are," Mrs. Parmer said. "And I finally realized
that I *want* her to have a complete report on everything that
happens so she knows my brother was laid to rest as properly as possible. Please notice how lovely Electra looks in
her white." Electra was too young to wear black mourning
clothes.

Sarah smiled at the sullen girl who was sitting across
from her, next to her Aunt. "Yes, she does."

Electra didn't smile back.

"And Leander looks quite handsome, doesn't he?"

Sarah looked at the young man sitting beside her. "Yes,
he does."

Leander pretended he hadn't heard.

Sarah managed not to sigh. This was going to be a long
day.

Sarah drew the line at sitting in the family pew. She took
a seat near the back of the church as the family filed down

the aisle to the front of the church where Mr. Wooten lay in state. She heard a buzz of reaction as people noticed Mrs. Wooten wasn't with them. The speculation would begin as soon as the service was over and people were free to talk among themselves. She wondered what Mrs. Parmer had decided to tell people when they asked, as they invariably would.

Sarah was watching the mourners file in and make their way up to view the dead man in his casket when a figure loomed beside her. She looked up to see Malloy staring back expectantly. She slid over in the pew to make room for him.

"What happened to your hair?" he asked with a frown.

Sarah touched it self-consciously. "Mrs. Wooten's maid arranged it for me."

"Don't let her do it again," he advised.

Sarah bit back a smile. "Do you see any likely suspects yet?" she whispered.

"At least a dozen," he replied solemnly.

She bit her lip to keep from smiling. "I suppose you're surprised to see me here."

"Yes, I am. I thought you had to stay with Mrs. Wooten."

"I did."

"Then why are you here?"

The lady filing into the pew in front of them gave them a disapproving glare.

"Mrs. Wooten ordered me to come," Sarah replied, lowering her voice. "She wants me to report back on everything that happens."

"Why doesn't she just ask her family to tell her?"

"I don't think she trusts them. They're a little angry at her right now."

Malloy nodded solemnly.

They sat in silence for a while, watching the crowd as the church filled almost to capacity. Malloy made a point of noticing every person who came in.

"Uh-oh," he murmured, startling Sarah.

"What is it?"

"It's the two Mr. Youngs, father and son."

"Mrs. Wooten's lover?" Sarah whispered, shocked. "Which one is he?"

Malloy indicated with a nod, and Sarah frowned. Not exactly what she had been expecting. He looked like a dreary young man already running to fat. He also looked as if he'd rather be standing before a firing squad than coming into this church.

The two men had words just inside the doorway, although the words were spoken too quietly for anyone else to hear. Mr. Young obviously expected to win the argument, but his son stubbornly refused to yield, shaking his head and stalking off to a rear pew on the other side of the church from where Sarah and Malloy were sitting. Mr. Young made his way to the front, where he viewed the body and spoke to the family members.

"He's probably afraid of causing a scene if he lets the family see him," Malloy remarked, staring at where Terry Young had seated himself. He was wiping his face with a handkerchief.

"He should be," Sarah replied. "I wouldn't be surprised if Leander challenged him to a duel."

"A little melodramatic, don't you think?"

"Leander tends to be melodramatic," Sarah said.

At last the service began, and they listened as the minister spoke of Mr. Wooten as if he'd been a saint, listing all of his good works and his devotion to his family and to the deaf through the Institution for the Improved Instruction of Deaf Mutes. After the appropriate amount of ceremony and music, the pall bearers, one of whom was Mr. Young and another of whom was Leander, carried the bier out of the church to where the shiny black hearse awaited.

"Are you going out to the cemetery?" Malloy asked as the family made their way down the aisle and the rest of the crowd began to follow them.

"Heavens, no. I shouldn't have even come here. I'm not riding in the family carriage again either. I'll walk back to the house."

"I'll see you there, then," he said and melted into the flow of mourners making their way down the aisle.

As she waited for the church to empty out, Sarah wondered how welcome Frank Malloy would be at the funeral dinner. Finally she left and headed back to the Wootens' house.

She found Mrs. Wooten in a state.

"What are you doing back so soon? Didn't you go to the graveside?" she demanded.

"No, I was worried about you."

"I'm fine! How am I going to know what happened there? Who can I trust to tell me?"

"Mr. Malloy will be there. He'll tell me whatever you want to know."

"Mr. Malloy? Who's that?"

"The police detective who's investigating your husband's murder."

"Good heavens! Nehemiah will turn over in his grave!" she exclaimed in horror. "What is this world coming to?"

Sarah needed a full half hour to finally calm her down and

only after answering dozens of questions about every detail of the service. She had to make up what she hadn't noticed or couldn't remember, because Mrs. Wooten wouldn't be satisfied with an "I don't know."

"You must go down when the guests arrive," Mrs. Wooten told her when she was satisfied that Sarah had told her everything. "I want you to sample the food and make sure everything is just as it should be. And tell me who's there, every single person."

"I won't know everyone who's there," she pointed out.

"Then find out!" Mrs. Wooten demanded irrationally.

Mercifully, she eventually exhausted herself and fell asleep. Luckily, the baby seemed to be sleeping pretty soundly, too. Sarah hoped he would stay that way for a while. She had only a few minutes to herself before she heard the carriages beginning to arrive outside. Leaving Minnie to sit with her mistress and the baby, Sarah went downstairs and found a place in a dark corner, where she could observe what happened without being noticed.

Mrs. Parmer, Leander, and Electra were the first to enter the house. Mrs. Parmer and Electra removed their hats, and the three of them took their places at the top of the stairs to greet the guests as they came up.

Sarah saw Mr. Young come in soon afterward, but his son was no longer with him. At least he'd had the sense not to come to the house, where Leander was even more likely to cause a scene. The trickle of visitors became a steady stream.

Sarah watched Electra Wooten as she accepted condolences from the black-clad mourners. "Where is your mother?" most of them asked.

"She was taken ill and cannot leave her bed," she said, the

words spoken even more tonelessly than usual, as if she were reciting sounds without even understanding the meaning.

If the visitor asked another question, seeking more details, Mrs. Parmer would reply, assuring the visitor that Mrs. Wooten was simply grief-stricken and would certainly make a full recovery and why didn't they go into the dining room and help themselves to some refreshment?

Sarah hadn't seen Malloy. He was probably making himself even more inconspicuous than she. The last of the mourners were climbing the stairs now, and Sarah saw Electra suddenly stiffen as she noticed someone on the stairs. Her resentful expression transformed in an instant to pure joy.

Sarah rose from her seat in the corner to see who had caught the girl's attention, and she noticed a young man staring back at Electra. He was slightly built for a man, but no less masculine for all that. His dark hair fell in unruly curls, and his soulful eyes seemed capable of only seeing beauty. His expression was cautiously hopeful, as if unsure of his welcome.

He should have been.

Leander saw the sudden transformation in his sister, and he, too, looked down to see who had caused it. "What's he doing here?" he demanded, but neither Electra nor the young man paid him any attention.

The young man quickened his step, pushing past the elderly couple ahead of him on the stairs and heading straight for Electra.

Could this be Mr. Oldham, Electra's suitor? The man Leander had hired to teach her to sign?

As if to answer her question, he started making rapid motions with his hands, and Electra's own hands began to move in reply.

What was he saying to her? No one else in this house would know, Sarah was sure.

"What's he doing here?" Leander asked again, nearly shouting now, as if by raising his voice he could make Oldham and Electra hear him. He must have realized the futility of that and grabbed his sister's arm, stopping her in midsign, but getting her attention at last.

"Why is he here?" he asked her more quietly.

"He came to comfort me," she told him, her voice loud enough for anyone to hear who cared to eavesdrop.

"He has no right to be here." He turned to Oldham. "Get out of my house!"

But Oldham didn't know how to read lips. He had no idea what Leander had said, although he could not have mistaken his thunderous expression. Oldham made some signs to Electra.

"He doesn't mean any harm," the girl said, moving to stand between her brother and her beau, as if to protect Oldham.

"What's going on here?" Mrs. Parmer asked, having finished with the last guests and turning her attention to the young people. "Who is this man?"

"He's Electra's *teacher*," Leander said with a trace of sarcasm, which Electra would not have heard.

"Leander, this is your father's funeral. You can't make a scene," Mrs. Parmer warned almost desperately.

Oldham had reached into his coat pocket and pulled out a small notebook and a wooden pencil. He began to scribble in the notebook, then held it up for Leander to read.

"I don't care—" Leander began to reply when he'd glanced at Oldham's message, but Oldham forcefully held out the pencil and notebook, reminding him that he needed to write his reply if he expected Oldham to understand. "Can't you sign to him?" Leander asked his sister in frustration.

"I don't know enough signs yet," she said, near tears. "Please, brother, don't send him away."

Leander snatched the notebook and pencil and wrote furiously, underlining something several times.

"Leander, please," Mrs. Parmer said, wringing her hands anxiously. "Don't do anything you'll regret."

"I already regret introducing this man to my sister," he said, handing the notebook back to Oldham, whose face flushed crimson when he read what Leander had written.

"What did you say to him?" Electra asked in alarm, reaching for the notebook, but Oldham was writing in it again.

"I told him he has no right to be here and that I forbid him to ever see you again."

Electra gave an anguished cry that attracted the attention of some of the mourners, and Mrs. Parmer quickly put her arm around the girl as if to comfort her. "It's been a difficult day for her," she told them, and tried to steer Electra away from her brother and Oldham, but Electra shook her off.

"I want him here!" she told Leander.

Oldham had finished writing, and he forced the notebook under Leander's nose again. Leander read what he'd written, and instantly calmed down.

"What did he say?" Electra demanded, trying to get the notebook again, but Leander snatched the pencil from Oldham and wrote a reply.

When he'd handed the notebook to Oldham, he said, "He apologized for offending me. He's going to leave."

"No!" Electra cried, grabbing Oldham's arm and making him drop the notebook. "Don't go!"

He couldn't understand her, but he must have guessed

her meaning from her desperate expression. He began to sign to her, slowly so she would be sure to understand.

"No, no!" she cried, shaking her head frantically so he'd understand her in return. She signed something, and he shook his head, too. Then he took her hand in both of his, making Leander gasp in outrage. Oldham and Electra were oblivious, though. Oldham lifted one of his hands and made a simple sign that turned Electra's face radiant again. She mimicked the sign back to him.

Sarah was afraid Leander was going to punch him or even push him down the stairs, but just in time, he released Electra's hand and turned to Leander again. He nodded politely and made a few signs.

"He says good-bye," Electra said.

"Good." Leander nodded stiffly back, and they all watched as Mr. Oldham turned and gracefully descended the stairs.

Even Sarah watched him go, thinking what a fine figure of a man he was, even though she didn't usually find the delicate, artistic type attractive. That's when she finally saw Malloy, who was waiting at the bottom of the stairs for him.

Oldham must have recognized him, and he stopped short for just a second before nodding politely and then going on, out of sight, toward the front door.

Everyone seemed to sigh with relief when he disappeared from view.

"Come, children," Mrs. Parmer said, holding Electra's chin in her hand to make the girl look at her. "We have to see to our guests."

They started off toward the dining room, but Leander said, "He forgot his notebook," and bent down to retrieve it.

Electra snatched it from him and held it possessively

to her breast. She gave him a defiant glare and then darted away, hurrying toward the stairs to the third floor and the sanctuary of her room before anyone could stop her.

SARAH WENT BACK TO CHECK ON MRS. WOOTEN several times during the afternoon, but the woman was still sleeping soundly. She must have exhausted herself with worry, Sarah surmised. So Sarah spent the time wandering around the house, among the mourners, trying to notice the things Mrs. Wooten would want described to her.

She caught Mrs. Parmer frowning at her several times, but luckily, the woman was too busy with her guests and too conscious of propriety to confront her about her presence. She was relieved to discover that she knew no one. The Wootens wouldn't socialize with the same exalted group of old money Brahmins that her parents did, she supposed. That saved her from having to explain her presence here. Whenever she encountered a curious look, she simply nodded, smiled, and moved on.

Avoiding conversation proved to be more exhausting than making it, she discovered as the afternoon wore on. She was looking for a place where she could hide for a few minutes when she noticed Leander and Mr. Young stepping into the small room she'd noticed earlier where Mrs. Wooten had her desk. Mr. Young's expression was determined, and Leander's was resentful. What could they have to discuss privately at a funeral?

Eavesdroppers seldom hear anything good about themselves, but Sarah doubted either of them would be discussing her. As casually as she could, she moved toward the door they had closed behind them.

"I really haven't decided anything," she heard Leander say.

"Your father would want you to finish your education," Young said.

"I really don't care what my father wanted anymore."

"Don't be a fool. There's no reason for you to get involved in the business just yet. You're young. You should enjoy yourself as long as you can and leave the business to me."

"So I should just let you and Terry run it into the ground?" Leander asked.

"I don't know what you're talking about," Mr. Young said gruffly.

"Don't you? I know what my father thought about you, and Terry's no better."

"Your father and I had our differences, but I would never do anything to hurt the company. It's half mine, you know."

"I don't know what I know," Leander said. "Look, this isn't the time or the place to talk about this."

"You're right. I'm sorry, but I wanted to know what your plans are. Maybe we could meet later . . ."

"Mrs. Brandt! There you are!"

Sarah looked up to see Minnie hurrying toward her.

"Mrs. Wooten is asking for you," she said.

Sarah sighed. She couldn't very well tell Minnie she had to stay where she was so she could finish listening at this door. She followed the maid upstairs.

Mrs. Wooten had been awakened by her hungry infant, and she was demanding to hear a report from Sarah. Sarah gave her one, including every detail she could recall but neglecting to mention Mr. Oldham's appearance. No sense in worrying her more than was necessary. Sarah was becoming concerned. Mrs. Wooten's color was high and her manner agitated, even after her nap.

"Mrs. Wooten, I think perhaps we should ask your doctor to pay you a visit, just to make sure everything is all right."

"No, I don't want to see him! I feel perfectly well. There's no reason to call that old busybody!"

"Then you must agree to calm down and rest. You're going to make yourself sick if you don't."

"I don't need a doctor," she insisted. "You'll stay, won't you? At least for another day or two? Until the wet nurse comes. I'll pay you twice whatever your normal fee is. Please! Don't leave me all alone, at the mercy of my family!"

In the end, Sarah agreed to stay for another day, not because of Mrs. Wooten's pleas but because she thought she might yet learn something that would help Malloy.

MALLOY FIGURED HE'D PROBABLY WASTED HIS ENTIRE day attending the Wooten funeral. Nobody acted at all strangely, unless you counted Oldham, who really had no business showing up at the Wooten house at all. You couldn't really blame him, though. If he wanted the girl, he'd be a fool to miss an opportunity to see her again. The next time he came to the front door, he might not be admitted.

The next morning Frank decided to return to Wooten's office. He'd been thinking about Sarah's theory that Wooten had been killed by somebody he was in business with. Not that Frank had any reason to believe that was true, but her remark had gotten him wondering. He'd looked at Wooten's appointments for Saturday, the day he'd been murdered, but it wasn't very likely his killer had scheduled the deed ahead of time so Mr. Wooten would write it neatly in his appointment book. The killer might, however, have visited Wooten earlier in the week and gotten into an argument with the man or received some bad news that made him come back at a later time, unannounced, to confront Wooten.

The clerk at the front desk wasn't happy to see Frank again.

"Mr. Young isn't in today," Peters informed his unwelcome visitor.

"I came to take another look around Mr. Wooten's office," Frank said.

"Didn't you already search it?"

Frank gave him a look that usually sent criminals running for cover.

"I . . . I'll check with Mr. Snodgrass," he decided and scurried away.

Frank remembered the head accountant from his previous visit. The older man had the dignity of a respected and valued employee, and he also wasn't happy to see Frank.

"Peters says you want to see Mr. Wooten's office again."

"I especially want to see his appointment book. I need to know who he met with last week and what they talked about."

"What could that possibly have to do with his death?" Snodgrass wanted to know.

Frank managed not to lose his temper. "I won't know that until I see the book, now will I? Now if you aren't interested in helping the police find Mr. Wooten's killer . . ."

Snodgrass sniffed, but he said, "Come with me."

He escorted Frank back to the office. The door was closed, and when Snodgrass opened it, Frank saw that the curtains had been drawn. Someone had worked very hard to clean up the bloodstains, but the carpet would have to be replaced.

The room had a musty, unused feel to it now that the former resident was gone. Would Leander use this office when he took over his father's half of the business? Frank wondered idly.

Snodgrass went straight to the desk, not allowing himself to look at the ruined area of the carpet. He pulled open a drawer and hesitated a moment before lifting out the ledger book and the stack of papers Frank had noticed on Saturday, the pages on which someone had been adding up columns of numbers. Snodgrass set them carefully on the desktop, off to the side, then retrieved the appointment book that Frank had looked at earlier. He laid it on the desk and found the correct page.

"Here it is," he said, stepping back so Frank could take his place and examine it.

"Tell me who these people are and why they met with Mr. Wooten that week," Frank said.

Snodgrass began with Monday and gave Frank the barest of information about each appointment. The early part of the week held nothing interesting or sinister.

"What did he and Mr. Young discuss here on Thursday?" Frank asked when Snodgrass tried to skip over that appointment.

"I'm sure I have no idea," he said, although the color rising in his face told a different story. "You should discuss that with Mr. Young."

Frank took a stab in the dark. "Is the business having problems?" Frank waited, watching Snodgrass's carefully expressionless face. "You'd know if it was," Frank guessed.

Snodgrass didn't flinch, but his gaze did dart, however briefly, to the ledger sitting on the corner of Wooten's desk. "I am not aware of any problems," he lied.

Frank pretended to believe him. He turned back to the appointment book and flipped the page to Friday.

"What's this?" he asked, squinting at the hurriedly scribbled name entered at the end of the day. "Does that say 'Oldham'?"

Snodgrass peered at the entry through his pince-nez. "I believe it does."

"Do you know Oldham?"

"I do not. He wasn't a client. I believe he was here on a personal matter."

"Did you see him when he was here?"

"Yes," Snodgrass admitted reluctantly.

"Was he alone?"

"I believe another gentleman came with him."

"Do you know the other man's name?"

"I wasn't introduced," he hedged.

"What did the other man look like?"

"Really, I didn't take any notice of him."

"An older man?" Frank tried, trying to figure out how to describe Rossiter. "Was he deaf?"

"I believe Mr. Oldham is deaf, yes," Snodgrass said.

Frank was ready to throttle him. "No, the other man."

"No, he wasn't," Snodgrass said. "Or at least he could speak and understand what was spoken to him. But Miss Electra is deaf, and she can speak . . ."

"Yes, I know, but you can tell she's deaf all the same," Frank said impatiently. "Did this man talk the way she does or did he talk like he could hear?"

"I believe he could hear. Mr. Oldham would make signs with his hands, and this gentleman would speak for him."

"Was his name Rossiter, by any chance?"

"It may have been," he allowed.

That would have been about right. Wooten would have received the letter from Higginbotham on Thursday evening, and he would have immediately questioned Electra and then sent for Adam Oldham. Wooten didn't understand signing, and Oldham couldn't speak, so Oldham would need an interpreter. He wasn't likely to bring his mother along on a visit like this, so Rossiter was the most logical choice since he'd been involved at the beginning.

Frank would give a lot to know what was said at that meeting. He might be able to find out, too, if he scared Rossiter enough. The man had lied to him about knowing Wooten, so Frank might be able to convince him he'd go to jail for obstructing justice or something.

"Did Mr. Wooten have any other appointments that aren't in the book?"

Snodgrass stiffened slightly before he said, "I'm not aware of any."

"I think you are," Frank said. "If I'm going to find out who killed Mr. Wooten, I need to know everything there is to know about what happened in the days before he died. You do want to see his killer caught and punished, don't you?"

"I don't know anything about who might have killed him," Snodgrass insisted.

But he did know something. Frank was sure of it. He wasn't going to betray his employer, even his dead employer, but someone else might.

"If you're finished here, I have work to do," Snodgrass said, hastily returning the appointment book, the ledger, and the papers back to the drawer where he'd found them. Then he went to the door and waited.

Plainly, he wasn't going to leave Frank alone in the office, which was exactly what Frank needed for him to do.

Frank allowed Snodgrass to escort him out. He thanked Snodgrass for his help and then lingered until he had returned to his office before turning back to the young clerk at the front desk. Peters was watching him the way somebody might watch a wild animal that had wandered in off the streets.

"Peters, Mr. Snodgrass said you'd know the name of the man who came in with Mr. Oldham on Friday afternoon."

Peters seemed relieved to be asked such an easy question. "Oh, yes, he told me his name was Rossiter. He didn't have an appointment, and I'm not supposed to take anyone back who isn't on the list, but Mr. Oldham is deaf, you see, and he'd brought Mr. Rossiter along to . . . to . . ."

"To interpret?" Frank supplied.

"Is that what you call it? Mr. Oldham made signs with his hands, and Mr. Rossiter told me what he was saying."

"Yes, that's what you call it," Frank said with a friendly smile, then leaned over and said softly, "I guess Mr. Wooten was pretty angry after they left."

Peters glanced over his shoulder to make sure no one else was nearby. "Oh, yes. He didn't get angry often, but when he did . . . He didn't shout or anything. That wasn't his way. He'd just get real quiet and cold, like he could freeze you to the spot with just a look."

"Did he ever get angry at you?"

"Once." Peters shuddered. "I made sure it never happened again!"

"If he wasn't shouting, how did you know he was angry that day?"

"He sent for me after they left, to send the telegram. When I saw his eyes . . ." He shuddered again.

"Who did he send a telegram to?" Frank asked idly.

"His son," Peters said without thinking, then caught himself, unsure of whether he should have revealed that bit of information.

Of course, Frank thought. Oldham would have told Wooten that Leander had hired Oldham to teach Electra. He'd want to deflect as much blame from himself as possible. It hadn't been his idea to meet Wooten's underaged daughter secretly. Her own brother had arranged it.

Frank nodded conspiratorially at Peters. "I guess he wanted to see Leander right away," he guessed.

"Oh, yes, *right* away. He told Leander to take the train up on Saturday morning and come straight to the office."

10

"Did Leander come on Saturday?" Frank asked.

"Not that I know of, but . . ." He glanced over his shoulder again. "I don't think he'd dare refuse."

Now wasn't that interesting? Leander Wooten had been summoned to his father's office on the very afternoon he'd been murdered. He'd also never mentioned that to Frank. Frank would have to ask him if he'd kept that appointment and what had happened when he did.

But first he had to check on one more thing.

"Could I use your lavatory before I go?" he asked.

"Oh, certainly," Peters said. "It's down the hall on the left, just before you get to Mr. Wooten's office."

Frank knew that already. After looking around to make sure he was unobserved, Frank slipped into Wooten's office, went straight to his desk. and found the ledger and the mysterious stack of papers. He slid the papers into the book, tucked the book under his arm, and made his way briskly back down the hall and past Peters's desk. The clerk was speaking with another man, and Frank nodded as he went by, not stopping even when Peters said something that might have been, "What do you have there?"

In another moment, Frank had melted into the crowd and vanished into the teaming city streets.

SARAH WAS ROCKING THE NEWEST ADDITION TO THE Wooten family in the chair the servants had brought over from the nursery when Betty Parmer entered the room un-announced. She hesitated a moment, looking to see if Mrs. Wooten was awake, before proceeding up to the bedside.

"Leander didn't come home last night," she informed Mrs. Wooten.

Even Sarah needed a moment to comprehend this amaz-ing statement.

"What do you mean, he didn't come home?" Mrs. Woo-ten asked, blinking in confusion.

"I mean he went out last night and never returned. I thought nothing of it when he wasn't at breakfast. He seldom is when he's at home, but when he didn't appear for lunch, I decided to rouse him. "None of the servants heard him come home last night, and his bed hasn't been slept in."

"Where on earth did he go last night?" Mrs. Wooten de-manded. "The evening of his father's funeral! Even Leander would know better than to go out on the town after such an event."

"I have no idea. He didn't confide in me," Mrs. Parmer said, obviously angry at the boy's impertinence. "It seems he didn't confide in anyone else either."

"How very like him to cause us the utmost concern at a time like this," Mrs. Wooten said wearily. "Well, I also have no idea where he might have gone, and I have no idea why you are burdening me with this now, when I'm weak and ill and can do nothing at all about it."

"I'm *burdening* you because I *thought* you might be concerned. He is your son, after all," Mrs. Parmer reminded her.

"I'm well aware that he's my son, which is why I'm sure he'll come home eventually. He always does. If you're worried, send someone around to his friends to find out whom he was with last night. He's most likely sleeping off his overindulgence at someone else's house, out of consideration for his poor mother."

With that, Mrs. Wooten sighed dramatically and pulled the covers up to her chin and closed her eyes, as if she simply couldn't keep them open another moment.

Mrs. Parmer made a rude noise and muttered something under her breath before slamming out of the room again.

When she was gone, Sarah said, "Does Leander often stay out all night?"

Mrs. Wooten opened her eyes and sighed impatiently. "Of course he does. He's a young man. That's what young men do. It was most inappropriate for him to go out last night, but without his father and his mother to guide him, I suppose he can be excused for making a bad decision. Have you heard anything from the agency about the wet nurse?" she added, surprising Sarah with the change of subject. "I don't know how much longer I will be able to take care of this child. I haven't slept two hours together since he was born!"

Sarah had no reply to this obvious exaggeration, but she

said, "I'll send another message to find out how much longer
they think it will be."

Seeing that the baby had drifted off, she laid him gently
in his cradle and went to do the errand. She encountered
Minnie coming up the stairs just as she was going down.

"Oh, Mrs. Brandt, that policeman is here, looking for Mr.
Leander. They told him he wasn't at home, so he's asked for
you instead."

Sarah hurried down to find Malloy waiting in the small
room just off the front hallway that was reserved for unwelcome visitors.

"Malloy," she said, absurdly glad to see him.

"Mrs. Brandt," he replied with a half-smile. "I'm surprised you're still here."

"Mrs. Wooten begged me to stay. She doesn't want to be
left alone with her family, and I don't blame her. She's done
nothing to endear herself to them lately."

"She might *never* have done anything to endear herself to
them," Malloy replied.

"You may be right. They said you were looking for
Leander."

"Yes, but they also said he's not home. Where is he?"

"That's just it. Nobody seems to know."

"I need to ask him a few questions. When do they expect
him back?"

"I don't think they do," Sarah said. "He didn't tell anyone
where he was going, much less when he'd return. He's been
gone all night, you see, and——"

"All night? Are you saying he went out carousing the
night of his father's funeral and never came home?"

"So it seems," she said,

Malloy shook his head in despair at the rich.

"What did you want to ask him?" she asked.

"Oh, nothing much," he said with feigned nonchalance. "Just what he and his father talked about when he went to his father's office the day he was murdered."

"What?" she asked in surprise.

"That's right. Turns out that Wooten had an appointment with Adam Oldham late on Friday afternoon. Mr. Wooten must have sent for him when he found out Electra was taking lessons from him. Mr. Rossiter came with him to interpret. I haven't spoken to Oldham or Rossiter, but I'm guessing they told him that Leander had hired Oldham."

"Oh, my, Mr. Wooten must have been furious at Leander!"

"He was, and he sent him a telegram, ordering him to leave school and appear at his office on Saturday."

"The day Mr. Wooten was killed!" Sarah exclaimed. "Did he come?"

"I don't know yet. If he did, he arrived after the rest of the employees had gone for the day. None of them saw him."

Sarah's eyes grew wide as she realized what this meant. "Could Leander have killed his father?"

"Whoever killed Wooten did it in a rage. He probably didn't plan it. He probably didn't even intend to harm Wooten when he went to see him. If he had, he would've brought along a more reliable weapon."

"Like a pistol or a knife," Sarah guessed.

"Instead, he got angry for some reason and grabbed the first thing that came to hand—one of the dozen trophies sitting on a credenza in his office."

"He must have intended to harm him then," Sarah pointed out.

"Probably, but maybe not kill him. We'll never know.

Maybe *he* doesn't even know. The point is, very few people could plan to kill a parent, but a lot of people accidentally kill a parent in the heat of passion."

"And I'm sure their argument was passionate," Sarah said. "Leander had betrayed everything Mr. Wooten believed in."

"Yes," Malloy agreed. "Getting someone to teach Electra to sign after they'd spent years teaching her to read lips and speak was the worst thing Leander could have done."

"Oh, no," Sarah disagreed. "Allowing her to fall in love with a deaf man was the worst. He'd taught her to lip-read and speak just so that would never happen!"

"So either of those things would have made Wooten furious, but both of them together . . ."

"I'm surprised Leander wasn't the one who ended up dead."

"Older men have usually learned to control their violent impulses," Malloy said. "Mr. Wooten was especially good at that. According to one of the clerks in his office, he never even raised his voice when he got angry."

"Oh, I hate people like that!" Sarah said. "I don't think I'd even blame Leander for bashing him on the head."

"If he's the one who did it," Malloy reminded her. "We still don't even know if he came back to the city on Saturday. That's why I need to talk to him."

"And of course you can't talk to him because he's not here. I think Mrs. Parmer was going to send one of the servants out to see if he was staying at a friend's house. I can send you word when he finally turns up."

"Don't bother. I don't know where I'll be, so I'll just plan to come back here this evening. Make sure Leander doesn't leave again before I get here."

"I'll do what I can," she promised.

"I'll see you later then." He picked up a large book that had been lying on one of the chairs and started for the door.

"What's that?" she asked.

He looked down at the book as if he'd forgotten he had it. "Some kind of ledger. I found it in Wooten's desk along with these." He opened the book and pulled out several sheets of paper on which someone had been doing sums with long columns of numbers.

"What does it mean?" she asked.

"I don't know, but the man at Wooten's office today got real nervous when he saw them in Wooten's desk, and even more nervous when I asked him if there were any problems with the company."

"Oh, I just remembered! Yesterday, at the funeral, I over-heard Mr. Young advising Leander to finish his education and leave him and his son to run the business for him. Leander made some remark about how his father hadn't thought much of Mr. Young's abilities to do that."

"Do you think Leander knew something specific?"

"If he did, he didn't say anything about it. He just sounded angry that Mr. Young would presume to tell him what to do and was getting back by insulting the man. But he did seem to think that his father didn't trust Mr. Young."

"Maybe with good reason. What else did they say?"

"Not much. Leander didn't want to talk about business at his father's funeral, which was understandable, and Mr. Young said they'd talk about it later. Then I was called away, so I didn't hear anything else."

"I wonder what this means," he mused, looking at the numbers written so neatly on the pages, but of course they meant nothing to him.

"My father always says that the numbers tell the story of a business," Sarah said.

Malloy frowned. "I prefer words."

"So do I, but I'll bet an accountant could tell you what this means."

"Do you know one?"

"My father employs a dozen of them, at least," she recalled. "Why don't you take this to his office? Ask for Mr. Colyer and tell him I sent you. He used to give me peppermints when I'd visit my father years ago. If anybody can make sense of this, he can."

FRANK HATED THE THOUGHT OF RETURNING TO THE OFfices of Felix Decker. He and Sarah's father had worked together on several occasions, and the experience had never been pleasant for either of them. At least he didn't need to see Decker this time.

The clerk at the front desk remembered him from his previous visits and was surprised when he asked for Mr. Colyer.

Colyer was a kindly version of Mr. Snodgrass. His thinning hair and his eyes were both the color of iron, and his expression was suspicious when Frank introduced himself.

"Mrs. Sarah Brandt sent me. Mr. Decker's daughter," he added in case Colyer didn't recognize the name.

Colyer's expression warmed instantly. "How is Mrs. Brandt?" he asked. "I haven't seen her in far too long."

"She's very well. She remembers that you used to give her peppermints."

He smiled at the memory. "She and her sister were such

sweet little girls. But you aren't here to talk about that. What is it you want?"

"I'm working on a murder case, and I found these in the dead man's desk," Frank said. They were still standing in the front lobby, under the watchful eyes of the clerk.

Colyer said, "Step over here."

They moved to the farthest corner of the room, where a sofa had been placed for guests who needed to wait. They sat down and Colyer took the ledger from him.

"Those papers were lying on top of it," Frank explained when he opened the ledger and found them.

Colyer glanced over them and then flipped through the ledger.

"Can you tell anything from them?"

"I'd have to study them," Colyer said. "What are you looking for?"

"I'm looking for a reason somebody might've wanted to commit murder."

"I don't have to ask whose ledger this is," Colyer said. "I read the newspapers. Why don't you just ask the accountants who worked for Mr. Wooten?"

"I did. He lied to me."

Colyer raised his eyebrows.

"Why would he lie?" Frank asked.

"I won't know until I figure out what these numbers mean," Colyer said. "Leave this with me, and come back tomorrow. I should be able to tell you something then."

FRANK'S NEXT STOP WAS THE NEW YORK INSTITUTION for the Deaf and Dumb. Rossiter didn't like being pulled out of his classroom a second time, but this time Frank noticed there was fear hidden beneath his outrage.

"I've already told you everything I know," Rossiter said. "You have no right to harass me."

"I have every right to harass you, Mr. Rossiter. You lied to me."

The surprise registered on his face before he could check it. "I have no idea what you're talking about," he lied again.

"You told me you'd never met Mr. Wooten, and now I find out that you and Adam Oldham visited him at his office the day before he died."

"I . . . I'm sure I never said I hadn't met the man. You may have asked me if I knew him, and of course I don't, not socially," he hedged.

"Met or knew or socialized, I don't care," Frank said, letting Rossiter see his anger. "I want to know what happened at that meeting with you and Oldham and Wooten."

"Just what you can imagine," Rossiter said defensively. "He'd found out that Adam was teaching his daughter how to sign. He was angry."

"How angry?"

"What do you mean?"

"I mean that Mr. Wooten is a man used to having his own way. You and Oldham had turned his own daughter against him."

"That's preposterous! We did no such thing. *I* did no such thing. I wasn't even involved."

"Except to recruit Adam Oldham because he stood a better chance of getting Electra Wooten to fall in love with him than you did."

"Mr. Wooten had no way of knowing that, and naturally, I did not mention it to him."

"He must have suspected it when he saw the two of you," Frank said. He'd never met Wooten, but he'd formed the opinion that he hadn't been a stupid man.

"I have no idea what he did or did not suspect."

"But I'm sure you know exactly what he threatened you with."

This time Rossiter couldn't hide the fear in his eyes. "Threatened? I don't know what you mean," he tried.

"You know exactly what I mean. Mr. Wooten would want to make sure neither one of you ever went near Electra again. He'd have the power to make sure that happened. What did he threaten to do?"

"I . . . You can't . . ."

"Yes, I can," Frank said. "I can even guess. Did he tell you he'd have your job? That he'd make sure no one ever hired you again at any deaf school in the country? It wasn't an idle threat. All he'd have to do is pass along the word that you had comprised his daughter. No parent would ever tolerate your presence in a school again."

"A teacher must be above reproach," Rossiter said, getting control of his fear. "I had done nothing wrong, but he would have ruined me anyway."

Frank thought it was a matter of opinion whether Rossiter had done anything wrong, but he decided not to argue the point. "And Oldham would have really been ruined. You might have found work someplace else, but as a deaf man, he didn't have a lot of options."

"Adam thought his best option was to marry Electra Wooten," Rossiter said somewhat bitterly.

"Did he tell Mr. Wooten that?" Frank asked with interest.

"Mr. Wooten already knew that Electra considered herself engaged to Adam. He made it clear to Adam that such a marriage would never happen."

"As long as he was alive," Frank remarked.

"What?" Rossiter asked in surprise.

"You heard me. Wooten would never allow his daughter to marry a deaf man, as long as he was alive to stop it."

"Believe me, Mr. Wooten's death was never discussed at that meeting," Rossiter hastily explained. "And it was certainly never considered, at least by me."

Frank thought that was likely. "Did you tell Wooten about his son's role in hiring Oldham to teach Electra?"

"We had to," Rossiter said, defensive again. "The alternative was to let Mr. Wooten think we had approached the girl and somehow coerced her into defying her father. Obviously, we couldn't allow him to think that."

"Obviously," Frank agreed. "So much easier to put the blame on Leander."

"The *blame*, if you can call it that, falls on Electra herself. She is the one who asked Leander to find a teacher for her in the first place," Rossiter reminded him.

"So all the men who could have refused that request must be completely innocent," Frank replied.

Rossiter had no answer for that, so he just stood there, fuming.

"I suppose Mr. Wooten was even more angry at his son than he was at you," Frank said.

"I don't believe it is possible to be more angry at anyone than Mr. Wooten was at us that day, although he never so much as raised his voice," Rossiter marveled. "I've never felt that cold before, not even on a February day."

"Did Mr. Wooten say how he intended to punish Leander?"

"Mr. Wooten is not the kind of man to reveal his plans to people like me," Rossiter said with more bitterness.

"I'm guessing he did make you both promise never to contact Electra again."

"Oh, yes. Adam was furious, of course. He kept professing his love for Electra and insisting he couldn't desert her. Luckily, Mr. Wooten doesn't understand signing, and I thought it wiser not to tell him what Adam was really saying."

"That must've made Adam pretty mad."

"He got over it after I explained to him how foolish he would be to defy a man like Wooten. Even if he and Electra were married, Wooten would make sure she was cut off without a penny."

"Did he really?"

"Did he really what?"

"Did he really get over it and decide he'd give her up forever? Because he showed up at the Wooten house after the funeral yesterday."

"He did?" Rossiter asked in surprise. Then after a moment, he said, "Well, I suppose he thought with Wooten dead, there was no longer any reason why he should stay away from her."

"It does seem logical, but from what I saw, Leander agrees with his father's decision that Electra shouldn't see Oldham anymore. He practically threw him out of the house."

"That's unfortunate," Rossiter said. "For Oldham, I mean. He genuinely cares for the girl, you know."

Frank didn't know, and he didn't care either. "Is there anything else you haven't told me, Mr. Rossiter, because if I have to come back again, I'll bring a Black Maria and cart you down to Police Headquarters in shackles."

"How dare you threaten me!" he blustered, but Frank saw the flash of fear again and knew he had Rossiter where he wanted him.

"Is there anything else?" he pressed.

"I . . . I don't think so. That was my only meeting with Mr. Wooten, I swear. When it ended, I promised him that Adam would have nothing further to do with Electra."

"Had Adam agreed to that?"

"Not yet, but he did later, when I explained everything to him, as I told you."

"Did you talk about it again when you saw him at your dinner party on Saturday night?"

"I tried, but he didn't want to discuss it anymore. He said everything was settled and more talking wouldn't change anything."

"If you remember anything else, be sure and send for me," Frank said. "I don't want any more surprises."

"Oh, no, you won't get any from me, I swear."

Frank was fairly certain that was true.

THE WET NURSE ARRIVED JUST BEFORE SUPPERTIME. She was younger than Sarah had expected. Most wet nurses were women whose own children were older. Perhaps her baby had died, as so many in the city did. Despite her youth, she had the same air of confidence they all acquired eventually. Because her role was so important to the household, she was a notch above the regular servants, who resented her exemption from anything unpleasant that might be remotely classified as work. She could demand whatever delicacy she wanted to eat and refuse to do anything she didn't like, saying it was bad for the milk. She didn't have time to so much as dust the nursery because she was caring for the mistress's child.

At least she was clean and knew not to gawk at the evidence of wealth all around her. Sarah took her right up to meet Mrs. Wooten.

"I'm very pleased to meet you, ma'am," Mrs. Fitzgerald said. All wet nurses called themselves missus, even though none of them ever seemed to have living husbands. "And is this the little gentleman?"

She scooped the baby up from his cradle and nestled him in her arms. "He's such a big fellow and so handsome! We'll get along just fine, won't we?" she asked him.

He merely stared back with wonder at this new person in his life.

"I shall be so grateful to you," Mrs. Wooten said. "He's been feeding every hour. I'm surprised I still have the strength to open my eyes."

Mrs. Fitzgerald looked questioningly at Sarah, who replied with an almost imperceptible shake of her head.

"You've been feeding him yourself?" Mrs. Fitzgerald exclaimed. "Mercy me, you should've sent for me sooner. You'll want to bind your breasts right away. That will stop your milk, you know."

"I'll take care of Mrs. Wooten," Sarah reminded her sternly, letting her know she might terrorize the servants but Sarah was in charge here.

"Oh, of course. I'm just glad you didn't start him on a bottle. It's so hard to get them to take the breast after that," she offered by way of amends. "I'll take this little one and get to know him, if you'll show me the way to the nursery."

In a few minutes, the servants had moved the cradle and

rocking chair back where they belonged, and Mrs. Fitzgerald was busy setting up her little kingdom.

Sarah hated binding a woman's breasts. The process of stopping a woman's milk after childbirth was painful and unnatural, but no one knew of a better way to do it. Usually, she had to do it because a baby had died, so at least this was a happier occasion.

Mrs. Wooten failed to appreciate that fact, however. She complained about the discomfort and the inconvenience, and berated Sarah and the agency for the delay in finding the wet nurse. Sarah decided not to remind her it was her own fault for having kept her pregnancy a secret. People like Mrs. Wooten didn't appreciate being reminded of their own faults.

"If you like, I can stay again tonight," Sarah said. "I'll show Minnie how to take care of you, and then plan to leave tomorrow."

Mrs. Wooten frowned. "I suppose you must leave sooner or later," she allowed. "Well, let's see how I feel in the morning."

"I'm sure you'll feel much better after a good night's sleep. I'll let you rest now. Just ring if you need anything."

"Oh, and find out where Leander has been. I want to see him later, when I wake up. I can't let him think he can run wild now just because his father isn't here to guide him."

Sarah pulled the drapes and left her.

She stopped in the nursery and found Mrs. Fitzgerald nursing the baby.

"Oh, good," she said when she saw Sarah. "Pull up a chair and have a chat. What on earth is going on here? They didn't know what to tell me at the agency, just that a lady needed someone quickly and the baby was already born."

"I don't know very much myself," Sarah said. She told

herself she was being discreet, not lying. If Mrs. Fitzgerald heard any gossip, it wouldn't be from her. "You see, Mrs. Wooten's husband was murdered on Saturday."

"Murdered! You don't mean it. Not here, in this house?" She glanced around fearfully, as if expecting a killer to jump out of a corner and attack her.

"No, he was at his office, alone, on Saturday afternoon."

"But a murder! Is it safe for me to be here, do you think?" She did look genuinely frightened.

"I'm sure no one has anything to be worried about. Whoever killed Mr. Wooten obviously had some sort of grudge against him, or maybe it was just a robbery gone wrong. But no one here has anything to fear, least of all you. No one here even knows you," Sarah reminded her.

"That's true enough, I guess. I've never known anybody who got murdered before, though. It's odd."

Sarah knew many people who'd gotten murdered, and she had to agree with her.

"Yes, well, getting back to Mrs. Wooten, the shock of her husband's death probably brought on her labor more quickly than she expected. She hadn't told her family about her pregnancy either. I'm not sure why she'd kept it a secret, something about being afraid she couldn't carry the baby to term because of her age, I think. In any case, she hadn't made any plans at all."

"She is a little old for this, but my mother had her last one at forty-two. One every two or three years since she was seventeen." Mrs. Fitzgerald shook her head.

"Mrs. Wooten's youngest is sixteen, so that's a bit different."

"A bit of a surprise, too, then! Poor thing, she probably thought the baby wouldn't live so why make plans."

"Yes, I'm sure that's it," Sarah said, a little surprised to hear how reasonable her own fiction sounded coming from someone else.

"Well, she's lucky. Looks like he wasn't too early. He should do just fine. What's his name?"

A knock startled them both, and Sarah went to open the door. Minnie was there, a worried look on her face. "That policeman is back, and he asked for you this time."

"Has Mr. Leander come home yet?" Sarah asked, excusing herself from Mrs. Fitzgerald and following Minnie downstairs.

"No, ma'am, he hasn't, and Mrs. Parmer is that worried."

"I'm sure she is," Sarah said. Where could he be? And how thoughtless to be gone so long without a word.

Malloy was in the small waiting room again.

"Leander hasn't come back yet," she told him.

"I know, the girl who answered the door told me. Did you say Mrs. Parmer sent someone to find him?"

"Yes, but I don't know what they found out. Let's ask if Mrs. Parmer will see us."

Mrs. Parmer was only too happy to see them. The poor woman looked as if she were at her wit's end.

"I haven't dared say anything to Valora, but we haven't been able to find any trace of Leander," she told Sarah the moment they walked into the parlor where she received them. "None of his friends have seen him since the funeral yesterday, and they swear he said nothing to them about having any plans last night."

"What time did he leave the house?" Malloy asked, pulling out his notebook.

"We aren't really sure, but it must have been after nine.

That's when I retired, and he was still here then. What could have happened to him?"

Sarah didn't dare look at Malloy. They both knew that any number of unpleasant things could happen to someone in New York City in the dark of night.

"Could he have just gone back to Princeton?" Malloy asked.

"I can't imagine he'd go without telling us," Mrs. Parmer said. "He didn't even take his bag. But we did telephone, just in case. They checked with his teachers and classmates, and no one has seen him."

"And you're sure none of his friends is covering up for him?" Malloy asked. "Maybe he has a lady friend or something, and he doesn't want you to know about it."

"Oh, I hope that's it. Is there any way you can find out?" she asked.

"If you give me the names and addresses of his friends, I'll question them again. They may tell me something they didn't want to tell your servant."

"Oh, thank you, Mr. Malloy. Yes, I'll make you a list. Please have a seat. I'll be back in a moment."

She hurried out, leaving Frank and Sarah staring after her.

"Do you really think he's seeking solace in the arms of a mistress?" she asked him.

"I hope so."

"But you don't think so."

"If he was going to be away this long, he'd have made up some excuse to leave. He would have known they'd go looking for him after a while. He probably expected to be back in an hour or two, before anybody even missed him."

"What do you think could have happened to him?"

"There are two possibilities."

"That he's either been hurt or killed," Sarah guessed.

"Or that our theory was right and he murdered his father. In which case, he's either run away or committed suicide."

II

It was still early enough that Frank was able to catch two of Leander's friends before they left for their evening's entertainments. The first was an obnoxious fellow with corn yellow hair that he'd slicked back with too much pomade and who reeked of too much scent. His clothing was remarkably ugly, considering that the house he lived in was big enough to accommodate the entire New York City police force. Money apparently couldn't buy good taste.

Frank had a little trouble convincing the servants to call young Master Armstrong Sterling to speak with him. He had to mention Leander Wooten by name, and only then did Armstrong reluctantly appear.

"What do the police care if Leander decided not to come home last night?" Sterling wanted to know.

"His father was murdered a few days ago," Frank reminded him. "His family is very worried about him."

"So I gathered when they sent the footman around looking for him. He wasn't here. I told the boy so already. He never said a thing to me about going out last night either. Would've talked him out of it if he had. Bad form. Very bad form. One may flaunt convention in certain things, but not this. This is too important. One's mother must be considered, after all. Women are sensitive. They feel things more than men do."

Frank doubted Mrs. Wooten felt much at all, but he didn't say so. "If he was going to stay out all night, where would he go?"

"No place! He wouldn't stay out all night."

"Well, he did stay out all night last night, and now we've got to find him. For his mother's sake," Frank added, managing to keep a straight face. "She's taken to her bed over this."

Sterling looked suitably horrified. "Has she? That's terrible! Leander should be ashamed. He's a bit of a stick-in-the-mud sometimes, but he's a good egg all around. To tell you the truth, I don't see him doing something like this. He's not the kind to go off and not say anything to anybody."

"When he does go out, where does he usually go?"

"Oh, lots of different places. Wherever we can find some good music and liquor."

"And women?"

"Women, too," Sterling admitted with a shrug, patting his slicked-back hair.

"Does Leander have a special woman, one he sees regularly?"

"Good God, no. Not Leander. First of all, his old man keeps him on a short leash. He couldn't afford to have a mistress, if that's what you mean."

"That's exactly what I mean. What about whores, then? Is there a regular place you go?"

Sterling's pale face bloomed with scarlet. "Really!" he tried, feigning outrage.

"If Leander is holed up in some brothel, I can take him home and put his family out of their misery," Frank reminded him gruffly. "So if he is, which one would it be?"

"I won't say we never visit those . . . such places," Sterling said, although admitting that cost him some of his outsized pride. "But again, Leander didn't have a lot of money to spend in places like that, and you don't get back in again unless you spend a lot of money."

Frank knew there were many "such places" that didn't require a lot of money to visit, but apparently, Leander and his friends didn't frequent them. He decided to test out another of his theories. "Is Leander the kind who would run away from trouble?"

"Run away? What do you mean?"

"I mean if he felt guilty about something, would he face up to it or try to get out of it?"

"Leander would never run away," Sterling said without the slightest hesitation. "He's more likely to get himself in *more* trouble by trying to explain. He did that more than once with his old man."

That had been Frank's impression, too, but he had been hoping to be wrong. If Leander had run away, he was likely safe at least. "If you had to guess where Leander might be, what would you say?"

Sterling looked genuinely puzzled. "I wouldn't say anything," he insisted. "What I mean is, I *couldn't*. I couldn't guess at all!"

Sterling looked at the list Mrs. Parmer had given Frank

and suggested his next visit should be to Percy Wilcox, who knew Leander better than anyone. Percy was a plump young man with a shiny face and protruding eyes that gave him a permanently startled look. He had no idea what could have become of Leander either.

"Not like him to disappear, is it? He's been away at school, though, so maybe he's developed some new habits, but why would he do it now? With his family all in an uproar over his father dying like that? Just not proper."

"Could he have a lady friend?" Frank tried. "Maybe he just decided it was nicer to stay with her than to go back to a house where everybody is in mourning."

"Leander's not much for the ladies. Oh, he likes to look at them and take a tumble once in a while, but he's never been one to fall in love. Not for more than a few hours at a time, if you know what I mean."

Frank did. "What might have kept him away from home this long?"

Percy considered. "His sister might. I mean, if she was in danger or in trouble, he'd do whatever he had to. Always has been protective of the girl. She's deaf, you know."

"Yes, I know," Frank said, "but she's not in danger. She's safe at home."

Percy shrugged. "Then I don't know where he'd be."

Frank tried the three other names on the list, but those young men were not at home, which meant Leander wasn't at their houses either. By then, the sun had set, and the city was settling into darkness. He wasn't going to be able to question anyone else until tomorrow, and that was a long time for Leander's family to wait. There was one more place he could look for Leander tonight. He'd tried not to think

about it, but he had no other options this evening. He raised
his hand to flag down a cab.

SARAH WAS LOOKING FORWARD TO A RESTFUL NIGHT,
since she didn't have to worry about the baby waking up.
The wet nurse would take care of him, and Mrs. Wooten
and Sarah would be able to sleep through the night without
disturbance. In the morning, she would finally be able to
go home and see Catherine and Maeve and sleep in her own
bed, at least until the next delivery. She was relaxing in Mrs.
Wooten's sitting room when Minnie came looking for her.

"That policeman is here again," she said. She didn't look
happy about it.

"Did he find Leander?" Sarah asked hopefully, setting her
book aside and rising from her chair.

"He didn't say nothing about Mr. Leander. He asked for
Mrs. Parmer, but he said to make sure you were with her
before they brought him upstairs."

Fear clenched in Sarah's stomach. He wouldn't need her
there to tell Mrs. Parmer good news. "Thank you, Minnie,"
she said, hurrying out.

She found Mrs. Parmer sitting in the back parlor, the
comfortable room the family used for gathering. She looked
up in surprise from her needlework when Sarah entered.
"Mrs. Brandt, is something wrong?" she asked when she saw
Sarah's face.

"Mr. Malloy is here," Sarah said, trying not to sound apprehensive. Maybe the news wasn't so very bad.

"Has he found Leander?" she asked, setting her work aside
and rising from her seat. "Has he brought him home?"

"I don't know," Sarah said, moving toward her.

"Mr. Malloy," the maid said in the doorway, and Malloy stepped into the room.

Mrs. Parmer's face lighted with hope until she saw his expression. "No!" she cried and her hand flew to cover her mouth.

"I'm sorry, Mrs. Parmer," he said, coming closer. "Maybe you should sit down."

All the color had drained from the woman's face, and she didn't resist when Sarah gently guided her back down into her seat. "Leander?" she asked in a whisper.

"I'm afraid he met with an accident last night."

"An accident?" she repeated, grasping the tiny shred of hope that offered. "Then he's . . ."

"He's dead," Malloy said. Although the words were harsh, his tone was amazingly kind.

"No, it can't be! There's been some mistake," she insisted, turning to Sarah as if looking for confirmation that a terrible error had been made.

"I saw his body," Malloy said. "He was found in the Bowery last night. He'd been robbed, so he didn't have any identification. That's why they hadn't notified you."

"No!" Mrs. Parmer cried again, her eyes filling with tears. "Not Leander, too!" Her voice caught on a sob, and then she was weeping piteously into her handkerchief. Sarah sat down beside her and slipped her arm around her, offering what comfort she could.

"I'm sorry, Mrs. Parmer," Malloy said after a few minutes. "Even though I'm sure it's Leander, someone will have to come down and make a formal identification, but that can wait until tomorrow. It doesn't have to be a family member either. One of the servants can do it for you."

Mrs. Parmer looked up, her eyes so dark with pain that

Sarah could hardly stand to look at her. "I'll go," she said. "I can't leave that poor boy alone. Someone from his family should claim him."

"Mrs. Parmer, please," Sarah tried. "You don't need to put yourself through that."

"He's my brother's child," she said simply. "And there's no one else to do it." She looked at Malloy. "Will you take me to him?"

"Now?" he asked in surprise.

"Yes, now. I won't be able to sleep until I've seen him for myself. I must be sure, you see."

"I'll go with you," Sarah offered, but Mrs. Parmer shook her head.

"Valora will want to know where you've gone, and I don't want her and Electra told until I've seen . . . until I'm sure it's him. I'll take my maid with me." She rose. "Please wait here, Mr. Malloy, while I get my things and order the carriage brought around."

When they were alone, Malloy ran a hand over his face. "She shouldn't do this."

"She's stronger than you think," Sarah told him. "And she won't believe it's him unless she sees for herself. What on earth was he doing in the Bowery?"

"Probably what everybody else does in the Bowery. He had a lot on his mind. I don't blame him for wanting to forget his troubles for a while."

"Wasn't he with his friends?"

"Not any of the friends Mrs. Parmer knew about, so we'll have to do some more investigating."

"How did he . . . ? You said it was an accident."

"If you call having somebody bash your head in an accident."

"That's how his father was killed," Sarah said, hugging herself against a sudden chill.

"Yes, it was."

She waited, and when he didn't say anything else, she asked, "Do you think they could be connected?"

"It's hard not to be suspicious, but he *was* in the Bowery. He's a rich man's son, wearing good clothes, drinking too much, and maybe flashing around a lot of money. He could've just been killed by somebody who wanted his watch."

"Poor Mrs. Parmer. Poor Electra," Sarah said, thinking how horrible this would be for the girl.

"What about poor Mrs. Wooten?" Malloy asked.

"I'm having a difficult time feeling much sympathy for her, but that's probably cruel of me. She'll certainly be devastated. Although . . ."

"Although what?"

"Leander told his mother that Mr. Wooten had changed his will so that Leander got control of all the money. He was supposed to take care of his mother and sister."

"So who gets it now?" he asked with a spark of hope. "Somebody who might've wanted him dead?"

"I'm sure it would be Mrs. Wooten or Electra, by law, unless Leander had a will, which seems doubtful since he's so young."

"You're probably right, and I don't see Mrs. Wooten or Electra following Leander down to the Bowery in the dead of night and hitting him over the head."

"Neither do I. Do you see anybody else doing it?"

"Mrs. Parmer?" he asked with a wry smile.

"What about Mr. Young?" Sarah asked, half-seriously. "He might have been worried Leander would find out he was . . . What was it Leander said? Oh, yes, running the business into the ground."

"That's insulting but not exactly illegal, and probably not serious enough to kill somebody over."

"Maybe it was. What did Mr. Colyer say when you showed him those papers?"

"He told me to come back tomorrow."

"So you really don't know yet. I told you before, people get killed over numbers all the time."

Malloy shook his head in dismay at her reasoning.

"Mrs. Brandt?" Minnie said from the doorway. "Mrs. Wooten needs you."

"I have to go," she told Malloy.

"Are you going home tomorrow?"

"I don't know now. I may have to stay if Mrs. Wooten is too upset. But I want to hear what Colyer has to say."

"I'll find you then."

Yes, she thought. Malloy always found her.

She hurried out to see what Mrs. Wooten needed.

SARAH WAITED UP UNTIL MRS. PARMER RETURNED. HER face was ashen as she climbed up the stairs. Her maid followed closely behind, her hands fluttering with the frustration of wanting to help and knowing that nothing could.

"I'm so sorry, Mrs. Parmer," Sarah said.

"Don't say anything to Mrs. Wooten or Electra until morning. They'll need their rest, and bad news always seems a little easier to bear in the light of day."

"Do you want to tell them yourself?" Sarah asked.

She seemed to wince at that, but she said, "I suppose I

must. We should probably call the doctor, too. Valora may need a sedative."

"I'll see to it tomorrow," Sarah promised. "Do you need anything?"

"Thank you for asking, my dear. You've been very kind under the circumstances. But I'll be all right. Someone must be strong for Electra. It's the least I can do for my brother's only living child."

Sarah thought of the infant lying in the nursery. He wouldn't enjoy the same devotion from Mrs. Parmer, and he might need it even more than Electra.

FRANK SLEPT FITFULLY THAT NIGHT. HE COULDN'T SEEM to banish the vision of Mrs. Parmer's face when she realized the body in the morgue was her nephew's. He'd grown to admire her after seeing the way she bore up under what must be unbearable. He'd very much wanted her to tell him he'd been mistaken and the young man he'd identified really wasn't Leander, but of course that hadn't happened.

Now all he could do for her was to find whatever justice was possible for the boy. The next morning, he didn't have any trouble at all convincing Captain O'Brien that he should investigate Leander Wooten's death as well as his father's. No detective had been assigned to the case yet, since nobody knew the body found in the Bowery was anyone important enough to investigate.

Mrs. Parmer had given him a photograph of Leander so he could show it around the bars to see if anyone remembered seeing him the night he died. He didn't hold out much hope, but it was worth a chance. He started in the alley where the body had been found, with the officer who had been called.

"He was laying right there," Kelly told him, pointing to a spot just inside the alley that ran between a bar called the Grey Goose and a pawn shop. They were both on Delancey Street. "Not real far in. Somebody saw his feet when they was passing by and told me a drunk was in there, passed out."

Kelly was what they called a whale, one of the enormous Irishmen who had been recruited by the police department to immigrate to New York. The idea was to get men so big on the force that they could handle anybody in a fight. They all stood over six feet tall, towering over most of the city's residents, and seemed almost as broad as they were tall, giving rise to the nickname of "whale."

Frank wasn't sure that the whales were really such good fighters. It was more that nobody wanted to find out the hard way, and so they fled at the sight of one of the oversized officers. Either way, their presence on the force helped keep the peace.

"You said he'd been robbed," Frank said.

"His pockets was turned out and empty. His watch was gone. Didn't have anything on him at all to say who he was. That's strange his father was killed just a few days ago."

"Yeah, it was. Did you find anybody who'd seen him?"

"He was in there," Kelly said, pointing at the bar next to the alley, "but nobody saw who he was with or nothing. He was alone when he come in, the bartender thought. Wasn't no big bunch of young swells out slumming or anything, not that he saw. They come down here in groups, looking for excitement. Sometimes they get it."

"I talked to some of his friends yesterday when I was looking for him. They said they weren't with him that night. It was the night of his father's funeral, and they were all surprised he went out at all."

"That don't seem right, even for a swell," Kelly decided. "Got to have some respect."

Frank had to agree. Leander didn't seem like the type of young man to go out carousing the same day he buried his father either, no matter how angry they were at each other on the day the old man died. "Did you find a murder weapon?"

"We think it was a piece of broom handle. We found it laying nearby with blood all over it. I sent it along with the body. They should have it down at the morgue."

"How do you think it happened?"

Kelly looked down at the ground where the body had lain, picturing it in his mind. "He was facedown, with his feet toward the street. I figure he was going down the alley and somebody comes up behind him and hits him over the head or at least knocks him down somehow. Then he hits him a couple more times when he's on the ground, just to make sure he won't get up very soon. Then he turns out his pockets and takes what he's got and runs off. The work of a minute or two at the most, and no one to see because it's so dark and nobody's paying attention to two men tussling in an alley in the Bowery because anybody who goes into an alley here deserves what he gets."

"That's the part that doesn't make sense to me," Frank said, looking around and trying to picture the street at night with half-drunk men coming and going. "Leander wasn't stupid. He wouldn't have gone down this alley without a good reason, and only a fool would go down it with somebody who might rob him."

"Maybe some girl lured him. That happens. The thief has a girl working with him. The swell thinks she's taking him back to her room, and he follows her down the alley."

That sounded reasonable, but Leander's friend had said he wasn't one for the ladies. Even if he was, would he take a chance on a two-bit whore down here when he could go uptown to some fancy house? None of this made any sense at all.

"According to his aunt, his watch was engraved. That should make it easier to find if somebody tries to pawn it," Frank said. "Here's the description."

He handed Kelly what he'd written out. "I'll have some men circulate it, see if anybody is stupid enough to try to get rid of it."

"I've got a photograph of the dead boy. I'll show it around and see if anybody remembers him from last night."

"You should wait until dark," Kelly advised. "Nobody who was here last night will be back until then."

"You're right," Frank said. He'd spend the day tracking down the young men on Mrs. Parmer's list and pressing them to tell him everything they knew about Leander Wooten that might explain why he was in the Bowery on a Tuesday night. And sometime today, he also had to see Mr. Colyer to find out if he'd figured out the ledger and the pages of numbers. He couldn't forget he was still investigating Mr. Wooten's death, too.

SARAH HAD SPENT A RESTLESS NIGHT, UNABLE TO SLEEP really soundly for worrying about what effect the news of Leander's death would have on the Wooten household. Mrs. Wooten was bound to be very upset, which meant her recovery was in jeopardy. She only hoped Mrs. Wooten's doctor knew what he was doing. So many didn't.

The one she was really worried about was Electra, though. The girl and her brother had obviously been close.

Shortly after the maid took away the breakfast tray, Mrs. Parmer came to Mrs. Wooten's room. She looked as if she hadn't closed her eyes all night.

"What do you want, Betty?" Mrs. Wooten asked impatiently. "I'm not in the mood for another one of your lectures, so if that's why you came—"

"That's not why I came," Mrs. Parmer said. "I have some news to tell you."

She looked so fragile, Sarah was afraid she might actually fall down. She hastily brought a chair to Mrs. Wooten's bedside for her. Mrs. Parmer sank down into it, casting Sarah a grateful look.

"Are you ill?" Mrs. Wooten asked with more annoyance than concern. "Because if you are, you shouldn't be in here. In my condition, the slightest illness could—"

"I'm not ill," Mrs. Parmer snapped, her patience hanging by a thread. "It's Leander."

"Leander? Has he come home?" Mrs. Wooten glared at Sarah. "I told you I wanted to see him the moment he came home."

"No, he hasn't come home," Mrs. Parmer said, her patience gone. "And he'll never be coming home again. He's dead, Valora. He was murdered the night of Nehemiah's funeral."

"What?" Mrs. Wooten cried. "What are you talking about? If this is some kind of macabre joke—"

"It's certainly not a joke," Mrs. Parmer said, furious now and rising to her feet. "How could you imagine I would joke about Leander's death?"

"You're trying to torment me, then," Mrs. Wooten said. "You want to destroy my nerves and make me ill so I'll die and you'll have Leander and Electra all to yourself! You've always been jealous of me," she accused. "You've always wished my children were your own!"

Mrs. Wooten was nearly hysterical now, and Sarah rushed over in an attempt to calm her.

"Please, stop this right now. This is no time for arguments. Mrs. Wooten, Mrs. Parmer is telling you the truth, I'm afraid. Mr. Malloy came to the house last night to tell us that they'd found Leander's body in the Bowery. Mrs. Parmer went down last night to identify it."

Mrs. Wooten's eyes grew wide as the truth began to dawn on her. "No, it can't be! What would Leander be doing in the Bowery? And Tuesday, did you say? That's the night of the funeral. He'd never go off like that on the day he'd buried his father!"

"I know it doesn't seem to make much sense," Sarah allowed before Mrs. Parmer could say something to set her off again. "But it's true all the same. Mr. Malloy is trying to find the answers to your questions, but until he does, you'll just have to accept that Leander is gone and start mourning him."

Mrs. Wooten stared back at her, too shocked to speak for a long moment. Then her eyes filled with tears. "Leander?" she said, the word so full of pain it was like a wail. "Oh, God, not Leander!"

She began to sob, and Sarah turned to Mrs. Parmer. "You can go now. I'll take care of her."

"Did you send for Dr. Smith?"

"Yes. I told them to send him up as soon as he arrives."

Mrs. Parmer looked at Mrs. Wooten with what might

have been pity if she had been less angry. Her sobs had become shrieks. "For once, I'm glad that Electra is deaf. At least she won't hear this."

She turned and walked out of the room, closing the door behind her softly, even though Mrs. Wooten was wailing too loudly to have heard it slam.

By the time the doctor arrived, Mrs. Wooten had exhausted herself and settled into a miserable stupor where every breath shook on a sob.

"Who are you?" he demanded of Sarah. He was an officious little man with sharp features and suspicious eyes. He looked her up and down and found nothing to like.

"I'm the midwife," she said.

"Midwife?" he echoed in surprise. "What on earth . . . ?" His suspicious eyes darted to Mrs. Wooten, ensconced in her luxurious bed.

"Mrs. Wooten gave birth to a healthy boy on Monday," Sarah said.

"Gave birth?" he exclaimed in horror. "That's impossible. I would have known! She would have sent for me."

"Well, she didn't send for you," Sarah said without sympathy. "She sent for me, and I delivered the baby. We've hired a wet nurse, although Mrs. Wooten had to feed the baby herself for the first two days until the agency found someone."

Dr. Smith looked at Sarah as if she were some strange creature he'd never seen the likes of before. "You allowed her to feed the child herself? A woman of her age? After she'd just sustained the shock of losing her husband?"

Sarah decided not to mention that losing Mr. Wooten hadn't been so very much of a shock to his wife. Instead she said, "Mrs. Wooten has just learned that her son Leander was murdered the night before last, and she's quite distraught."

"Leander? Good God! What happened?" Dr. Smith asked, forgetting he was outraged at Sarah.

"He was robbed in the Bowery," Sarah said, figuring that was all the explanation he needed. "And Mrs. Wooten needs something to settle her nerves."

He looked at his patient again, taking in her shuddering body and red-rimmed eyes. "Naturally, she does," he said. "And I will need to examine her to make sure she isn't suffering any aftereffects of a botched delivery," he added, giving Sarah another withering look.

Sarah merely smiled back. Arguing with doctors like him rarely accomplished anything.

"If you'll send for her maid, you can leave," he told Sarah.

"No," Mrs. Wooten said weakly. "I want her to stay!"

Plainly, Dr. Smith was offended by this request, but he said, "Whatever you wish, Mrs. Wooten. Now I need to make sure the afterbirth was properly expelled . . ."

He examined Mrs. Wooten, and to Sarah's relief, he appeared to know what he was doing. He seemed almost disappointed to find his patient perfectly well. He gave her a dose of something he mixed up in a glass of water. In a few minutes, her shuddering subsided, and she fell into a deep sleep.

"Give her this whenever she becomes agitated," he said, handing Sarah a bottle. "The dosage is written on the label." He glanced at Mrs. Wooten again and shook his head. "I can't believe she didn't tell me she was expecting. I've been her doctor for over twenty years." He looked at Sarah as if she was supposed to explain it all to him.

But she remembered what Mrs. Wooten had said about
Dr. Smith being a gossip. "I'm afraid you'll have to ask Mrs.
Wooten. All I know is that when her labor started, they sent
for me."

He waited, and when she offered nothing else, he said,
"How is Electra? She must be equally distraught."

"I don't know," Sarah said. "Mrs. Parmer was going to
tell her after she told Mrs. Wooten, but I haven't been able
to leave Mrs. Wooten."

"Then I'd better see her before I leave," he said and was
gone without another word.

Sarah was also worried about the girl, but she had to remind herself that she had no official position in this household and what happened here was really none of her business.
A few minutes later, however, Minnie came up and told her
Mrs. Parmer wanted to see her.

Leaving the maid with Mrs. Wooten, Sarah went downstairs to the family parlor. To her relief, Dr. Smith was gone.
She found Mrs. Parmer sitting on the sofa with Electra. The
girl was remarkably quiet. She sat with her legs drawn up,
hugging her knees and rocking back and forth. She didn't
look up when Sarah entered, as if she'd retreated so far into
herself that she was no longer aware of her surroundings.

"She wants to see Mr. Malloy," Mrs. Parmer said with a
puzzled frown. "She won't say why, but I'm sure she wants to
know the details of Leander's death. I don't think that would
be good for her to know, do you?"

Sarah had no idea if it would or not. In Electra's place,
she'd want to know everything, no matter how horrible. Of
course, she could never really be in Electra's place. She had
no idea what it was like to be deaf or to have been so shel-
tered and protected all her life because of it.

"What did you tell her?" Sarah asked.

"That he'd been in an accident."

Electra suddenly seemed to realize someone else was in the room. She looked up at Sarah and then at her aunt. Sarah realized she was looking to see if they were talking, trying to read their lips. When Electra looked back at her, Sarah said, "I'm sorry about Leander."

"What happened to him? Why won't she tell me?" she asked desperately.

"He had an accident," Sarah said. "He hit his head."

Her eyes filled with tears, but she blinked them away furiously. "Where did it happen? I need to know!"

"I don't know exactly where."

Electra didn't believe her. "I want to see Mr. Malloy," she said with a frustrated frown. "Send for him!"

"I don't know how to find him," she said, "but he did say he'd visit me later today."

"We must warn him not to upset her," Mrs. Parmer said.

"What did you say to her?" Electra demanded of her aunt, who'd turned her head away so Electra wouldn't see.

Mrs. Parmer shook her head, as if to say it didn't matter, but Electra disagreed. She turned back to Sarah. "What did she say?"

"She doesn't want you upset."

"I'm already upset! Brother is dead!" she wailed.

"Dr. Smith left some medicine for her," Mrs. Parmer said to Sarah.

"No! I don't want to go to sleep!" Electra protested. "I won't take it! I want to see Mr. Malloy."

"I'll let you know as soon as he gets here," Sarah promised.

One of the maids knocked on the door, and when Mrs. Parmer bade her enter, she said, "I know you're not receiving, but there's a gentleman here to see Miss Electra, and he won't go away until I tell her."

Electra stiffened at this news and unfolded herself, putting her feet back on the floor.

"A gentleman?" Mrs. Parmer was saying. "Who is he?"

"He wouldn't give his name. He said he's Miss Electra's teacher."

Electra was on her feet now and moving toward the door. Before she could reach it, a man came in. It was the fellow Sarah had seen arguing with Leander at the funeral.

"Adam!" Electra said joyously, hurrying to meet him.

12

THIS TIME FRANK STARTED AT THE BOTTOM OF THE LIST Mrs. Parmer had given him of Leander's friends. He already knew the first two young men on that list hadn't seen Leander and claimed not to know where he'd gone on Tuesday night.

The hour was early for young men who had spent most of the night out on the town, but Frank managed to frighten the servants at each house into waking their young masters. The first two he visited knew no more than the ones he had visited last night, so Frank didn't hold out much hope for this last one.

Nathan Parkhurst was a handsome young fellow, or he would have been if he'd taken the time to shave and comb his hair. He was glaring at Frank through bloodshot eyes as he entered the parlor where the maid had directed Frank to wait.

"The girl said something's happened to Leander Wooten," he said in a tone that indicated he held Frank personally responsible for such an outrage.

"I'm sorry to inform you that Mr. Wooten was killed in the Bowery on Tuesday evening."

Parkhurst stared at him stupidly, rubbing his head as if trying to wake up his brain to comprehend what Frank had just told him. "*Leander* Wooten? Are you sure?"

"His aunt, Mrs. Parmer, identified him."

This was even more incomprehensible. "In the Bowery, you say?"

"Yes, in an alley next to a saloon called the Grey Goose. I know young men from good families sometimes go down to the Bowery on a lark. Did you and Leander ever—"

"Oh, yes," Parkhurst said, obviously happy to have a subject he knew something about. "We've done that, but not for weeks now and never *alone*! That would be foolish!"

"Very foolish," Frank said, thinking of Leander with his pockets turned out and his head bashed in. "Did you ever go to the Grey Goose?"

"I don't remember it, but we could have. One never pays attention to the name of the place."

Frank thought that very likely. "Can you think of anybody who might've gone out with Leander that night besides the names on this list?" He showed Mrs. Parmer's list to the young man.

He shook his head. "Tuesday night, did you say? Wasn't that the day of the funeral?"

"Yes, it was."

Parkhurst frowned. "If he'd asked one of us to go with him, we would've turned him down. Not proper and all that. Maybe he was just feeling low and needed some fun." But even Parkhurst didn't look like he believed that.

"Would he have gone with a girl he met in one of those places?"

Parkhurst looked at him as if he were insane. "And risk a case of the clap? Not likely! That's not the worst of it either. They all have pimps who try to run some game on you. Like they burst in at the worst possible moment and pretend to be the girl's outraged husband who's going to bring charges against you unless you pay him some outrageous sum."

"Or the panel game," Frank offered, "where he's hiding behind a panel, and while you're busy with the girl, he opens the panel and gets your wallet out of your pants that are hanging on a chair."

"I didn't know about that one!" Parkhurst exclaimed.

"There's a lot of them. Just steer clear of the Bowery from now on."

"After what happened to Leander, I think we all will!" Parkhurst vowed.

"So you think Leander wasn't likely to have gone off with some girl, then."

"Not if he was sober enough to be thinking straight. Of course, if he was drowning his sorrows, who knows?"

Frank would have to find out how heavily Leander was drinking that night. "Can you think of any other reason Wooten might have gone to the Bowery alone on the night of his father's funeral?" he asked one last time in desperation.

Parkhurst shook his head, rubbing it as he had before, as if to stimulate his brain to work harder. "Unless . . ."

"Unless what?" Frank asked eagerly.

"Unless it had something to do with his sister. He'd run into a burning building for his sister."

"The Bowery isn't a burning building," Frank said.

"But it's dangerous, isn't it?" Parkhurst reasoned.

"His sister wasn't in the Bowery," Frank said. "She was at home, safe and sound."

"Then there was no reason for Leander to be out, was there?"

Frank was very much afraid this was true.

ADAM OLDHAM STOPPED JUST SHORT OF TAKING ELEC-tra in his arms, although Sarah could see that was what they both wanted. The longing in Electra's beautiful eyes was startling. Oldham, on the other hand, simply looked desperate.

He began to move his hands, speaking to her in the language only she could understand.

"What is he doing here?" Mrs. Parmer demanded. "What is he saying to her?"

Sarah, of course, had no idea.

Electra was signing, replying to whatever he had said to her, and paying no attention to her aunt.

Mrs. Parmer went to Electra and took her by the arm, capturing her attention. Electra turned to her impatiently. "What does he want?"

"He heard about Leander," she said. "He came to comfort me."

"How did he hear about Leander?" Sarah asked, but of course Electra couldn't hear her.

Mrs. Parmer relayed the question, since she had Electra's attention.

"He saw the newspaper this morning," the girl said.

"Good heavens, could it be in the newspaper already?" Mrs. Parmer asked Sarah.

"If someone at the morgue told a reporter last night," Sarah said. "I believe they pay for tips like that."

"How horrible," Mrs. Parmer murmured. Then she noticed that Oldham and Electra were signing to each other again. "What is he saying?" she demanded when she'd captured Electra's attention again.

"None of your business," the girl said defiantly.

"It most certainly is my business!" Mrs. Parmer informed her. "You are still a child, Electra, and it's my responsibility to protect you."

"I don't need to be protected from Adam," she said. Oldham touched her arm and signed a question. He probably wanted to know what Mrs. Parmer was saying. Electra answered him.

"Stop that!" Mrs. Parmer said in frustration. "I can't have you conversing with this man unless I know what you're talking about!"

"Adam can't speech-read, and he can't speak," Electra said, just as frustrated. "How else is he supposed to talk to me?"

"He's not supposed to talk to you at all!" Mrs. Parmer said. "I distinctly heard Leander say he wasn't welcome here any longer."

"Leander is dead," Electra said, her voice catching on the tears she was fighting. "He can't tell me what to do anymore."

Sarah was trying not to interfere, but she could see that someone needed to. "Perhaps if Electra could tell you what they are saying when they sign," she suggested.

Mrs. Parmer frowned. "She doesn't have to tell us the truth," she pointed out.

No, she didn't, Sarah thought, then she remembered something else. "He wrote in a notebook when he was talking to Leander."

Electra had been following this conversation, and she quickly signed something to Oldham.

The look he gave Sarah was usually reserved for meddling busybodies. Sarah had seen it before. But he reached into his coat pocket and pulled out a notebook and a pencil and held them up rather defiantly for Sarah to see.

Sarah gave him a look to rival the one he'd given her.

"You could sit on the sofa," Sarah quickly suggested, "with Mrs. Parmer in the middle so she can see what each of you is writing."

Electra didn't like that arrangement at all, but she interpreted it to Oldham, who nodded his agreement. The three of them trooped to the sofa and Oldham waited until the two ladies were seated before taking his place beside Mrs. Parmer.

Sarah knew she should probably leave them to it, but she was much too curious to go voluntarily. Instead, she took a seat out of their line of sight in hopes they would forget she was there.

Oldham wrote something and showed it to Mrs. Parmer, who said, "You're welcome," before remembering Oldham couldn't read what she was saying, only what she wrote. She took the pencil from him and wrote her reply. Apparently, he had thanked her for not throwing him out.

Thus began their strange conversation. Sarah realized that eavesdropping here was a waste of her time. Except for an occasional murmur from Mrs. Parmer, no words were spoken, and she couldn't see what they were writing.

Mrs. Parmer read what each of them wrote as they did so, then passed the notebook to the other to read and reply.

"A very nice sentiment," Mrs. Parmer remarked at one point when observing Oldham's progress. Then later, "Electra, you cannot say that to a gentleman," and she tore the page from the notebook and crumpled it in her fist, refusing to relent even when Electra pouted.

After that, Oldham and Mrs. Parmer had an exchange of messages that weren't passed to Electra, although the girl was straining to read them over Mrs. Parmer's arm. Sarah could see Mrs. Parmer's manner changing ever so slightly during this conversation. She no longer seemed quite as protective, and by the end of it, she was actually smiling at Oldham. Even more importantly, he was smiling back, and Adam Oldham's smile was, Sarah realized, something few women could resist.

She remembered what Malloy had told her about all the females at Brian's school being in love with him—even Malloy's own mother. Now she understood why. He was using his considerable charm to soften Mrs. Parmer's disapproval. If she was so easily won, Mrs. Wooten—who was the only remaining authority over Electra's future—would stand no chance at all. Electra's only concern would be if Mrs. Wooten decided she wanted Oldham for herself!

Although Electra seemed annoyed that her aunt was monopolizing her communication with Oldham, even she was smiling by the end of the visit. Something to which her aunt had agreed pleased her very much.

Oldham took Mrs. Parmer's hand and bowed over it formally as he took his leave. Then he took Electra's hand in his right and made a small, quick sign with his left that brought the color flooding to Electra's cheeks. It was the same sign Sarah had seen him make to Electra on the day of the funeral that had made her so happy.

This time, Mrs. Parmer had seen it, too. "What did that mean?" she asked Electra suspiciously.

"He was just telling me good-bye," she said blithely.

Mrs. Parmer was right. Electra would lie about what the signs meant if she didn't want them to know.

AFTER LEAVING THE PARKHURST HOUSE, FRANK REALIZED he needed to get to Mr. Colyer before it got too late in the day. He still needed to call on Sarah before returning to the Bowery later that evening to see if anyone remembered seeing Leander the night he was killed.

To Frank's surprise, the clerk at the front desk greeted him by name, as if he'd been expected.

"Mr. Malloy, Mr. Decker would like to see you. He left instructions that he was to be interrupted no matter what he was doing when you arrived."

Frank couldn't help the feeling of foreboding that came over him. How often had he been left kicking his heels, waiting for the great man to find time for him even when he'd had an appointment? Sarah's father had no love for his daughter's policeman friend. Decker probably wanted to rake him over the coals for asking his head accountant to do a favor for the police. He should have taken the ledger somewhere else.

By the time the clerk came back to escort him up to Decker's office, Frank was fuming and mentally composing a defense that would absolve Colyer of any blame Decker tried to impose on him.

Decker's office wasn't at all what Frank had expected on his first visit here. The room was comfortably but not extravagantly furnished, and everything looked slightly worn, as if it had been there a long time but the occupant saw no reason to replace it unless it was truly worn out.

To Frank's surprise, Colyer was already in Decker's office, standing behind Decker's desk, just to Decker's right. To Frank's great relief, Colyer's expression was solemn, but he showed no indication he had been chastened in any way.

"Mr. Malloy," Decker said by way of greeting. "You caused Mr. Colyer quite a bit of concern."

"I didn't mean to," Frank said honestly. "And I never intended for you to be bothered, Mr. Decker. I hope I didn't cause trouble for anybody."

Decker exchanged a glance with Colyer, but Frank had no idea what silent message was exchanged. "Mr. Colyer said my daughter had suggested consulting him."

Frank also didn't want to get Sarah in trouble. "I didn't know what the numbers meant, and she said if anybody could make sense of them, it would be Mr. Colyer."

"She remembered I used to give her peppermints when she was a girl," Colyer said to Decker with a small smile, and Frank relaxed. Frank might be in trouble, but Colyer wasn't.

Frank wanted to ask what there was about the ledger that had caused Colyer concern, but he waited, knowing Decker would tell him when he was good and ready. He probably enjoyed making Frank wait.

"Mr. Colyer believes this ledger belongs to Mr. Nehemiah Wooten," Decker said.

"I found it in his desk, along with those papers that I brought with it."

"What did you think it meant?"

"I didn't know what it meant, but it was in a drawer of the desk of a man who'd just been murdered. I don't know much about running a business, but in the normal course of things, I'd expect to find the ledgers in the accountant's office. I needed to know what it was and why it was there."

"And what did you *hope* it was?" Decker asked with interest.

"I hoped it was a reason for somebody to want Mr. Wooten dead."

"It is."

Frank blinked in surprise. "It is?" he asked.

"Yes," Decker said mildly. "That's why it caused Mr. Colyer so much concern. That's why he brought it to me, to make sure his conclusions were correct and to ask me what he should do about it."

"I guess you think his conclusions were correct," Frank said.

"Mr. Colyer is rarely wrong when it comes to numbers, Mr. Malloy."

"That's what I've heard," Frank said. "What are his conclusions?"

He figured he'd probably made a mistake in asking outright like that, but he was getting tired of Decker's games.

Decker looked up at Colyer. "Why don't you tell him what you've found, Mr. Colyer?"

Colyer cleared his throat. "The ledger, as you probably know, represents the official accounting of Young and Wooten for this year to date. It shows the income, the expenses, and the profits or losses of the company. Somehow, Mr. Wooten must have become aware of some discrepancies, or perhaps he just became suspicious. Businessmen often develop a feel for how much money their company should be earning, and he may have wondered why his expectations weren't being met. He may also have had some additional documents, probably invoices to other businesses for work

Wooten's company had performed for them. That is what he was figuring on these other sheets." He picked up one of the sheets covered with columns of numbers.

Decker couldn't stand it. He had to take over. He took the sheet from Colyer's hand. "Wooten apparently was adding up these missing invoices here." He pointed to one column, and Frank stepped closer to the desk so he could see it. "Mr. Colyer could find no record of these particular amounts entered into the official ledger as income. Then Wooten added that sum to the actual amount listed in the ledger as income for each month, and the totals are the numbers he circled."

Frank nodded his understanding. "The missing invoices were paid, but that income was never officially recorded, so . . ."

"So Mr. Wooten wasn't receiving his share of it," Decker said.

"Who was?" Frank asked.

"We can't tell from this," Decker said carefully.

"Could it be the accountant? He acted strange when he saw the ledger in Wooten's desk."

Decker looked at Colyer, who said, "The accountant may be the one who actually found the discrepancies and brought them to Mr. Wooten's attention."

Frank considered this information. "That doesn't make sense. I was there, investigating Mr. Wooten's death. I asked him outright if there were problems with the business, and he denied it. All he had to do was tell me."

Decker looked at Colyer again.

"Mr. Wooten is dead," Colyer said, making Frank frown.

"I know he is."

"And his other employer, Mr. Young, is still very much alive. If Mr. Young is the one who was stealing from the company, and if he killed Mr. Wooten to cover his crime, and if you can prove it and make sure Mr. Young goes to prison, then the accountant has a reason to help you."

"Can you do that, Mr. Malloy?" Decker asked.

Frank could see the problem clearly. "Without Mr. Wooten to bring charges, I'd have a hard time getting proof that somebody embezzled money from the company, and without proof of that, I'd have a hard time proving Mr. Young had a reason to kill Wooten."

"We all know that even if you had proof that Young killed Wooten, for *any* reason, you would have a difficult time even bringing charges against him," Decker said.

He was right. Rich men didn't stand trial for anything in New York, not even murder. A nice fat wad of bills in the right pocket would ensure that.

"And the accountant isn't going to give evidence against his sole surviving employer," Frank concluded. "He'd lose his job, and nobody would ever hire him again."

"I told you he would understand," Decker told Colyer. Frank wasn't sure if that was a compliment or not. Decker looked back at Frank. "We still might be able to bring Mr. Young to justice, however."

"Not so fast," Frank said, surprised Decker would even care about such a thing, much less take it into his own hands. "You're right, I don't have proof that Young killed Wooten, although this gives him a pretty good reason to want him dead. He still might be innocent, though, and there are other people who wanted him dead for different reasons."

"Oh, I didn't mean justice for murder," Decker said, dismissing it with a wave of his hand. "I don't even care who killed Wooten. I mean justice for stealing from his partner.

Everyone bends some rules in business, Mr. Malloy, but if we allow men to steal from their partners with impunity, none of us is safe."

Sarah had occasionally mentioned the ways in which the rich punished those who broke the rules they held sacred, things that may not actually be illegal but were offensive nonetheless. "What are you going to do?" Frank asked with interest.

"First of all, I'm going to hire a new accountant, if you will be so kind as to tell me the name of the gentleman who acted so strangely when he saw this ledger in Mr. Wooten's desk."

THE MAID WAS WAITING TO SEE MR. OLDHAM OUT, AND no sooner had he left than Mrs. Parmer said, "Oh, wait, he left a notebook here the day of the funeral." She touched Electra's arm to turn her attention from Oldham's retreating figure. "You should return his other notebook."

Electra looked at her aunt for a long moment and then moved away with no response, as if she hadn't understood. She went to the window, where she could observe Oldham as he left the house and walked down the street.

"That girl," Mrs. Parmer murmured, then said to Sarah, "She probably wants it as a keepsake."

Sarah thought she was probably right. "Mr. Oldham seems like a well-bred young man," she observed, trying to encourage Mrs. Parmer to express her own opinion.

"He certainly does," she agreed with more enthusiasm than Sarah had expected. "I don't know what I expected, but I think I was judging him by Leander's opinion. Now that I remember, it was Leander who caused the scene at his father's funeral. Mr. Oldham had done nothing to provoke him."

Except make Electra fall in love with him, Sarah thought, although in all fairness, he had probably been unable to prevent that. "I gather he expressed himself well," she tried.

"Oh, yes," Mrs. Parmer said. "He gave me his condolences on the loss of my brother, and apologized for the unpleasant scene at the funeral. As soon as he realized Leander objected to his presence, he made his excuses to Leander and left. I can't really blame him for wanting to comfort Electra. He apparently cares very deeply for her, so naturally, he'd want to be with her when she's grieving."

Electra suddenly turned away from the window and back to them. Mr. Oldham must have gone out of sight.

"You like him, don't you?" she said to her aunt.

Caught off guard by such a direct question, Mrs. Parmer needed a moment to frame an answer. "He seems like a respectable young man," she said diplomatically.

"I saw you smiling at him," Electra said. She wasn't teasing, just stating a fact. "You like him. Why wouldn't Leander like him?"

"Leander was just worried about you. He didn't want anyone to take advantage of you."

"Adam loves me," Electra said. "He wants to marry me."

"You're too young to be thinking about marriage," Mrs. Parmer said. "And a rich girl always has to be concerned when a poor man wants to marry her."

"Adam doesn't care if I'm rich or not," she insisted.

"Then he won't mind waiting until you're of age, will he?" Mrs. Parmer argued.

Electra turned to Sarah.

"I need to see Mr. Malloy," she said. "You won't forget?"

"No, I won't forget," Sarah promised.

Electra wandered out of the room without another word.

"It's so difficult to teach her proper manners. She has no idea what the things she says sound like," Mrs. Parmer observed. "I'm sorry to have involved you in all of this."

"I'm happy to help, if I can. All of you have been through so much lately."

Mrs. Parmer's eyes filled with tears, which she hastily blotted away with her handkerchief. "I don't know what will become of Electra with only Valora to watch over her."

Sarah shared her concern. "I understand Mr. Wooten didn't approve of Electra being courted by a deaf man. Does Mrs. Wooten share his opinion on that?"

"I have no idea what Valora thinks. My brother wasn't the kind of man to consider the opinions of others when forming his own. He expected his wife and children to obey him regardless, and they learned not to bother disagreeing."

"Do *you* share his opinion on this?"

Mrs. Parmer had to think about this. "I really don't know," she said after a few moments. "I hadn't ever given it much thought, but after seeing Electra with Mr. Oldham, I can see that there would be certain advantages in marrying someone who bore the same burden, so to speak. Of course, there's the problem of the children. That was Nehemiah's concern. He was worried that when deaf people marry each other, they produce deaf children."

"And yet," Sarah said, "very few of the students at Mr. Oldham's school have even one deaf parent."

"Is that true?" Mrs. Parmer asked in surprise.

"Yes, it is, and neither one of Electra's parents were deaf," Sarah reminded her, feeling silly for pointing out the obvious, but Mrs. Parmer's expression showed she hadn't thought of it that way before. "And Mr. Malloy's son is deaf, but he and his late wife weren't."

"But there is still the issue of Mr. Oldham being poor and Electra being so young. I believe that was what concerned Leander."

"He was certainly justified in that," Sarah agreed. "But as you said, if he truly does care for her, he'll wait."

"I can't imagine why she wants to see Mr. Malloy," Mrs. Parmer said. "You must instruct him not to tell her what really happened to Leander. It's enough that she knows her father was murdered."

"I'll be sure he understands that," Sarah promised. She just wondered if Malloy would share Mrs. Parmer's concern or if he might have a reason for telling Electra the truth.

FRANK LEFT FELIX DECKER'S OFFICE WITH THE LEDGER and the pages of numbers. Decker had no objections to Frank's returning them to where he'd found them. Decker had no further need of them, and Frank might find them useful in some way.

Decker's plan, as Frank understood it, was to try to hire the accountant, Snodgrass. If Snodgrass gratefully accepted the offer of a new position, Decker would know he was not only innocent of involvement in the embezzling but eager to escape an uncomfortable situation. If he refused, Decker would know Snodgrass was involved in the crime. What he would do from there involved a lot of quiet conversations in gentleman's clubs that would slowly strangle Terrance Young's reputation.

Now that Frank had time to think about it, the pieces were starting to fall into place. Young and Wooten had met on Thursday. Snodgrass had tried to skip over that appointment when he'd been describing each of Wooten's meetings that week. When Frank had asked outright what the two men had discussed, Snodgrass had claimed ignorance, but Frank had suspected he was lying even then. Young had claimed not to have seen Wooten since then. He'd left the office and not returned, according to him. If Wooten had accused him of embezzling at that meeting on Thursday, Young wouldn't have dared show his face at the office again. Unless he'd returned on Saturday, after everyone had left, to plead for another chance. Wooten, however, wasn't the kind of man who gave second chances.

Would Wooten have brought charges against him? Probably not. Nobody wanted the scandal of a trial, and Wooten wasn't the kind of man to publicly admit he'd been taken advantage of. But he'd certainly dissolve the partnership. He'd never have given Young another chance to cheat him. And he'd have told everyone why he'd broken with Young. If Felix Decker could destroy Young's reputation, Wooten could have done so even more quickly and easily.

At least he'd convinced Decker to wait until Frank was finished with his investigation before taking any action against Young. He needed to know if Young was guilty of more than just embezzlement. He wouldn't be able to prosecute Young if he did kill Wooten, but at least he'd know for sure and could make certain no innocent person was charged.

Sarah had told him that Young had approached Leander at the funeral and tried to convince him to continue his education and leave running the business to Young and his son. That could have just been the surviving partner showing a natural concern for the dead man's son. That was what Young would most certainly say. But Leander hadn't been grateful. He'd been angry and lashed out. Had Leander known about the embezzlement? More importantly, had Young thought he did? Because if he did and Young had killed his partner, he'd also have to kill the partner's son. And of course, he couldn't forget about Terry Young. He also had a good reason for wanting Wooten dead, even if he hadn't known Mrs. Wooten was pregnant. And did he know his father was stealing from the company? Or maybe Terry Young was the one stealing.

Unfortunately, he couldn't just confront either Young, father or son. Men that powerful would have his job if he overstepped his bounds. He'd need to be sure. He'd need more evidence. And he'd need to know that the same person who'd killed Wooten had killed Leander. It was still possible that Leander had killed his father, then gone down to the Bowery to drink himself into a stupor out of guilt on the night of the funeral, and been beaten and robbed by some stranger. He needed to find out where Leander had been last Saturday when his father was killed.

Which meant he needed the names of Leander's college friends so he could send someone to New Jersey to question them. And that, of course, meant another visit to the Wooten house.

SARAH HAD JUST CHECKED ON MRS. WOOTEN, WHO HAD refused to eat more than a few bites of toast before demanding another dose of the medicine Dr. Smith had left for her. Sarah couldn't blame her for preferring oblivion to facing the loss of her son. She was in Mrs. Wooten's sitting room when Minnie came in looking for her. Sarah had been expecting

Malloy's visit today, so she wasn't surprised, but Minnie's expression told her something was amiss.

"I'm sorry to bother you, Mrs. Brandt, but I don't know what to do."

"What is it, Minnie?"

The girl was literally wringing her hands. "Mr. Young is here. Mr. Terry Young. He . . . Well, Mrs. Parmer won't see him and Mrs. Wooten can't see him and I don't think Miss Electra should see him, but he won't leave until . . ."

"Until what?" Sarah asked in amazement.

"He wants to see the baby."

"Oh, dear."

"Yes," Minnie agreed. "The rest of the staff don't know what to do with him!"

Sarah's mind was racing. Malloy had asked her to find out if Terry Young was the baby's father. She was now certain he was, but might she find out something more if she observed Mr. Young with his new son? "Where is Mrs. Parmer?"

"She's in the family parlor. I already asked her, and she—"

"I'll speak to her," Sarah said. "Stay here in case Mrs. Wooten needs anything."

Sarah found Mrs. Parmer fuming. "Did you know that Terry Young had the effrontery to come here and demand to see Valora's baby?" she asked Sarah.

"Yes, Minnie told me. She also told me you refused to admit him, but he has still refused to leave. This has put the servants in a difficult position."

"Refused to leave? How dare he?" she asked in outrage. "He can't possibly expect any consideration from anyone in this house!"

"I know how you feel about him, and I certainly sympathize with you, but perhaps it would be crueler to allow him to see the child than to refuse."

Mrs. Parmer stared at Sarah, uncomprehending. "What do you mean?"

"You are thinking that it would be kind to allow him to see the baby, and you have no wish to be kind to Mr. Young. However, I'm thinking that allowing him to see the child, knowing he can never claim him as his son, would actually not be kind at all. It is exactly the sort of punishment your brother would have wished on the man who cuckolded him."

"Oh, Mrs. Brandt, you are so right! And exactly what he deserves. Of course, we are assuming Terry Young possesses the normal human emotions."

"He must possess some of them, or he wouldn't care about seeing the child," Sarah said. "The easiest thing for him to do now would be to never return to this house and never see Mrs. Wooten again. The family isn't going to tell anyone what happened, and if he keeps away, there will be no gossip to betray him. Instead, here he is at your door to see his child."

Mrs. Parmer nodded her agreement. "Mrs. Brandt, would you take Mr. Young up to the nursery? He may only stay for a few minutes. We don't want the child and his nurse disturbed."

"I would be happy to," Sarah said.

She found Terry Young waiting in the same unwelcoming room where they usually put Malloy. He rose the instant she entered, then frowned when he didn't recognize her. She introduced herself to him as the midwife.

"Mrs. Parmer has given me permission to take you to the

nursery for a visit," she told him. "But you cannot stay long. We don't want the baby or his nurse disturbed."

"Of course, of course," he quickly agreed. "I just want . . . Well, I was curious, you know, to see him. It's a boy, I understand."

"Yes, it is. Please follow me."

She led him up to the third floor and made him wait outside while she consulted with the nurse. "A family friend is here to see the baby."

"He's just been fed," the nurse said, exercising her authority. "He shouldn't be jostled at all."

She admitted Mr. Young, who looked around the room as if he'd never entered a nursery before. Perhaps he hadn't since the days when he'd been a resident of one himself. The nurse was holding the baby. She'd dressed him in a long white gown and a bonnet more suitable for a stroll in the park than for an afternoon at home. She turned him so Mr. Young could see his little face.

"He's . . . very small," Mr. Young managed, his voice a bit hoarse.

"He'll grow," Sarah said. "Would you like to hold him?"

His eyes widened with terror. "Oh, no, not at all! I wouldn't know what to do. I just . . . Well, I wanted to make sure he's sound."

"He's perfectly sound," Sarah assured him.

Mr. Young admired the boy for a few more minutes, then pronounced himself satisfied and thanked Sarah and the nurse for humoring him. Sarah escorted him out of the room and back down the stairs to the second-floor landing. Sarah had to admit he looked shaken. She had been right that seeing his son under such circumstances had been very unsettling and much more traumatic than he had expected. She was wracking her brain, trying to think what Malloy would want her to ask him and coming up with nothing.

He turned to thank her again and take his leave when one of the maids approached her. "I'm sorry, Mrs. Brandt, but Mr. Malloy is here to see you."

"Oh, thank you," Sarah said, but the girl was looking at Mr. Young.

"He said he also wants to see Mr. Young before he leaves."

13

Frank couldn't believe his luck in finding Terry Young at the Wooten house. He would have bet a week's pay that Young wouldn't ever darken the door here again, but he would have underestimated Young's audacity. The man apparently had no shame at all.

When Sarah ushered him into the small waiting room, however, he looked as if he felt nothing but shame. Sarah, on the other hand, was trying hard not to smile. "Mr. Malloy, how nice to see you again," she said.

"Mrs. Brandt," he said by way of greeting. "Would you mind leaving me alone with Mr. Young for a few minutes? I have several questions to ask him."

"I can't imagine what you want to ask me," Young said nervously, his eyes darting around as if looking for a means of escape. "I've already told you everything I know."

"Just send the maid for me when you're finished," Sarah said and discretely withdrew, closing the door behind her.

"Mr. Young," Frank began, "when the maid told me Mrs. Brandt was with you just now, I remembered something I've been meaning to ask you about. You told me you were going to meet with Mr. Wooten on Saturday afternoon about something, but that you changed your mind."

"I . . . I believe I did, yes," he allowed.

"What was it you were going to discuss with him again?"

"I . . . It was about Electra. I'd learned she was seeing some deaf man secretly. But then I found out he already knew."

"And how did you find out about Electra and this man?" That was what had been bothering Frank, the thing he hadn't been able to feel comfortable about.

"What?" Young asked in surprise.

"Who told you that Electra was seeing this man? You see, only a few people knew, and I was wondering which one of them would have told you about it."

"I really don't . . . I mean, what does it matter? Someone told me, and I thought Mr. Wooten should know."

"But surely you remember who told you. Something that shocking? I wouldn't forget who told me. The only people who knew were Leander, Electra, the man himself, and another teacher. Which one of them was it?"

Young's eyes were darting again as he thought frantically. "It was Leander," he decided, probably because Leander was no longer able to confirm or deny it.

Frank nodded as if he believed him. He wouldn't even bother to ask why Leander would have confided this dangerous secret to a man he would have no reason to trust. "When did he tell you?"

"What do you mean?"

"I mean when did you see him? He was away at school, I understand, and had been for several weeks."

"He . . . he told me before he left for school."

"And you kept the secret for several weeks?" Frank asked, feigning surprise. "Why did you suddenly decide to tell Mr. Wooten on that particular day?"

"I just did. I felt he needed to know." Young was starting to feel more comfortable with his lie.

"I don't believe you, Mr. Young."

Fear flashed in his eyes, but he raised his chin defiantly. "It doesn't matter whether you believe me or not."

"Yes, it does, because I'm trying to figure out who did go to see Mr. Wooten that afternoon he was killed."

"Stop toying with me. You know perfectly well that I did have an appointment with him that afternoon. I just didn't keep it," Young said. Sweat was beginning to bead on his forehead.

Frank suddenly realized how odd it was that Young had volunteered that information the first time he'd questioned him. If he hadn't kept the appointment and therefore hadn't been at the office that afternoon, why mention it at all? "And how did I know that?" he asked.

"Do you think I'm a fool? You must have seen it in his appointment book," Young snapped. "He always wrote everything in his appointment book."

But for some reason Wooten hadn't written this one down. Young had been afraid Frank would find the appointment scheduled and believe Young had been there, so he'd made sure Frank knew he hadn't kept it. But why lie about the reason for the meeting?

Because the real reason was too embarrassing.

"You were afraid I'd see that you had an appointment with Mr. Wooten at . . . one o'clock," he guessed, remembering that Higginbotham's had been at two. "And you wanted me to know you didn't keep it, so you couldn't have been there when he was killed."

"I didn't! I wasn't!" he insisted.

"And it doesn't really matter why you had to see him, I guess. Unless you were going to talk to him about the money that's missing from the company, the money *he'd just discovered* was missing from the company." Frank let his gaze drift to the chair where he'd laid the ledger.

Young's eyes widened when he saw it. "No, that's not true! Nothing is missing! It's all a mistake," he said, really sweating now.

"Is that what you told him? That it was just a mistake all those invoices were never entered into the books?"

"I didn't tell him anything! I never had a chance!"

"Why? Because you got so angry that you picked up a trophy and smashed it into his head first?"

"No, because I never saw him!"

"Why not?" Frank asked with interest. "You did go to the office, didn't you? You did keep the appointment."

"Yes, but . . ." He pulled out his handkerchief and mopped his face. "Someone was already there, in the office with him."

"Who was it?"

"I don't know! I didn't see. I just saw that the door was closed, and I heard Wooten's voice."

"What was he saying?"

"I couldn't hear the words, just his tone. Mocking. He was mocking somebody, the way he did when he thought he was right and you were stupid." Terry had obviously heard that tone many times.

"You must have heard the other man's voice," Frank said. "Who was it?"

"I didn't! I didn't stay long enough. I heard Wooten, and I decided I didn't want to see him after all. I left. And I'm leaving now. If you ask me about this again, I'll say that I was never there, and you can't prove otherwise. Good day, Mr. Malloy."

He didn't try to stop Young from leaving. There was no point. The man had already given him all the information he intended to. Actually, he'd given him *more* information than he'd intended to. But what did it mean?

And he was lying. Frank knew he was lying, but what part of the story wasn't true?

Frank was still trying to figure that out when Sarah appeared in the doorway.

"He left in a hurry," she observed.

"He got tired of telling me lies," Frank replied with a small grin.

She came in and closed the door. "What did he tell you?"

"That he had an appointment with Wooten on Saturday at one o'clock."

Her blue eyes widened in surprise. "That's interesting."

"Yes, especially because he lied about it the first time I talked to him. He'd made the appointment with Wooten, but for some reason Wooten didn't put it in his appointment book. He usually did write them down, though, so Young thought I had seen it and believed he'd been back to meet with Wooten at the time he was killed."

"Did he keep the appointment?"

"At first he told me he didn't. He said he'd just found out—yes, that *is* what he said," Frank mused, remembering.

"He said he'd *just* found out that Electra was secretly seeing a deaf man, and he was going to tell Wooten about it. Then he found out Higginbotham had already told him, so he didn't keep the appointment."

"But he did keep it," she guessed.

"Yes, but I couldn't figure out why he'd lied about the reason for the meeting, and that's how I caught him. See, I'd believed him the first time when he said he didn't keep the appointment, but something was bothering me. Today I realized it was the reason he gave me. He couldn't have known Electra was seeing Oldham unless somebody told him."

"Maybe somebody did."

"Who? It could only have been Leander, Electra, Oldham, or Rossiter. He doesn't even know Oldham or Rossiter. Electra wasn't going to tell, and why would Leander?"

"I see. But he did know about it."

"He knew about it when I questioned him on Monday. Anybody could've told him about it by then, even Mrs. Wooten. They were together when I got here, remember."

"I remember! But why go to such pains to make up a phony reason for the meeting?" Sarah asked.

"Because he needed a logical reason to explain why he didn't go to Wooten's office that afternoon, even though he'd made an appointment."

"So what do you think the real reason for the meeting was?"

"Oh, I haven't had a chance to tell you what Colyer found out. We'd better sit down." He moved the ledger from where he'd left it and set it on the floor.

"I hope you gave Mr. Colyer my regards."

"He sends his in return, and so does your father," he added wryly.

"My father? Did you see him, too?"

"Oh, yes. What Colyer found was so interesting, he felt he had to show it to your father. It seems somebody was embezzling from the company."

"See? I told you it would involve trouble with the business. Who was it?" she asked eagerly.

"Probably one of the Youngs," he said. "Terry wasn't surprised when I mentioned it just now, so he knew. So either he's protecting himself or his father or both of them."

She considered this information. "So you think Terry went to this meeting with Mr. Wooten, they argued about the embezzlement, and Terry killed him."

"That's one theory, but Terry claims he never saw Wooten. He says when he got there, somebody else was already in the office with Wooten."

"Who?"

"He says he doesn't know, but if he's telling the truth, and he didn't do it himself, it was probably the killer."

"And he didn't hear a voice or see anyone?"

"He says not, but he's lying about something. I know he was lying about the embezzlement and about not keeping the appointment. He also might be lying about not knowing who was with Wooten."

"Especially if it was his own father."

"Or he could be lying and nobody else was there at all because he's the killer. Or he could be telling the truth about everything except the reason for the meeting, and he really doesn't know who was with Wooten. Because there's a good chance it was Leander, and Terry would have no reason to protect *him,* so he'd tell us if he knew it was him."

"How do you intend to sort it out?" she asked in amazement.

Frank sighed. "First I have to find out if Leander came to see his father that day. That's the main reason I'm here, to get the names of his friends at school."

"I guess that means you have to go there to question them."

"I was going to send somebody else, but you're right, I think I'd better go myself."

The door opened, and Electra burst into the room, bringing both of them to their feet. "You promised you'd tell me when he came!" she said to Sarah. Her cheeks were flushed with anger.

"I was going to. I needed to speak with him, too."

She wasn't interested in Sarah's excuses. She turned to Frank. "What happened to my brother?"

Frank looked to Sarah for guidance.

"Mrs. Parmer doesn't want her to be upset," she said.

"Aunt Betty won't tell me what happened to him!" Electra said. "She said he had an accident and hit his head. Where was he?"

"He was in the Bowery," Frank said, feeling his way. He wasn't sure what part of the story Mrs. Parmer thought would upset her, and he wasn't getting any guidance from Sarah either. She just stood there looking as puzzled as he felt.

"Where is that?" Electra asked.

"A dangerous part of the city," he said. "Someone hit him on the head and robbed him."

Electra closed her eyes and released her breath in an enormous sigh. Then her whole body seemed to go limp, and both Frank and Sarah reached to catch her before she could fall. They managed to get her down into one of the chairs.

Sarah began chaffing her wrists. "Electra, are you all

right?" she was asking, forgetting the girl couldn't hear her. Her eyes were still closed.

After another moment, she opened them. "Thank you," she said to Frank. "I was so frightened."

"Why were you frightened?" Sarah asked when she'd gotten the girl's attention.

She seemed surprised at the question. "I . . . I was afraid because they wouldn't tell me the truth. But now I know." Tears flooded her eyes, and she began to weep. "Poor brother!"

Frank shook his head. Girls never made any sense to him. He stood back and let Sarah comfort her. The weeping only lasted a few minutes before she was able to get control of herself again. She wiped her eyes with a handkerchief she had pulled from her pocket. When he judged her calm enough, he asked her one final question, the one no one had been able to answer so far.

"Do you know why Leander went out that night?"

She just stared at him in that way she had, then rose from her chair, turned, and walked out of the room. He looked at Sarah for an explanation.

"I think she does that when she doesn't understand what someone has said to her."

Or, Frank thought, when she didn't want to answer a question.

"You need the names of Leander's friends at school," Sarah said. "I'll ask if Mrs. Parmer can see you." She started out of the room, then paused. "Oh, I almost forgot, do you know what this sign means?"

She made a sign with her hand, holding up some fingers and her thumb, and Frank grinned. "Has some deaf man been courting you, Mrs. Brandt?"

She quickly closed her hand back into a fist. "Of course not! What does it mean?"

"It means *I love you.*"

He was still grinning, and she grinned back. "I saw Oldham make it to Electra."

"Well, just be careful who *you* make it to."

"I will," she promised.

FRANK FIGURED HE HAD ENOUGH TIME TO TRAVEL TO New Jersey and back and still be able to find possible witnesses in the Bowery that night. The Bowery would just be getting started after nine that night, and if he didn't get there until midnight, so much the better.

He was lucky and didn't have to wait too long for a train. The neat little town of Princeton wasn't really far from New York City, but it might as well have been on another planet. The rolling fields stretched away in every direction, greening back up now after the summer heat. The stone buildings of the newly renamed college sat placidly in Gothic splendor, their tall windows seeming to point toward heaven. Frank had to ask several young men for directions to the residential college where Leander Wooten had lived. His classmates were just returning from their dinner and were shocked to find a policeman waiting for them.

Victor Patton was the one Frank wanted to speak with first. He'd been Leander's roommate. He looked very much like the friends Frank had questioned in the city, with his expensive clothes and his phony sophistication. Except these young men already knew Leander was dead, and they were feeling shock, if not genuine grief.

"Is Wooten really dead?" the young man wanted to

know before Frank could ask a single question himself. "We couldn't believe it when they told us." They were sitting in the room Patton had shared with Leander, a messy place that smelled like dirty socks. Frank had been given one of the two desk chairs to sit on, after Patton had removed a pile of dirty clothes. Patton had chosen a bed.

"He's dead," Frank confirmed bluntly, figuring that shocking these rich boys was the quickest way to get their attention "He was down in the Bowery, where he had no place being, and somebody hit him over the head and robbed him."

"Good God," Patton said. "Poor Woo Woo. That's what we called him. Woo Woo. We all have nicknames."

Frank decided not to comment on this. Or to ask Patton what his nickname was. "I'm trying to trace Wooten's movements from the day his father died. I understand Mr. Nehemiah Wooten sent his son a telegram on Friday night."

"Oh, yes, there was quite a folderol about that, I'm afraid. Woo Woo was in a state. The old man was angry about something. It was the sister, you know. What's her name? I never can remember."

"Electra," Frank supplied.

"Oh, yes, a fool for the Greeks. The old man, that is. Gave his children the silliest names, but what can you do?"

Frank didn't point out that Woo Woo was pretty silly, too. "So the telegram was about Electra?"

"I don't think so. At least, it didn't say anything in particular. The old man wasn't going to put his daughter's name in a telegram that anybody could see, was he?"

Frank didn't suppose he was.

"He wanted Leander to come home right away. That's about all it said, but it didn't need to say much else. We all know what it means when the old man sends for us, don't we? It's never good news. The old man never sends a telegram to say, 'Come on home, son, I want to raise your allowance,' or something like that. Oh, no. It's always when you've been caught out and he's calling you on the carpet."

Frank's father had never sent him a telegram to tell him anything, so he couldn't judge. "So Leander thought his father was calling him on the carpet?"

"He was sure of it. Something about his sister. She was going to be in trouble with the old man, too, or at least that's what Woo Woo thought. They were in it together anyway. I'm sure of that. He was more worried about her than himself. She's deaf. Did you know?" Frank nodded. "And he was scared. I don't know what he thought the old man was going to do, but he was scared."

He had every reason to be, Frank thought. "So when did he leave for the city?"

"On Sunday morning, after he got the message that the old man was dead."

"What?" Frank asked, confused.

"On Sunday morning, after—"

"But his father wanted him to come on Saturday," Frank said. "Isn't that what his telegram said?"

"It is, but that's what all the folderol was about. You see, we were out on Friday night. We were out quite late, which isn't unusual, and when we got back, we were . . . well, quite drunk. Neither one of us noticed the telegram. Somebody had slipped it under the door, you see, and one of us stepped on it or something. We didn't even turn on the lights when we came in. Fell into bed with our clothes on. Slept until afternoon the next day."

"So Leander didn't even get the telegram until Saturday afternoon," Frank said.

"No," Patton confirmed. "I found it sticking out from under my bed when I finally woke up. Woo Woo was in a state. He knew the old man was already pretty angry, but he'd be livid when Woo Woo didn't show up. Not seeing the telegram because you were too drunk isn't a good excuse either, let me tell you."

Frank didn't suppose it was. His mind was racing. "Are you sure Leander didn't go to New York on Saturday?"

"Oh, no," Patton said. "We were both passed out here until after lunch. They sent somebody up to check on us when we didn't appear. I told Woo Woo he should just clean himself up and catch the next train. That was all he could do, wasn't it? He did go to the dean's house and ask to use the telephone. He tried to phone the old man, but he didn't get an answer, so he decided not to go. Really, I think he was just too hung over to make the trip."

"Did he phone his father's house?" Frank asked.

"I don't think so. Somebody would've answered there, wouldn't they? A servant at least. It must have been the office. He wanted Woo Woo to meet him at the office, I think. Wait, the telegram might still be here on his desk."

Patton jumped up and rummaged around for a moment and came up with the telltale yellow sheet of a telegram from among the stacks of books and papers Leander Wooten had left behind. "Here it is."

It said simply, "TAKE TRAIN HOME SATURDAY STOP MEET MY OFFICE STOP FATHER." Exactly the allowable ten words. Nothing really ominous unless you knew you'd violated your father's most sacred desires and arranged for your deaf sister to learn to sign. And Leander had missed his appointment. He hadn't even gone to the city that day.

He hadn't killed his father. So who had? And who'd killed Leander?

FRANK TOOK TWO UNIFORMED OFFICERS WITH HIM TO the Bowery that night. He didn't want to end up like Leander Wooten, dead in an alley with his pockets turned out. Leander's death still might have nothing to do with his father's, still might be an unfortunate coincidence, but Frank didn't believe things happened by accident. When two bad things happened together, they were usually connected in some way.

The Grey Goose was a lively place by the time Frank arrived near ten o'clock. He wanted nothing more than to head home to his own bed, but he had to find out if anybody remembered seeing Leander Wooten on Tuesday night. If he waited much longer, he'd have no chance at all. To those who frequented places like the Grey Goose, one day was pretty much like another.

He started with the bartenders, who wouldn't even look at the photograph until he'd paid for an expensive drink he didn't receive. One of them remembered Leander, mainly because he'd bought only one beer. Young men like that came to the Bowery to get drunk, and they usually came in groups and had lots of money to spend. The bartender had been happy to see a rich young blade stepping up to the bar until he'd looked around and realized he was alone.

"He only had one drink?"

"He only had one here," the bartender clarified.

"Did you see him talking to anybody?"

The bartender gave him a withering look. "It's not my job to keep track of who talks to who. I got work to do."

Frank gave it one last shot. "Did you see him leave?"

"No, I didn't. I didn't see him do anything but pay for his drink and walk away. Stupid fool, and then he gets himself killed almost on the doorstep. Now I ask you, what swell in his right mind will ever come down here again?"

Frank figured the world was full of foolish young swells who'd forget Leander's death in a few weeks, but he didn't comfort the bartender. He showed the photograph around to some of the patrons, but nobody remembered seeing Leander. If he'd met someone here, that man probably wasn't here now and wouldn't admit it if he was.

By midnight, Frank gave up his fruitless quest and went home. His mother would fuss at him for coming in so late, but she'd fix him something to eat. Then he could sleep for a few hours before starting all over again.

SARAH WAS BEGINNING TO WONDER HOW LONG THEY would allow her to stay on at the Wooten house before someone noticed that her services were no longer needed. She was starting to feel too comfortable being a confidante to so many wounded people here. Mrs. Wooten was finally coming out of her grief-induced stupor. That morning, she had informed Mrs. Parmer that she would make the plans for Leander's funeral herself, even though Dr. Smith had told her she must not exert herself in the slightest for at least two full weeks after the birth.

Mrs. Parmer was bearing up under the burden of having lost her brother and her nephew in just a few days' time, although she was beginning to show the strain. Electra kept to her room most of the time, probably grieving in her own way.

"Mrs. Wooten," Sarah said when she had finished helping her change into a clean nightdress and get settled again, "I should probably leave today. Unless you need me to stay on," she added for courtesy. She didn't really want to stay. She wanted to go home and see Catherine. She missed her daughter dreadfully.

"Are you sure it's safe? I mean, I'm still in such pain from my breasts being bound, and Dr. Smith doesn't want me to lift a finger. You warned me yourself that I need to be careful, and there's so much to do with the funeral . . ." Her voice broke on the word, and Sarah began to feel guilty.

Still . . .

"You're doing very well, and Minnie knows how to take care of you now. The baby is thriving with his nurse, and I'm afraid I'm beginning to feel like an intruder here. There's really nothing left for me to do. You can always send for me if you need me," she added, hoping that would convince her.

It did. "I will miss you, Mrs. Brandt," Mrs. Wooten said. It was the closest she would come to acknowledging the important role Sarah had played during one of the most stressful times of Mrs. Wooten's life. "I've been very impressed with your work."

Sarah thanked her, packed up her things, and went to say good-bye to Mrs. Parmer.

"I'm sorry to see you go," Mrs. Parmer said with a sad smile. "It seems I've come to depend on you. You're always so levelheaded and sensible about everything."

Sarah smiled. "It's easy to be levelheaded when you're dealing with other people's problems. I just hope I was some help to you during this time. I know it's been very difficult for you."

Mrs. Parmer sighed. "Yes. Our lives will never be the same again. And poor Electra. I don't know what will become of her. Not many families would allow their sons to marry into a family where two people had been murdered." She dabbed at her eyes with her handkerchief.

"Electra is beautiful and charming. I'm sure someone will find her irresistible," Sarah said, although she didn't add that he might be the deaf man Electra's father had wanted to avoid.

"I hope you're right," Mrs. Parmer said, sighing again. "She deserves some happiness in her life."

"A woman can be happy, even if she isn't married," Sarah reminded her gently.

Mrs. Parmer smiled. "Yes, but it's a lonely life. Electra should have children, too."

Mrs. Parmer arranged for Sarah's fee to be paid to her and summoned the carriage to take her back home. Sarah could have taken the El, but she enjoyed the trip in the luxurious vehicle, and she knew her neighbor, Mrs. Ellsworth, would be in a tizzy of excitement to see such a fine conveyance coming down Bank Street.

Mrs. Ellsworth had long been the neighborhood's main source of information. A widow whose son worked long hours, she'd had too much free time and had spent it keeping track of her neighbors' business. Now that Sarah had a family, however, Mrs. Ellsworth no longer had time to notice what other people were doing. She was too busy teaching Catherine and Maeve the domestic arts. So Sarah brought a little excitement to her neighbor's life by arriving in the Wootens' carriage.

By the time the footman had opened the door and helped her out, Catherine, Maeve, and Mrs. Ellsworth were on the front stoop to greet her. Catherine went flying down the front steps and into Sarah's arms.

"Mama, I missed you!" she said, her eyes shining with happiness as Sarah covered her small face with kisses.

"I missed you, too, my darling girl. Have you been good for Maeve and Mrs. Ellsworth?"

"I was good as gold," she bragged. "Wasn't I, Maeve?"

Maeve gave her a mock frown. "Maybe good as brass," she allowed, "but I'm not so sure about gold." Catherine giggled delightedly.

"Oh, she was pure gold," Mrs. Ellsworth insisted. "Now let your mama come inside. She must be exhausted!"

The footman brought Sarah's bag inside, and the girls watched the carriage rolling down the street from the front window until it was out of sight.

"Your patient must have been very wealthy," Mrs. Ellsworth remarked, watching over their shoulders.

"Yes, for a change," Sarah said. The wealthy seldom used midwives anymore.

"You must tell me all about it," Mrs. Ellsworth whispered. "After Catherine goes to bed."

But it was hours until then, so Sarah allowed the girls to make a fuss over her and tell her everything they had been doing in the days she had been away. In general, she just enjoyed being home again. Mrs. Ellsworth took her leave shortly after Sarah arrived, explaining that she did occasionally have to return to her own house next door and do some things there, but she promised to come back later.

Sarah saw her out.

* * *

"HAS CATHERINE HAD ANY MORE OF THOSE SPELLS?" Sarah asked when they were out of earshot of the girls.

"No, nothing out of the ordinary at all. She's been perfectly normal."

Sarah sighed with relief. "I've been worried about her."

"I'm sure you have, but there's no need. And now that you're home again, I'm sure she'll be fine."

Sarah walked her to the front door.

"Was it the Wooten family you were called for?" Mrs. Ellsworth asked her when they reached the foyer. "I saw the newspaper stories about Mr. Wooten being murdered, and I thought that must be the case Mr. Malloy was working on."

"Yes, Mrs. Wooten went into labor, probably from the shock."

"How terrible," Mrs. Ellsworth said. "That poor man will never see his child."

"Perhaps it isn't terrible at all," Sarah said in a tone that made Mrs. Ellsworth's eyes gleam.

"Well, then, I will definitely be back to hear all the details."

"I suppose you also saw that their son, Leander, was killed on Tuesday night as well."

Mrs. Ellsworth looked surprised. "How terrible! No, I hadn't heard. Tuesday night, you say? I get a newspaper every morning, but I didn't see a story about it."

"Oh, they didn't identify his body until Wednesday night, but I thought it was in the newspapers yesterday morning."

"Maybe it was the afternoon papers, but I never buy

them. I always think one dose of bad news a day is enough. And how awful for the family. First the father and then the son. Has Mr. Malloy figured out what happened yet?"

"Not yet. He was going to New Jersey yesterday."

"New Jersey? Whatever for?"

"The son attended college there, and Malloy had to find out something about him. I think they said he goes to Princeton University."

"Oh, yes, they changed the name of the College of New Jersey to Princeton, didn't they? It sounds much more elegant, doesn't it?"

Sarah agreed and Mrs. Ellsworth took her leave, promising to return later to hear Sarah's story.

FRANK FIGURED HE SHOULD CHECK IN AT POLICE HEAD-quarters and give them an update on his progress. The desk sergeant was glad to see him.

"You got a message about the boy that was killed in the Bowery on Tuesday night." He handed Frank a note.

It was from Officer Kelly, the one who had found Leander's body. Someone had tried to pawn Leander Wooten's watch.

14

THE FELLOW WHO HAD TRIED TO PAWN LEANDER WOO-
ten's watch was a sorry specimen. Kelly was holding him at
the station house, and he looked a little the worse for wear.
Fresh bruises marked his face, and he seemed to be suffering
the effects of alcohol withdrawal. They'd brought him to
one of the interrogation rooms, and he looked up with bleary
eyes when Frank walked in with Kelly.

"Stand up, then," Kelly commanded. "Show some respect
for your betters."

The man tried to rise, but plainly he couldn't quite manage it.

"That's all right," Frank said in a friendly tone. He
glanced at Kelly, giving him the silent message that he'd
decided this was the role he would play in their little drama.
"Sit down. Have they been treating you well?"

The man glanced up warily at Kelly, who was maintaining his angry expressions. "Yeah, sure," the man said guardedly.

Frank took a seat across the scarred table from him. "What's your name?"

"Battersby," he said, wiping his mouth with the back of his hand. "Albert Battersby."

He was a wizened little creature, shrunken inside his filthy clothes. His grimy face was wrinkled and drawn, making him look ancient, although the arrest report said he was only thirty-six. His trembling hands were knobby from hard work, but he would no longer be capable of that. He wouldn't be able to earn enough for liquor and food both, so he'd choose liquor most of the time. He'd sleep on the streets, beg when he could, and steal what he could. Frank tried to imagine Leander Wooten going into an alley with this man.

He couldn't.

"You were caught trying to pawn a watch," Frank reminded him. "Where did you get it?"

"I told them a dozen times, I found it!" Battersby insisted, giving Kelly a glance to see if he was going to get mad about it. Kelly's expression remained grim, but he stood back, giving Frank the opportunity to work.

"*Where* did you find it?" Frank asked conversationally.

"I . . . I don't remember. On the street somewhere."

"You were lucky, I guess," Frank said. "Being the first to spot it. Something like that wouldn't be there very long, would it?"

"No," Battersby agreed with pitiful enthusiasm. "I was lucky."

"Except I guess they told you the watch belonged to a dead man."

Battersby glanced at Kelly again. "They said. They think I killed him, but I never! I was in a bad way that night. I couldn't've hurt nobody."

"You were in a bad way?" Frank asked. "You needed a drink, you mean?"

"I hadn't had anything in almost two days!" Battersby said. "I had the shakes so bad, I could hardly walk. Kind of like now," he added with another glance at Kelly.

Frank nodded his understanding. "You were hanging around the saloon, waiting for somebody to come out and toss you a coin."

"Yes, yes, that's right!"

"But nobody did, because your luck has been bad," Frank guessed.

Battersby's rheumy eyes widened in surprise. "That's right," he again confirmed.

"So you were excited when you saw that swell come out of the saloon and go down the alley, and you followed him, and—"

"No, no, it wasn't like that!" he insisted.

"What was it like?" Frank asked, leaning forward as if he was really interested. "Did you bring the broom handle with you, or did you find it?"

"I didn't have no broom handle! I didn't have nothing!"

"You did, Albert," Frank said with a disapproving frown. "We found it by the body, right where you left it."

"I didn't leave it! I didn't leave nothing!"

"So you saw him come out and go down the alley and you followed him because he was a little drunk and all alone—"

"He wasn't alone!"

The hair on the back of Frank's neck stood up, but he just said, "He wasn't?"

Battersby glanced at Kelly again. Seeing no threat of violence, he said, "He wasn't alone. There was two of them."

"Two men?" Frank asked.

"Two swells. I called out to them, but they just went right on by. Never gave me nothing!"

"Is that why you followed them?" Frank asked.

"I didn't! I told you, I never followed nobody! I just sat there, trying to get somebody to stand me to a drink, but nobody paid me any mind. And then I saw one of the swells come out of the alley. He looked around, up and down the street, like he was looking for somebody, and then he walks away, kind of fast and still looking around."

"Then what did you do, Albert?" Frank asked.

Battersby licked his lips. "If I could just have a drink. Maybe you've got a flask on you, Mr. Detective . . ."

"If you tell me the truth, I'll make sure you get a drink, Albert. What did you do next?"

Battersby leaned forward, across the table, close enough that Frank could smell his fetid breath. "I waited a bit, to see if the other one come out, and when he didn't, I went to see. To see if he needed help, don't you know? I thought the other fellow might've done him some harm."

Frank nodded. "You're a Good Samaritan, aren't you, Albert?"

"That's it, a Good Samaritan," Battersby eagerly agreed.

"And I guess you helped him," Frank said.

Battersby rubbed his mouth again. "I sure could use that drink . . ."

Kelly reached out without a word and slapped Battersby upside the head.

"Hey, what was that for?" he complained, rubbing the side of his head.

"To remind you that you need to tell me the truth," Frank said mildly. "And the truth is that when you saw these two swells go into the alley, you went to see what they were up to."

"Oh, no, I—" Kelly moved as if to slap him again, and he quickly added, "That is, maybe I did. I was curious, don't you know? I wondered what they was up to, like you said. You see some strange things in the Bowery."

"And what did you see?"

"I couldn't see much. It was dark as pitch, but I could hear. It sounded like one of them was getting a beating. I know what that sounds like, right enough." He gave Kelly a black look, which the policeman returned in kind.

"And did you try to stop it?" Frank asked.

"Not likely! I ain't crazy. I tried to run away, but I fell. I wasn't too steady on my feet, like I said. I fell down, and I thought for sure he would've heard me, the one doing the beating, but it was noisy, from the saloon, don't you know? And when he come out and looked around, I just laid still on the sidewalk, like I was passed out, and he never noticed me. Then he run off, like I said."

Frank considered his story. "What did you do when he was gone?"

Battersby seemed to shrink even further. "I ain't proud of this, but I was dying. You don't know what it's like, needing a drink so bad . . ."

"No, I don't," Frank agreed. "But I can imagine. You knew some swell was in the alley, all by himself and beaten pretty bad. So you decided to see if the other swell had left anything in the other man's pockets for you."

"He was dead," Battersby defended himself. "If not right ther., he soon was. He never even moved when I turned out his pockets." He shook his head. "I should've left the watch, but he didn't have much on him. Ten dollars and some silver is all. I figured the watch would bring that and more. Now about that drink . . ."

"What did this other man look like, the one who ran away?"

"I don't know. I didn't pay no attention to what they looked like," Battersby protested.

"Tall, short, fat, thin?" Frank pressed him.

Battersby swiped at his mouth. "One was taller than the other, I know."

"Which one came out of the alley, the tall one or the short one?"

"I don't know! Please, I really need that drink . . ."

"Did you see them go into the saloon?"

"No, I hadn't been there long when they came out. I never saw nothing. Please, mister . . ."

Frank stood up. "I'm finished with him."

"Wait, come back! You promised me a drink!" Battersby was hollering as Frank and Kelly left the room. Kelly told an officer waiting outside to lock Battersby back up.

"You believe him?" Kelly asked as they made their way upstairs.

"His story makes sense. Battersby has the watch, and he admits he took it off the dead man. I can't imagine the dead man going into an alley in the Bowery with Battersby, or even going in alone. Wooten was young and healthy and athletic, so I don't think Battersby could've taken him by surprise, even if he'd been strong enough, which he isn't, even when he doesn't need a drink."

"But what was Wooten doing at the saloon, and why did he go into the alley?"

"I don't know yet, but Wooten must've had a reason for being in the Grey Goose that night. If he just wanted to get drunk, he could've done that in a safer place, so he must've been there to meet somebody. If he did meet somebody, he might've left with that person. I doubt he would've left the bar with somebody he didn't know, and if somebody in the bar had spotted Wooten as an easy mark and followed him into the alley, he would've robbed him, but Battersby found money in his pockets and his watch still there."

"So if Battersby didn't kill him—and I think you're right about him not being able—then whoever killed him just wanted him dead," Kelly summarized. "That means he must've known his killer. Do you know who that might be?"

Frank sighed. "I'm very much afraid I do."

FRANK HAD BEEN DREADING THIS MOMENT. HE'D PUT the evidence together, and it all pointed in one direction. Nehemiah Wooten had discovered that his partner was embezzling from their company and confronted him on Thursday of last week. On Saturday, Young had returned to their office for some reason. Maybe he hoped to convince Wooten not to make the theft public. Wooten had refused, enraging Young, who'd picked up an old loving cup from Wooten's athletic youth and clobbered him with it.

Then Young had hoped to keep Leander Wooten away from the business for a while, maybe for years, while he either bled the company dry or covered up his tracks. But Leander had made Young think he knew the whole story. Young had somehow arranged to meet him that night and lured him out into the alley. Sarah had even heard Young telling Leander they would talk later. Leander would have felt perfectly safe with Young, a man he'd known all his life. Then Young had repeated the little scene he'd had several days earlier with Wooten's father, leaving Leander dead and himself safe from discovery.

Until Frank had found the ledger and the mysterious arithmetic that pointed to embezzlement. He couldn't arrest a man like Young for murder, but he could make sure he was guilty. Then he could turn Mr. Decker loose on him.

Peters, the clerk at the front desk, showed Frank into Mr. Young's office and left him there. Frank had wrapped the ledger up in brown paper, so Young wouldn't see it first off. He probably knew by now that Frank had taken it, but Frank wanted to keep some element of surprise.

Young had risen from his seat to greet Frank. "Sit down, Mr. Malloy," he said in a surprisingly friendly tone. "I've been expecting you."

"You have?" he asked as he took the offered chair in front of Young's desk.

"Of course I have. We're both men of the world, Mr. Malloy. I knew it was just a matter of time before you paid me this visit."

Frank figured he might as well get to it. He was still holding the ledger in his lap. He placed it carefully and purposefully onto Young's desk.

"What do you have there?" Young asked with a frown.

Frank sat back in his chair and watched Young's face carefully. "It's a ledger. I found it in Mr. Wooten's desk."

Young didn't look the least bit alarmed. Or guilty. "Peters told me you'd taken it. That's how you figured out the money was missing."

Frank nodded. "And I knew you and Mr. Wooten had

argued on Thursday. That's when he figured it out, wasn't it?"

"You know it is, Malloy. You spoke with my son. He told me all about it." He folded his hands on his desk and stared intently at Frank. "You've done an excellent job of sorting all of this out, Mr. Malloy. You're quite clever. I've often thought that it's a shame the city of New York doesn't pay its law enforcement officers what they're really worth. If Mrs. Wooten weren't indisposed, I'm sure she would have had the presence of mind to offer a suitable reward for the satisfactory conclusion of this case. I'm afraid women can't always be depended upon to understand how these things work, however."

Frank wasn't sure whether he should agree or disagree, so he just waited to hear the rest of what Young wanted to say.

"Now then, we should get down to business. I *am* prepared to offer you a suitable reward for a satisfactory conclusion to this case. A donation to the police benevolence fund, if you will."

Frank knew what Young was talking about. He was offering Frank a bribe. People politely called them rewards or even donations, but everyone knew what the real purpose was.

"What would you consider a satisfactory conclusion to the case?" Frank asked, really wanting to know.

"This is getting very tiresome, Mr. Malloy," Young said, no longer quite so congenial in the face of Frank's challenge. "You know very well what I would consider satisfactory. I want to protect my son. Would five thousand dollars do that?"

Frank wasn't sure what surprised him more, the

amount—which was nearly a year's salary for him—or the fact that Young was talking about protecting his *son*. Why would Young be willing to pay that much to keep Terry's affair with Mrs. Wooten a secret when Young himself had committed murder?

Because, Frank realized with stunning clarity, what Young wanted to protect his son from had nothing to do with adultery. Nobody would pay five thousand dollars to protect his son from a simple scandal. *Terry* was the one who had stolen the money, and *Terry* had gone to Wooten's office that day to plead for mercy. And *Terry* had killed Nehemiah Wooten!

And Mr. Young was willing to pay Frank five thousand dollars to forget he knew it. Except Frank had already decided Terry Young wasn't the killer.

"Where were you when Mr. Wooten was killed, Mr. Young?"

Young stiffened. "Me? How dare you ask me that!"

"I have to know where you were," Frank insisted in the voice he used to intimidate hardened criminals. He shouldn't risk offending Young, but he couldn't make another mistake about this. If there was any chance Young was guilty . . .

"If you must know, I was with a lady all afternoon. She would vouch for me, although I have no intention of giving you her name—"

Before he could finish, the office door burst open, and Terry Young was standing there. His face was red and his eyes wide. "What's going on here?" he demanded, glaring first at Frank and then at his father.

"Get out of here, Terry. This doesn't concern you," his

father said, jumping to his feet. He looked more alarmed than angry.

Frank decided to try an experiment. "Your father is trying to bribe me," he said.

Terry's gaze shifted to Frank. He looked alarmed as well. "Bribe you?" He looked back to his father. "He can't prove anything. I already told him I didn't hear your voice, so I don't know for sure that you were there."

"Me?" Mr. Young asked, confused now. "When did you hear my voice? What are you talking about?"

"When Nehemiah was killed!" Terry said, exasperated. "I didn't hear you or see you there, so nobody can prove you did it!"

"Of course they can't prove *I* did it, because *you* did it!" his father replied, equally exasperated.

Terry Young blinked in surprise. "No, I didn't! I . . . I thought you did!"

Father and son stared at each other for a long moment, stunned. They'd been trying to protect each other, and neither was guilty.

Frank sighed and stood up. "I guess this means I won't be getting my five thousand dollars."

The two men looked at him as if they'd never seen him before. Neither made any move to stop him as he strolled past Terry Young and out of the office, leaving the incriminating ledger behind. He'd be sure and let Mr. Decker know that Terry Young was the embezzler. As much as he disliked Mr. Young, he couldn't in good conscience allow him to be ruined for his son's transgressions.

Frank wondered what Terry had used his ill-gotten gains for. Maybe he'd entertained fantasies of running off with

Mrs. Wooten to some foreign land where no one would know them. It was a disturbing thought.

SARAH AND THE GIRLS HAD JUST FINISHED CLEANING up their lunch dishes when they heard the front doorbell. All three groaned in disappointment, certain Sarah was being summoned to a delivery.

"I'll get it," Maeve said, hurrying out to answer it. Catherine followed on her heels.

Sarah followed more slowly, not anxious to leave again so soon, until she heard Catherine giggling and the rumble of a familiar voice. She quickened her steps as much as dignity allowed.

Malloy had lifted Catherine up into his arms, and she was laughing at something he'd said to her. "Mrs. Brandt," he said when he caught sight of her.

"Mr. Malloy," she replied, unable to keep herself from smiling. "What brings you here? Have you caught the culprit?"

"I'm afraid not," he said. "I guessed completely wrong, and now I have to start all over again."

"Oh, dear," Maeve said. "Don't you have any ideas at all?"

"I have one or two," he said. "But I needed to consult with Mrs. Brandt first."

"My mama is very smart," Catherine informed him.

"I know she is," Malloy said with a grin.

Sarah hated the heat she felt rising in her cheeks, but she was grinning back. "I'm always happy to assist the police whenever I can," she said.

"We just finished eating," Maeve said. "Are you hungry? I can fix you a sandwich."

"I would appreciate that very much," Malloy said. "Could you help Maeve, Miss Catherine?"

Catherine nodded vigorously and allowed Malloy to set her down on her feet again.

Maeve and Catherine headed for the kitchen.

"What happened?" Sarah asked him when the girls were gone.

"I was sure Mr. Young had done it. He and Wooten argued over the embezzlement on Thursday, right after Wooten found out about it. I figured he'd come back on Saturday afternoon. Terry Young had an appointment with Wooten at one o'clock that day, but when he arrived, someone was in the office with Wooten already, so he left. I thought Young was the one stealing from the company, so I figured he had another argument with Wooten and killed him."

"That makes perfect sense," she said. "Come in and sit down," she added, leading him over to the two easy chairs sitting by the front window.

"Yes, it does make sense, except that Young wasn't the one stealing. It was his son, Terry."

"Terry? Why on earth would he need to steal?"

"Who knows? He's got a mistress, you know. Maybe he was saving up to be able to keep her in style once she left her husband for him."

"She never would've done that!" Sarah said, shaking her head.

"Maybe she wouldn't've had any choice. If Wooten found out about them, he would have thrown her out."

"That's true. So Terry was planning for the future. But he didn't kill Mr. Wooten?"

"No. It's very disappointing. His father was prepared to pay me off to make sure I kept quiet about it, too."

"How dishonest of him," Sarah said, shaking her head in mock dismay.

"Yeah, well, I don't think either of them are too worried about doing what's right. In any case, neither of them killed Wooten or Leander, so who did?"

"Are you sure the same person killed both of them? I thought Leander was robbed in a dangerous part of the city."

"He was, but the fellow who robbed him didn't kill him. He wouldn't have been any match for a healthy young man. Which means that the fellow who killed him didn't rob him, because he still had money and his watch on him when the robber came along."

"How do you know who robbed him?"

"He tried to pawn Leander's gold watch. It was engraved, so the pawnbrokers were watching for it."

"Do they help the police?" Sarah asked in surprise.

"When it's important, they do. Most of the time, they don't care if the goods are stolen or not. They'd be out of business if they did. But when it's a murder of somebody important, and they'll get in trouble if they don't, then they're amazingly helpful."

"I see," Sarah said. "So if the same person killed both of them, who could it be?"

"Somebody who had a reason to want both of them dead."

She gave him a look. "I figured that out, but who wanted both of them dead?"

"I've been thinking that Adam Oldham had a reason to want both of them out of the way."

"Not Adam," Sarah protested. "He's such a nice young man."

"Don't tell me you've fallen in love with him, too," Malloy said with a frown.

"Not in love exactly," Sarah said, "but you must admit, he's very handsome."

Malloy made a rude noise, and Sarah managed not to laugh.

"All right," she said. "I'll admit that Adam had a good reason to want both Leander and his father out of the way, but how could he have lured Leander to a saloon? They never even saw each other. Could he have sent a letter or something?"

Malloy was frowning again. "But they did see each other, at the funeral."

"That's right," Sarah remembered. "But just for a few moments. And they couldn't speak to each other. Leander doesn't understand signs, and Mr. Oldham doesn't read lips."

"But they did have an argument," Malloy said. "Leander told him to leave the house and never come back or something like that. I couldn't see exactly what happened. Did you?"

"Yes, I saw it all. Mr. Oldham had a notebook that he was writing in. He uses it when he has to communicate with people who don't understand his signs. He wrote something to Leander. It must have been an apology, because Leander calmed right down."

"Did Leander write something back?"

"I think so. They both wrote in the book, at least. I'm sure of that."

"I wish I could see what they wrote," Malloy mused.

"You can!" Sarah remembered. "In the excitement, Mr. Oldham dropped the notebook, and Electra picked it up.

Her aunt reminded her to give it back to him when he called on her the other day, but she didn't. We thought she wanted it as a keepsake or something. Girls are so sentimental . . . What is it?"

Malloy had jumped to his feet. "I need to see what they wrote in that book."

"Mr. Malloy, your sandwich is ready," Maeve called from the kitchen.

"Take a minute to eat," Sarah said. "I'll get ready and go with you."

"You don't need—"

"You're dealing with a young girl," she reminded him. "What if she refuses to let you see the notebook? Are you going to go charging upstairs and search her bedroom for it?"

Malloy could see the problem. "But she might let you see it," he guessed.

"Or at least I could go to her room and look for it if she doesn't. I won't be long."

By the time Sarah had changed into a street dress, Malloy had gobbled down his sandwich and was pacing impatiently. The girls were watching him curiously, as if he were a specimen in a zoo. The moment he saw that Sarah was ready, he hurried to the front door, snatching his hat off the rack where Maeve had hung it when he came in, and held the door open for her.

"I don't know when we'll be back," Sarah called after her as Malloy took her elbow and propelled her down the front steps.

"It'll be faster to take the El," Malloy said, referring to the elevated train that ran up Ninth Avenue. They headed down Bank Street, then up Hudson to the Little Twelfth Street Station.

As they reached the station, Sarah saw a newsboy trying to sell the last of his early papers before the afternoon editions came out. "Malloy, I just remembered, Mrs. Ellsworth said the Thursday morning newspapers didn't have the story about Leander's death in them."

"It's not likely they would," Malloy said, still holding her elbow as they climbed the long stairway up to the station. "Mrs. Parmer didn't identify his body until late on Wednesday."

"But you don't understand. When Mr. Oldham arrived at the Wooten house to see Electra on Thursday morning, he already knew Leander was dead. He claimed he'd read about it in the paper, but it wasn't in the paper yet."

Malloy's expression grew even grimmer, and he quickened his pace even more, until Sarah was practically running to keep up with him.

GETTING TO THE WOOTEN HOUSE SEEMED TO TAKE FOR-ever, although she kept reminding Malloy that Oldham didn't know they'd figured it out. He'd be working at the school today, as usual, thinking he was safe, and he wouldn't be a danger to anyone else. Both men who might have kept him away from Electra were already dead.

Sarah still couldn't seem to calm Malloy's anxiety, and her own began to grow. By the time they reached the Wootens' house, she had to resist the urge to pound on the door when the maid didn't answer their knock as quickly as she wanted.

"We need to see Mrs. Parmer immediately," Sarah told the startled maid.

"The family is in mourning and—"

"I know, I know," Sarah said impatiently. "But we must see her. Mr. Malloy has some information for her."

"I'll see if she's home," the girl said doubtfully, as she was trained to do when unexpected and possibly unwelcome visitors arrived.

"Calm down," Malloy said to Sarah while they waited, although she noticed he was still fidgeting, too.

When the maid returned to escort them upstairs, Sarah had to force herself to walk at a reasonable pace and not to push past the girl and go charging into the parlor.

Mrs. Parmer was on her feet when they entered the room. "Mrs. Brandt, Mr. Malloy, this is a surprise. Do you have some news for me?" she asked hopefully.

"Mrs. Parmer, we're so sorry to bother you," Sarah hastened to say, cutting off whatever Malloy might have said. "But Mr. Malloy needs to see the notebook that Mr. Oldham left here on the day of Mr. Wooten's funeral."

"The notebook?" Mrs. Parmer asked. "You mean the one he was writing in?"

"Yes, that's the one. Electra took it to her room, I believe. Remember, you suggested she return it to him when he called on her yesterday, but she ignored you."

"That's right, I do remember." She turned to Malloy. "Why do you need to see it?"

Malloy looked at Sarah, silently asking her to frame a suitable reply that wouldn't alarm Mrs. Parmer unnecessarily.

"He thinks there might be some clue in it about why Leander went out that evening," Sarah said carefully.

Mrs. Parmer wasn't a stupid woman. She only needed

a moment to figure out the implication of what Sarah had said. The color drained from her face. "Do you think—?"

"We don't know anything for sure," Malloy hastened to explain. "I just thought that Oldham might have suggested a meeting. He might not have," he added diplomatically. "And if he did, that would at least explain why Leander went out that night. It wouldn't necessarily mean that . . . Well, I just need to know for sure."

Mrs. Parmer's eyes were wide with apprehension as she considered the possibilities. "Please, wait here. I'll go find Electra and have her get the notebook." Mrs. Parmer left the room, her back rigid as she fought to hold her fears in check.

"Do you really think Mr. Oldham could have killed Mr. Wooten?" Sarah asked.

"He could've gone to see Mr. Wooten at his office. I don't know how he would've known he'd be there, but maybe he was just lucky."

"You said Terry Young heard someone in the office with Wooten, but he couldn't have heard Mr. Oldham speaking. Mr. Wooten wouldn't have been speaking to Oldham either," Sarah realized.

"Terry said he heard Wooten's voice, but he didn't understand the words, just the tone. He said it was the tone he uses when he thinks he's smarter than you are or something like that."

"Oh, my, Mr. Wooten couldn't have been a very pleasant man to know."

"Or to do business with. I can't really blame Terry for stealing from him."

"Or Mrs. Wooten for betraying him?" Sarah asked archly.

"Well, I'd have to think about that one, I guess."

Sarah considered what Malloy had said. "So Terry didn't hear the other person speaking?"

"No. He assumed it was his father, and that his father had killed Wooten in an argument, but Young thought Terry had done it and was willing to pay me a fortune to protect him, so I have to assume Young is innocent, too."

"Still, his not hearing the other person's voice is interesting," Sarah said. "Mr. Oldham doesn't speak."

"But why would Wooten have been talking to a deaf man?"

Sarah considered this. "But you do, don't you?" she mused. "From habit. I noticed the family here even speaks to Electra when she can't see their faces. After all these years, they still forget sometimes that she can't hear them."

"Probably because she usually acts as if she does, replying when they speak to her because she watches their lips."

"And that's what Mr. Wooten would've been used to, a deaf person who can understand what he says."

"Which could explain why Terry heard Mr. Wooten speaking but not the other person."

Malloy nodded. "So I guess we've convinced ourselves that Oldham could've killed Wooten, and we'll soon know if he lured Leander out to that saloon."

"I hope we're wrong," Sarah said, "for Electra's sake. She'd be devastated if the man she loves is the one who killed her father and her brother."

"And what about all those other poor females who are in love with him, too? Even my own mother," Malloy reminded her. "I won't be able to go home again if I have to arrest him for murder."

Sarah smiled in spite of herself.

The sound of footsteps in the hallway silenced them, and they waited expectantly as Mrs. Parmer appeared in the doorway. Her face was pale and her eyes were terrible.

"What's wrong?" Sarah asked, hurrying over to her.

"It's Electra," she said. "She's gone."

15

"WHAT DO YOU MEAN, SHE'S GONE?" SARAH ASKED, HUR-
rying to her.

"She isn't in the house. I had the servants check when she
wasn't in her room. No one saw her leave, but she's taken a
carpet bag and some of her clothes are missing. Where could
she have gone?"

"I'm guessing she's run off with Oldham or she's hoping to," Malloy said. "The question is, did Oldham put her
up to it or is she doing it on her own? Did you find the
notebook?"

Mrs. Parmer shook her head absently. "You mean she's
eloping? She's only sixteen," she said to Sarah, as if that were
a valid argument against such a possibility.

"Mr. Malloy could be wrong about that," Sarah said, giving him a warning look. "Come and sit down."

"May I search her room, Mrs. Parmer?" Malloy asked.

"There might be something that will tell us where she went."
Sarah knew he was thinking about Oldham's notebook.

"Yes, yes," Mrs. Parmer said. "Have the maid take you
upstairs and show you where it is."

Malloy hurried out.

"Is there a friend she might go to?" Sarah asked. "Someplace she might feel safe?"

"If she went to her friends, their parents would send us
word, I'm sure. Oh, Mrs. Brandt, what shall I do? We must
find her. If anyone discovers that she's run off with Mr. Oldham, she'll be ruined!"

That, Sarah realized, might be just what Mr. Oldham
was thinking, too. He didn't have to actually marry her
now. He only had to take her someplace and be gone overnight and her reputation would be ruined. No respectable
man would have her, then. A deaf girl with a ruined reputation would be hopeless indeed. She'd have to marry Oldham or no one.

Sarah and Mrs. Parmer waited for what seemed like an
hour but which the clock on the mantle said was no more
than ten minutes. Finally, Malloy came back, his expression
grave.

"I found this in her room," he said, handing Mrs. Parmer
an envelope. "It must've been delivered this morning."

It was addressed to Electra with no return address and no
stamp, so it hadn't been mailed. How had Electra received
it? Mrs. Parmer started to open it, but Malloy said, "It's
from Oldham. He says he wants to marry her." Mrs. Parmer
gasped. "He tells her to pack for an overnight stay and meet
him at Grand Central Station. They'll run away and elope
and surprise everyone."

"Oh, Mr. Malloy, I can't allow this. My brother . . . This

was what he wanted to avoid at all costs. Electra was never to marry a deaf man, and certainly not a man who stole her away against the wishes of her family! How do we know he even cares for her at all? Surely, if he did, he'd treat her with more respect than to ask her to sneak out and run away!"

"You're right, Mrs. Parmer," Malloy said. "We can't let him do this. How long has she been gone?"

"She came down for luncheon," Mrs. Parmer remembered. She glanced at the clock on the mantle. "Less than two hours, even if she left immediately after that."

"Then we might catch her. At least we should be able to find out where they were going. Somebody would've noticed a young couple like that, especially if they're deaf and talking with their hands."

"I should go with you," Mrs. Parmer said, rising from her seat.

"No," Sarah said. "If you were to go to the train station asking about her, that might cause talk. You should stay here in case she comes home. And we'll send you word the instant we know anything, I promise."

"Oh, Mrs. Brandt, you're right, of course, but I can't ask you to do this."

"You aren't asking me. I'm offering. I know Mr. Malloy will go after them, but he'll need a chaperone for Electra. She knows me, and she'll trust me, I'm sure."

"You are too kind. How can I ever thank you?"

"Don't thank me yet," Sarah said. "Thank me when we bring Electra home."

Malloy took the letter from Mrs. Parmer and tucked it into his pocket.

"I should get the carriage for you," Mrs. Parmer said. She was near tears.

"We can go faster without it," Malloy said. "We should get started, Mrs. Brandt."

"Try not to worry," Sarah told her. "We'll do everything we can."

"God bless you," Mrs. Parmer said as they hurried out.

Once again, they decided to take the El. They had to wait only a few minutes for a train, and were able to get seats a little removed from the rest of the passengers so they could talk.

"Did you find the notebook?" Sarah asked.

"No, and the reason I didn't let Mrs. Parmer read the letter herself is that he asks Electra to bring it with her."

"Maybe he just wanted it back," she suggested, trying to come up with an innocent explanation, although neither of them really believed it.

"Maybe," Malloy allowed. "We won't know for sure until we see what's in it."

Sarah shivered with a sudden chill. "But why would he have killed Leander?" she asked. "Or Mr. Wooten, for that matter?"

"We don't know that he did, of course, but the most obvious reason would be that he wanted to marry Electra, and they would never have allowed it."

"Then he must really love her," Sarah said.

Malloy shrugged. "Who knows? He could have other reasons for wanting to marry her."

"You mean he just wanted her but didn't love her?"

"Or something not romantic at all," he said with a grin at her determination to make this about desire. "Oldham was a smart young man. He had a college education, and he was good looking and charming. If he hadn't been deaf, he could've been very successful in life."

"But he *was* successful. He had a good job at the school," Sarah said.

"Teachers don't make a lot of money, not compared to people like the Wootens, and the deaf teachers get paid less than the ones who can hear," Malloy said.

"What?" Sarah said in outrage. "That's terrible!"

"I'm sure Oldham would agree with you. He must've been frustrated and angry. Then Rossiter—that's the teacher Leander first approached about teaching Electra to sign—he realized that if he put Oldham and Electra together, they'd probably fall in love. Rossiter knew Mr. Wooten was trying to convince the school board to stop teaching deaf children to sign at all, and he wanted . . . Well, I'm not sure exactly what Rossiter really wanted. He said he wanted Electra and Oldham to marry and have children who weren't deaf, to prove Alexander Graham Bell's theories were wrong, but that all seems kind of . . . I don't know, far-fetched, I guess."

"Yes, it does, and it would take so very long," Sarah said.

"Yeah, I think that's what was bothering me," Frank said. "Not many people would be willing to wait years to get revenge or whatever it was Rossiter was hoping for."

"Yes, and his plan sounds almost high-minded, until you think about how many people could be made unhappy. If Electra and Oldham married, her family would have been unhappy. If her family disowned her, Electra would be unhappy, and if her family managed to keep them apart, the lovers would be unhappy."

"And even if they did marry, there's no guarantee *they* would be happy together, especially if Oldham just married her for her family's money."

Sarah signed. "This is horrible."

"The only good thing is that we have a chance of catching them before he gets her away."

"Do you think he really plans to elope with her?"

"No, do you?"

"No. I didn't want to say anything in front of Mrs. Parmer, but he probably just plans to be away with her someplace overnight. With Mr. Wooten and Leander no longer around to protest, Mrs. Wooten would almost certainly agree to a hasty marriage to prevent a scandal. She doesn't seem likely to care what her husband might have thought about it either."

"I'm sorry I didn't get to know Mrs. Wooten better," Malloy said with a sly grin. "She must be an interesting woman."

They'd reach their stop, and they hurried off the train and down the stairs to the street. The walk to Grand Central Station left no time or breath for conversation. Malloy set a brisk pace, and Sarah didn't protest. She was as anxious as he to get there.

The station was relatively quiet in the midafternoon, but still many people sat on the benches in the enormous arched waiting area, where the autumn sun shone downward through the skylights above. Some of the people would be waiting for their trains to be called. Others were waiting for someone to arrive. Still others had no place else to go and found the station to be a cool, comfortable place to spend the day.

After quickly scanning the people in the room and seeing no sign of Oldham or Electra, Malloy approached the ticket windows, leaving Sarah to keep watch in case the couple appeared. Sarah heard some shouted protests as Malloy pushed in front of those waiting in line, but the protests ceased when he informed them he was with the police and was trying to catch a kidnapper.

He described the couple to the ticket agent. Sarah saw the man shake his head and then call over the other agents. They consulted and one of them explained something to Malloy. Malloy reached into his pocket and purchased a ticket.

Sarah felt her stomach drop. They were too late. Oldham had gotten her away.

Malloy came over to where she was waiting. "The ticket agent remembered them. He thought it was funny that the girl did the talking, and he noticed her voice sounded strange, too. They bought tickets to White Plains."

"White Plains! I should have remembered. The Wootens have a summer cottage there. They'd just been there for the month of August, I believe." Many wealthy families went to that area to escape the city's unbearable summer heat.

"That makes sense. Oldham probably knew about it, and Electra knows the area, and they'd have a place to stay that wouldn't cost them anything. Oldham doesn't have a lot of money for hotels, and he might attract attention taking such a young girl to one. Desk clerks at decent places ask questions."

"You bought yourself a ticket," she said.

"I got us *both* a ticket," he corrected her. "If you'll agree to accompany me, Mrs. Brandt," he added with a teasing glint.

"Are you trying to get me to elope with you, Malloy?" she teased back.

"If I was, I'd plan it a little better," he replied. "Chasing after a spoiled rich girl and her fortune hunter abductor doesn't seem like the best way to start an elopement of your own."

"No, it doesn't," Sarah replied. "And I have to say, I'm impressed that you understand that."

The look he gave her was meant to imply he understood a lot of other things as well, and Sarah felt the heat that had started elsewhere in her body rising in her face. "How long until our train leaves?" she asked to turn the conversation in a safer direction.

"Half an hour," he said, not fooled at all. "We have time to get a drink at the lemonade stand."

As they sipped their drinks, grateful for the refreshment after their hasty trip downtown, Malloy said, "The ticket agent said Electra seemed very happy. He didn't believe she was being kidnapped."

"I'm sure no one else will either. We need to make up a better story."

"In White Plains, they probably know her, too, so we have to be careful of gossip. What do you suggest?"

Sarah considered. "I doubt they'd believe we're relatives, not the way we're dressed. We could be teachers from her school. I doubt they'd ask us to sign for them."

"They don't use signs at Electra's school, remember?" Malloy reminded her with some amusement.

"Well, then, that's what we'll say. I forgot to ask, how much of a head start did they have on us?"

"Over an hour, but they don't know they're being followed, so they won't be in a rush. I'm just worried about how long it'll take us to find the Wootens' cottage once we get there."

"I'm sure the people at the station will know where it is. It's a small town, and they probably depend on business from the rich families who have homes there. I just hope . . ."

"What?" Malloy prodded when she hesitated.

"I hope Oldham hasn't already seduced her. If he really is the killer, she may never get over it."

The trip to White Plains wasn't particularly long but the miles seemed to crawl by. Sarah and Malloy could find nothing to talk about that would distract them from their mission, although they tried several times. By the time the train pulled into the White Plains station, they'd been sitting in silence for a long time.

The stationmaster knew exactly where the Wootens' cottage was.

"Miss Electra and her young man already arrived," he told them. "She didn't say nothing about expecting more guests, though. We would've had a cart waiting."

"You know how careless young people are," Sarah said, the lies coming easily now. "The rest of the party won't arrive until tomorrow. We came early to help get things ready."

"Can you get someone to drive us out?" Malloy asked, a little more anxious than a true guest should have been. Luckily, the stationmaster didn't appear to notice.

"I'll have somebody here in no time. Just sit yourselves down."

Sarah hoped he wouldn't notice that they had no luggage. Or that Malloy was pacing impatiently. And that they weren't in a very festive mood.

By the time a young fellow arrived with a dog cart to take them, they were the only people left in the station. Even the stationmaster had gone home for his supper.

"Nobody said there was people coming," the boy informed them defensively when they were on their way. "I always take people out to the Wootens' house when they tell me they've got guests coming."

"Did you take Miss Electra out earlier today?" Sarah asked.

"Oh, yes. She and her young man. They was doing the strangest things with their hands that I ever saw. Miss Electra said he was deaf, too, only he can't read people's lips when they talk, so she talks to him with her hands. Making signs, she called it."

"How did you know he was her young man?" Sarah asked.

"She told me. Said they was getting married real soon. I believed her, even though she's pretty young, a year younger than me, in fact. I wouldn't want to be getting married just yet. But she looked real happy about it. Girls do get excited about such things, I guess."

The sun was beginning to set when the cart turned in between two brick pillars that marked the entrance to the driveway. Stately trees lined the half-mile-long approach to the imposing brick house.

"This is a *cottage*?" Malloy murmured for Sarah's ears alone.

"Oh, yes," she said. "A cottage is a house that can be operated with only three servants."

"Miss Electra said the servants was coming up with her family, in the carriage," the boy said. "I guess they ain't here yet." No lights shone in any of the windows, although a thin trail of smoke drifted from one of the four chimneys.

"Good thing we came ahead," Sarah said. "We wouldn't want Miss Electra to be here unchaperoned." That, at least, would stop any gossip.

"Do you want me to wait?" the boy asked. "Just to make sure you can get in?"

Sarah had already gone to the front door, which fortunately, was unlocked. "We'll be fine," she called back, while Malloy gave the boy some money.

"Let's wait until he's out on the main road again, in case Electra causes a scene," Sarah said to Frank. "We don't want him coming to her rescue." They stood on the front stoop until the cart was gone.

When they stepped inside, the house was strangely silent and dim, since all the drapes had been drawn when the family had left last month. In the fading light they could see that the furniture had been draped with dustcovers. The place smelled musty and unused.

They stood still, listening for some indication of where the missing couple might be. Sarah hoped they wouldn't find them upstairs in bed.

"We don't have to be quiet," Malloy said in a normal voice, startling her. "I just realized they can't hear us. Come on."

Sarah followed as he led the way down the center hall toward the back of the house. They found them in the rear parlor, a cozy room. They'd started a fire to ward off the evening chill, and spread one of the dustcovers on the floor for an impromptu picnic. The remains of their supper had been gathered into a pile, dishes and cutlery and scraps of food, and Oldham, in his shirt sleeves, was lying on the floor with his head in Electra's lap. They were making slow, lazy signs to each other, the visual version of billing and cooing, unaware that they were being observed.

Sarah stepped forward with Malloy right behind her, walking toward them until Electra caught sight of them. She looked up in surprise, and Oldham followed her gaze. When he saw them, too, he sat up, then jumped to his feet.

By the time Sarah and Malloy reached them, he'd helped Electra to her feet as well.

"I wasn't expecting you for hours yet," Electra said, surprising them.

"You were expecting us?" Sarah asked in surprise.

"Not you in particular, but I knew Aunt Betty would send someone after us. I didn't think they'd miss me until suppertime, though."

Malloy waved his hand to capture her attention. "We were looking for the notebook."

Electra smiled. "You figured it out!" she said with satisfaction. "I was beginning to give up hope."

Oldham was signing frantically, trying to get her attention. She signed something back to him impatiently.

"What's he saying?" Malloy asked.

"He just wants to know how you found us and some other stuff about how he'll never let me go," she said dismissively. "He doesn't know I left the note for you to find."

"That was careless of you," Malloy said.

Electra shook her head. "I had to make sure someone could follow us. How else were you ever going to figure out who the killer was?"

"So Adam did kill Leander and your father," Malloy said, glancing at Oldham, who was signing frantically again. Electra was still ignoring him. Not at all what Sarah would have expected from a besotted young girl.

"How did you know he was the killer?" Sarah asked after capturing Electra's attention.

"He told me he killed Father," she said without the slightest expression.

Sarah and Malloy gaped at her.

"When?" Sarah managed, wondering how long the girl had known this horrible truth.

"The day Mother had the baby. Brother took me out so I could meet Adam. He said I needed to break it off with

Adam. It wouldn't be right to continue with my lessons with Father dead. Adam told me what he did."

"And Leander wouldn't have known what they were talking about because he didn't understand signing," Malloy murmured to Sarah.

Oldham had given up trying to get a response from Electra. He'd found his jacket, which was draped over the sofa, and pulled out a notebook and pencil. He'd been scribbling in it and now handed it to Malloy.

"He wants to know what we're talking about," Malloy said after reading it. "What should I tell him?" he asked Electra.

"Tell him you figured out he killed them," Electra said.

Malloy wrote something and handed the notebook back to Oldham.

The shock registered on his handsome face, but he quickly recovered. He wrote something and handed the notebook back to Frank with a very confident smile.

"He says I have no proof." Malloy looked at Electra. "He's right. I can't prove he met Leander that night."

Electra turned and walked away, or at least that's what Sarah thought she was doing, but she was actually going to the carpetbag sitting on the floor nearby. She stooped down, rummaged around for a moment, and then rose with something in her hand. She carried it back and held it out to Malloy with a confident smile of her own. It was a notebook just like the one Oldham had been using. The notebook Oldham had dropped the day of the funeral. The notebook that contained whatever message Oldham had given Leander on the day he was murdered.

Oldham made a strangled sound in his throat and dove

to intercept the notebook, snatching it away from Malloy's
fingertips. Oldham turned on Electra, his face a mask of
outrage and horror and indescribable pain. He was signing
quickly, awkwardly, because he still clutched the notebook
in one hand.

Malloy tried to snatch it away, but Oldham dodged him
and lunged for the fireplace, where the flames were lazily
licking at a log. He managed to open the book, fanning the
pages as he tossed it into the fire.

Malloy tried to push him aside, but Oldham turned and
grabbed Malloy's arms, catching him off balance so that they
both fell to the floor. While they struggled, Sarah grabbed
the poker that stood in a stand beside the fireplace. Hastily
skirting the writhing bodies on the floor, she managed to
catch the notebook with the tip of the poker and toss it away
from the flames to the safety of the hearth. It was charred
and half-burned and still smoldering, and she stamped on
it to smother any remaining embers and stop any further
destruction. Perhaps there was still enough left to provide
the proof Malloy would need, but she doubted it.

Malloy had finally succeeded in subduing Oldham or else
Oldham had simply ceased to struggle. Perhaps he figured
the notebook had been destroyed by now. A glance at its
sad remains brought a satisfied sneer to his beautiful mouth.
Malloy was on his feet, panting slightly, and Oldham sat up,
draping his arms over his knees as he caught his breath.

After a moment his gaze found Electra, who stood there
shaking her head in disgust. "I know what it said," she told
Malloy. "It said to meet him at the Grey Goose Saloon on
Delancey Street."

But Adam couldn't hear her. He was scrambling for the
notebook and pencil he'd been using earlier. He scrawled

something across a page and handed it to Malloy in triumph. Sarah could read it easily.

"No proof," it said.

Malloy stared back at Oldham with a sneer of his own. He dropped the notebook, reached into his jacket pocket, and pulled out something that glinted golden in the firelight. It was two short cylinders. He held one up in each hand for Oldham to see.

Sarah had no idea what they were, but Oldham did. The blood drained from his face. Malloy turned slightly to show them to Electra. "Do you know what this is?"

She stared at them in wonder. "Adam's mechanical pencil. His mother gave it to him when he graduated from college. He told me he lost it."

"He did," Frank said. "In your father's office on the day he was killed."

To Sarah's amazement, Electra smiled.

Oldham couldn't understand what they were saying, but he did understand that Electra had betrayed him. The look he gave her sent a shiver up Sarah's spine. For a moment they were all frozen, as if in a tableau, and then Oldham sprang, quick as a cat.

Before anyone could guess his intent, he'd snatched up a knife from the pile of dirty dishes and leaped to his feet. Instinctively, Malloy threw himself between Oldham and Electra, but Oldham had turned to Sarah. Grabbing her arm, he twisted it up behind her back and placed the blade of the knife to her neck.

She cried out in pain, and Malloy lunged for her, but a warning sound from Oldham stopped him cold. Oldham couldn't explain his intentions, but he didn't need to. They were crystal clear. The blade of the knife felt as if it were burning her skin where it pressed threateningly, and the pain in her arm brought tears to her eyes.

Terror turned Malloy's eyes coal black, and he raised his hands in a sign of surrender. Then he started looking around for something. He found the notebook and the pencil lying nearby where Oldham had dropped them. Moving slowly, making his intentions clear, he bent over and retrieved them, then wrote something in the notebook and held it up for Oldham to read.

Sarah saw it, too. "Don't hurt her. I will let you go."

She couldn't see Oldham's face, but Malloy must've been satisfied with the response. He raised his hands in the sign of surrender again, even though he still held the notebook and pencil. Oldham started tugging on her arm, and he took a step backward, forcing her to do the same. He was backing them toward the door.

"Don't let him get away!" Electra cried.

No one paid her any mind.

Sarah and Oldham were making slow progress, but Malloy hadn't moved. He stood there glaring, as if the very force of his anger could protect her. Sarah's mind was racing. She wasn't going to leave the house with him, no matter what. And she wasn't going to allow him to kill her either. Amazingly, she realized she had a weapon. A very deadly weapon.

"Poker," she said to Malloy, hazarding only that one word. She knew Oldham couldn't hear her, but she wasn't sure if he could feel the vibrations of her voice if she tried to say more.

She saw Malloy's gaze flicker to her right hand, where she still clutched the poker she'd used to rescue the notebook from the fire, and his eyes widened in comprehension.

"Don't take any chances," he said, barely moving his lips.

"You can't let him go!" Electra cried again and started toward Oldham.

Sarah felt Oldham tense, and the knife dug painfully into her neck, but Malloy caught Electra's arm and stopped her, holding her fast as she struggled.

Behind her, Sarah heard Oldham make a sound that might have been a sob. She'd been right about one thing: Oldham had loved Electra. But she'd been so wrong about how the girl felt about him. She had a thousand questions for Electra. She only hoped she'd have a chance to ask them.

Once they were out in the hallway, Oldham quickened his pace. Sarah had to struggle not to stumble as she fought her skirts and the terror of the knife at her throat and tried to keep the poker from bumping Oldham and revealing her secret weapon. Sarah's mind was racing. How could she use the poker? She'd have to decide soon, before they reached the door.

He would probably either release her hand or remove the knife from her neck in order to open the door, unless he turned her around and made her do it. If he released her arm, she might be able to spin around and hit him with the poker, but she wouldn't have much time or much room, and if she didn't hurt him the first time . . .

At the end of the hallway, Sarah could see a shadow in the doorway to the room they'd just left. Malloy had moved up, ready to come after them the moment he heard the front door open. Even still, he was much too far away to save her if Oldham decided to slit her throat.

She felt Oldham's breath on her ear and realized how close his face was, just over her right shoulder. He was slow-ing down, and they passed the doorway into the front parlor. They were almost to the front door. She had to act now or be totally at his mercy.

Sarah braced herself, tightening her grip on the poker. Bending her elbow, she lifted the metal rod slowly, making no sudden move to alert Oldham to her intentions. The poker was straight out at waist height, and then she felt his breath again and she quickly lifted her arm, sending the poker back over her shoulder and straight into his face.

She felt the impact. Oldham made a horrible sound and released her instantly. Now free, she spun around, slapped her left hand over the right on the poker handle, and raised it up just as Oldham recovered and lunged at her with the knife. She brought the poker down with all her might, not aiming or hoping or planning, just praying it would stop him.

This blow landed even more solidly on his shoulder, eliciting a satisfactory grunt of pain. She heard something clatter to the floor. The knife? She couldn't be sure. She raised the poker and brought it down again. By the time she'd raised it a third time, Oldham was on his knees, cringing, his arms over his head, and before she could bring the poker down again, someone grabbed it.

"I'll take it from here, Mrs. Brandt," Malloy said. Using the pressure of his hand, he forced her to lower it, and then he picked up Oldham by the scruff of his neck and punched him solidly in the stomach.

Sarah winced at the violence of it, completely forgetting she'd been about to bash Oldham's brains in just a moment earlier, but she instantly saw the wisdom. Oldham wasn't hurt, but with the wind knocked out of him, he was completely incapacitated.

"See if you can find someplace where I can lock him up," Malloy said as Oldham writhed and gasped for breath. "I'll need to go find the local police, and I don't want to take a chance of him hurting you again."

Finding herself unable to speak, Sarah handed him the poker and went in search of Electra, who had been watching everything from the far end of the hallway. The girl was helpful enough to show Sarah the pantry, a windowless room about eight feet square and lined with shelves that were almost bare at the moment. The door could be locked and the key hung conveniently nearby, since the room contained nothing of value at the moment.

At Sarah's call, Malloy dragged Oldham back to the kitchen, threw him into the pantry, and locked the door.

"Did I hurt him?" Sarah asked.

"I think you might've broken his collarbone, but nothing serious." He looked at the key, looked at Sarah and Electra, who was still watching everything with avid interest. "I think I'll keep this," he said and dropped the key into his own pocket.

Oldham began pounding on the door and trying desperately to turn the knob. That lasted for a few minutes and then they heard the sounds of what might have been sobbing. Sarah winced again.

"That's why I'm keeping the key," Malloy said with disapproval. "I've got to walk back to town and try to find somebody in authority to take him into custody. I'll probably be gone several hours, so don't let him out, whatever you do."

"He had a knife to my throat," Sarah reminded him indignantly, raising her hand to touch the skin that was still stinging. "I'm not going to let him go!"

"Oh, my God, you're bleeding," Malloy said in alarm, "Sit down." He pulled out a kitchen chair and forced her down onto it.

Meanwhile, she was feeling the injury. "It's just a scratch," she protested. "I'll take care of it. You should get going. It'll be dark soon."

But Malloy insisted on washing the blood away at least, to satisfy himself that she was right and it wasn't serious. Sarah sat patiently, allowing him to fuss over her and reveling in the opportunity to see a side of him he seldom revealed. His large hands were amazingly tender as they wiped the blood away.

When he was satisfied that she was all right, he left, armed with a crudely drawn map from Electra of the shortcut footpath he could take to town.

By then, Oldham had fallen silent. Sarah couldn't help wondering what was going through his mind. Locked in his silent world, he would have no idea what to expect. For all he knew, they'd locked him in there and intended to leave him to die. Sarah briefly considered writing him a note and slipping it under the door, but then she felt the wound on her neck again and changed her mind. Instead, she turned her attention to Electra, not quite certain if she could be trusted or not.

"Let's go back in the other room," Sarah suggested. Electra shrugged and followed Sarah back into the small parlor where the two lovers had held their picnic.

Sarah went to where the charred notebook still lay on the hearth. It had cooled enough to be handled, but when Sarah picked it up, she realized that the flames had done their work. They would have only Electra's word now for what it had said.

Electra had found the other notebook and pencil where Malloy had discarded them earlier and was idly flipping through it. When she looked up, Sarah asked, "Did you ever love Adam?"

The girl's face wrinkled with distaste. "A little, at first. But he is just a teacher. And he killed Brother."

Sarah could only think of one of the thousands of questions she'd had earlier. "Why?"

Electra studied Sarah for a moment, as if considering whether she was worthy of an explanation. Apparently, she decided she was. She walked over to the sofa from which they'd pulled the dustcover for their earlier picnic and flounced down onto it. She opened the notebook and began to write.

By the time Sarah had joined her, she'd already written several lines, and the words kept flowing.

"I wanted to learn to sign, so I asked Brother to find me a teacher. Adam was like all the other deaf boys I know. They all fall in love with me. He said he wanted to marry me, but I had to tell him my father would never allow it. I told him all about how my father wanted me to act like a girl who could hear and marry a man who could hear so I wouldn't have deaf children. I told him how my father would hate him and would forbid him to ever see me again if he asked for my hand. He got very angry. And then my father found out he was teaching me to sign. He made Adam come to his office. Father threatened him with all kinds of things if he ever saw me again."

When she stopped, Sarah took the book and wrote, "Why did Adam go back to see your father on Saturday?"

Electra smiled like a good student who is pleased to hear a question to which she knows the answer. "He wanted to change Father's mind. He wanted to show Father he was good enough for me. But Father made fun of him because he couldn't talk and he couldn't understand what other people said to him. He made fun of the way he wrote in his notebook. Adam lost his temper and hit Father with one of his trophies. He said he didn't mean to kill him," she added and shrugged.

"Why didn't you tell Mr. Malloy all this?"

"I didn't want to get Adam in trouble. I still loved him, and I wasn't mad at him for killing Father," she wrote, her gaze clear and innocent.

No, Sarah thought, she wouldn't have been. Malloy had told her that Electra's reaction to her father's death had been almost exultant. The man who had ruled her life and ordered her days was gone and would cause her no more inconvenience. "Did you know Adam was going to kill Leander?" Sarah asked.

Electra considered this. "No. If he hadn't killed Brother, I never would have betrayed him."

Epilogue

"I CAN'T BELIEVE HOW WRONG WE WERE ABOUT ELEC-tra," Sarah said to Malloy.

It was Sunday afternoon, two days after they'd confronted Electra and Oldham. Malloy had spent most of Saturday questioning Adam Oldham and closing up the case. They were sitting on a bench in Central Park, where Malloy had invited Sarah and her girls to meet him and Brian. Maeve was pushing Catherine and Brian on the children's swings nearby. The park was crowded, as usual, so the noise of screaming children and chattering adults gave them privacy for this very interesting conversation.

"I should've known something was wrong when she seemed glad her father was dead," Malloy said. "I overlooked it because she's deaf and . . ."

"And because you felt sorry for her?" Sarah asked.

"I guess. That's probably how she's gotten away with a lot in her life."

"I'm sure. She told me so many things that night in White Plains while we were waiting for you to come back. She said she really did want to learn to sign, but not especially because she wanted to be able to speak to other deaf people. She mostly wanted to defy her father, I think."

"Oldham said she talked about her father all the time, about how she hated him and how she'd never be able to marry him as long as her father was alive. He'd saved the notebooks where they'd written things back and forth in the beginning, until she learned to sign better. His mother brought them to me to read. I guess she hoped it would help somehow."

"Did Electra actually ask him to kill her father?" Sarah asked in surprise.

"No, not outright or at least not in writing. Who knows what she may have signed to him, though. I don't suppose she said anything to you about that?"

"No, of course not. She was trying to blame Oldham for everything, so naturally she wouldn't. I believe she told him how much she hated her father. Girls that age often do. She also admitted that she purposely let her teacher catch her practicing her signing and then follow her to her meeting with Oldham, so her father would find out. She wanted a confrontation between Oldham and her father."

Malloy whistled. "I wondered how the teacher was able to follow her so easily. Do you think she was hoping Oldham would kill Wooten?"

"I wouldn't go that far, but she certainly wanted her father to find out she was learning to sign, and she must've known how angry he would be at the person responsible."

"But why did she want Leander to die?"

Sarah considered that. "She didn't, but Oldham thought he was going to be as strict with her as her father had been. From Oldham's point of view, Leander had made it clear he wasn't going to allow Oldham to see Electra again. Leander felt guilty for being the one to bring them together, and he thought Oldham had taken advantage of her innocence."

Malloy made a rude noise. "That girl hasn't been innocent for a long time. Did you know she was the one who wrote the note I found in her room?"

"The one asking her to run away with him?" she asked in surprise.

"Yeah, that one. Oldham swore he didn't send it, and he showed me the one she'd sent him, asking him to meet her. She apparently tried to copy his handwriting from the notebook. She didn't do a very good job, but it didn't look like hers either, so I was fooled."

Sarah was trying to make sense of this. "Why did she write herself a note and leave it for someone to find?"

"She said it herself that night—she wanted someone to come after them. She had no intention of eloping with Oldham. She'd sent him a letter, telling him to meet her at the station, but she knew her aunt would send someone looking for her when she turned up missing. They'd know from the note that she'd taken the train somewhere. Anyone could've done what we did and found out where they went. They were a couple that people would remember."

"She was just surprised we got there so quickly."

"But why go to so much trouble?" Malloy asked with a frown. "She had the notebook. She could've just given it to me."

"She wasn't sure it was enough to prove Oldham killed

Leander. She wanted him to be guilty of kidnapping her, too. At least that's what she said."

"She did seem to enjoy all the attention."

"What I find really disturbing is how much she enjoyed humiliating Oldham. She took the notebook and kept it to use against him."

"She really was cruel to him," Malloy agreed. "He loved her, and she used that for her own purposes."

"I was afraid he was right and you didn't have any more evidence when he burned that notebook," Sarah recalled. "I never had a chance to ask you about that thing you had in your pocket, the thing Electra said was a mechanical pencil."

"I found it in Wooten's office the day he was killed. Somebody had broken it in half. The pieces were on opposite sides of the room when I found them, like somebody had tossed them away. I asked all the employees, but nobody had ever seen it before. It was expensive, made out of brass and ivory, so I figured it was Wooten's and stuck it in my pocket. I almost forgot I even had it."

"What made you remember?"

"The way Oldham kept writing in his notebook. I'd never seen him do it, but I knew that since he couldn't read lips or speak, that's the only way he could communicate with people who couldn't sign. It made sense that somebody who had to do so much writing would invest in something fancy. The fact that a mechanical pencil didn't need to be sharpened would be an advantage, too. I wasn't sure it was really his until I showed it to him, but if he was the killer, it had to belong to him."

"How did it get broken?"

Malloy shook his head. "Funny thing about that. It's

what got Wooten killed. According to Oldham, he went to see Wooten alone that day. He didn't want Rossiter to know what they talked about, and he suspected Rossiter didn't always correctly interpret what Oldham said to Wooten."

"You mean Rossiter purposely lied?" Sarah asked in surprise.

"No, Rossiter admitted to me that he'd be more diplomatic than Oldham intended, and Oldham had guessed that. Anyway, Oldham wanted to talk to Wooten alone, so he had to use his notebook and write messages back and forth."

"Mr. Wooten must've hated that!"

"He did. He made fun of Oldham because he couldn't speak or understand what was said to him. When Adam tried to respond, Wooten grabbed his pencil—the pencil his mother had given him when he graduated from college because she was so proud of him—broke it in two, and threw it on the floor. Then Wooten laughed, because Oldham was helpless and couldn't make himself understood without it."

"I can't even imagine how angry that must have made Oldham," Sarah said. "No wonder he struck Wooten."

"It's still against the law to kill somebody, no matter how obnoxious they are," Malloy reminded her.

"And Leander wasn't obnoxious," Sarah pointed out. "He was justifiably concerned about an older man taking advantage of his sister. Oldham had no business trying to court Electra."

"And he had no business killing Leander."

They sat for a moment, mulling over the strange facts of the case and watching the children play.

"What will happen to Oldham?" she asked.

"He'll go to prison, at least. He may get the electric chair. He certainly planned to kill Leander, even if killing Wooten was an accident. What about Electra? Did you tell her mother what you found out about her part in all this?"

"Her mother claimed to be too upset to see me. I tried to tell Mrs. Parmer, but she adores Electra and couldn't bring herself to believe anything evil about the girl. It is hard to understand how such a young girl could have caused such havoc."

"Young girls have been doing that for centuries," Malloy observed mildly.

"I suppose you're right. But that night at the house, while we were waiting for you to get back, she was writing all the things she told me in Oldham's notebook."

"She was?" Malloy asked with interest. "What happened to it? You should show it to Mrs. Parmer."

"Electra burned it," Sarah said. "She threw it in the fire when I wasn't looking."

Malloy's face twisted with frustration. "That girl is too clever for her own good."

"But not as clever as I," Sarah said. "I'd already torn out the pages she'd written and stuck them in my pocket. I gave them to Mrs. Parmer yesterday. I just hope they'll convince her that Electra isn't the innocent child she pretends to be."

"That's all you can do." Malloy slapped his hands on his thighs. "Now, that's enough of this. It's a beautiful day. Let's take the children and get some ice cream."

"What a wonderful idea, Malloy."

When they rose from the bench, Malloy offered her his arm, and Sarah took it, slipping her hand through his elbow. For one moment, their eyes met, and Sarah felt all the differences between them slipping away.

Well, for this one afternoon, at least.

Author's Note

MANY THANKS TO ALL THOSE WHO HAVE WRITTEN TO ME
with information about the Deaf and their unique issues.
Some have shared historical information they learned from
family members, and others have simply shared their personal stories or those of loved ones. All were grateful that
I had included a deaf character in the Gaslight Mystery
Series.

I've learned more about this subject through the years
I've been writing this series, and I felt the time had come
to address it. My research taught me many things I didn't
know, especially about the movement in the late nineteenth
and early twentieth centuries to eliminate the teaching of
American Sign Language (ASL) in favor of teaching deaf
children to speechread and speak. The theories I attribute
to Alexander Graham Bell were actually his. He dedicated
a great portion of his life and personal fortune to advance

them, and he had great success in doing so, very nearly eliminating the teaching of ASL. Only the efforts of the Deaf community preserved this important method of communication, although the debate over which method should be taught still rages today.

I have been careful not to offer an opinion on which method of instruction I feel is better, because this is an issue I feel very strongly is one of the few in which both sides are equally right in their arguments. Each method of instruction is right for particular individuals, and I believe both should continue to remain available.

I have tried to be as accurate as possible in my depiction of the deaf characters in this book. If I have erred in any way, I apologize. It is my own ignorance at fault, and I'm sure my knowledgeable readers will correct me. Some of the terms I have used are not correct by modern standards but were correct in the time period in which Frank and Sarah lived. Others I purposely misused because the person speaking would not have known the correct terms.

Please let me know if you enjoyed this book. I will also put you on my mailing list and send a reminder when the next book in the series comes out. Contact me through my website at: victoriathompson.com.